## *"Majesty...?"*

"Lord Pendragon?"

"I must have my brother's sword." Mallory held out his right arm to the air, palm up in supplication. And, before the King could reply, pointed toward the table on which Henry had set the gleaming weapon.

It rose up. Point downward.

The dragons on its hilt unfurled their golden wings.

And the sword flew sedately through the air to Lord Mallory's hand. A moment later, he resheathed it. Bowed, and, turning, strode from the chamber.

It was an uncertain silence that followed his departure...

# THE BLIND KNIGHT

## GAIL VAN ASTEN

ACE BOOKS, NEW YORK

THE BLIND KNIGHT

An Ace Book/published by arrangement with
the author

PRINTING HISTORY
Ace edition/July 1988

ISBN: 0-441-06727-1

Ace Books are published by The Berkley Publishing Group,
200 Madison Avenue, New York, NY 10016.
The name "ACE" and the "A" logo are trademarks
belonging to Charter Communications, Inc.

PRINTED IN THE UNITED STATES OF AMERICA

10  9  8  7  6  5  4  3  2  1

I grew up with a profound love
For ancient times . . .
Their mystery,
Romance and magic,
Sheer elegance.
Now I am a Mind Traveller,
Free to wander where I will . . .
To touch with adult sophistication
The complexities of other worlds,
Other souls . . .
Come. Share with me
This fairy tale for grownups.
This elegant dream I had. . . .

G.S. Van Asten
March, 1985

# ONE

1145 A.D.

The grave was dug, making a long, opaque gash of dark earth, a wound in the center of the fairy ring of toadstools gleaming silver in the moonlight. The gnarled old man picked up the stiffening corpse of his lady, and, stepping over the boundaries of the circle, knelt again beside the trench he had prepared for her. He laid the body with great tenderness in the damp, darkly silent earth, and placed her cold, lax hands upon her breast. Gently, he smoothed the folds of her gown to conceal the damage that lay beneath . . .

And, for the last time, touched the flaxen silk of her hair.

Even in death, his lady had that fey translucence he had well nigh worshipped since he had wed her. Her white face gleamed with ephemeral serenity in the cool moonlight, and he could feel her spirit sigh approval at his choice of resting place. His lady . . . The last of her line, descended, as he was himself, from the spirit people—the Druids of ancient times.

The old man's mouth tightened. Aye. Before the Romans came . . . Before the Danes. And the Saxons. And, long before these cursed Normans had come to rape the land again. He had seen it all. His mind, his memory, stretched back more than a thousand years.

Carefully, he moved the soft, compliant earth from the mound beside the grave and sprinkled it evenly over his lady's body. Muttering ancient prayers and incantations, he watched her form disappear slowly into the embrace of the mother from whom she had drawn her material being.

She had been a gentle soul, his lady. At one with growing things, her essence had been like the renewal of each spring-time. Innocent of the darker knowledge he contained. She had been incapable of harming any manner or form of creature. She had been a celebration of life itself.

Likewise, she had been entirely unsuspecting of the Norman lord who spied her in the woods, then bent on rape, pillaged her body. Killed her hideously.

Lord Wilfred of Wodensweir smoothed the last of the soil into place, then stood up. He flung back the folds of the voluminous cloak that both concealed and amplified his stooped and aged form, and looked up at the full moon that shone brilliantly overhead.

He drew a deep breath, summoning power—and extended hands that lost their gnarled, root-like appearance, and fleshed out into the straight-fingered confidence of a young and powerful man. He straightened, and seemed to grow much taller. The lines and creases of impenetrable age faded from his face as the skin tightened into the appearance of vigour. The sparse hair on his scalp thickened, darkened from threads of silver into a lush, midnight hue. And his hawk brows drew together in reflection of the thunder forces that were gathering within him.

He gestured imperiously to a point some distance beyond the fairy ring, and a strangely convoluted staff of some six feet in length, polished to a reflective sheen by ageless handling, rose from the grass and moved with sedate obedience through the air toward his right hand. His fingers closed about it, and his eyes gleamed amber fire as he raised the staff and pointed it toward the moon.

"Heed me, spirits!" he called out, his voice echoing deep, like distant thunder. "Hear my summons, for I am Merlin's brother. I am the last High Warlock of this realm! I do call thee to thy duty to me . . .!" The tip of his staff pointed like a fingertip toward the moon, silver light slithering toward him along its twisted length as it wove circles of beckoning around the lunar perimeter. His other hand stretched out, palm up in the night air for spirits to touch as they answered him.

A cool wind gusted abruptly across the woodlands that surrounded him. Leaves rustled. Branches swayed, and the warlock's lips flickered in a grim smile as he felt the response of the elements.

He looked up, watching the appearance of the first, silver-edged clouds that glided toward the moon in answer to his call. He moved the staff to direct them, and the clouds darkened, condensed, as they wafted in a circle around that perfect orb . . . gathered together, deepened.

He uttered an incantation.

Lightning flashed. Energy filled the air.

Ephemeral beings reached out to touch his fingertips in delicate homage, then drew back, gathering about him to listen to his will.

Thunder rumbled softly.

"Aye. Thou answer promptly. I am well pleased!" The warlock's voice caressed the night. "Do heed my summons to serve vengeance upon the Norman lord, Robert De Cheiney, now Earl of Wallenford, which is by rights, mine own demesne! This lord hath ravaged my lady to ease his lust. And he has slain her who knew not even thought of harm to any mortal soul." His voice gained power at it permeated the darkness.

"So...I do right this vile wrong by a curse upon his house." Menace slithered through the air with serpentine agility as his eyes searched the company of illusions about him, seeking out particular servants for the specifics of the task he had in mind.

He raised his staff high overhead. Lightning flashed downward from the stormclouds that boiled together to obscure the moon, touched the point, and spun into a fireball.

He tossed the fireball into the air and caught it in his other, outstretched palm, then glared into its depths.

"Do thou, in the duty of kindred, seek out this lord and poison his seed that he may not beget any fruit upon the wombs of women," he hissed. "Do thou, likewise, seek out the infant that grows in his lady's womb, and, as I command it, make of this child a creature of alabaster with eyes of scarlet hell, incapable of any sight of the mortal world.

"Such is my curse. Lord Robert will look upon his son and know the white innocence he hath destroyed. He will see in the scarlet eyes of this one who is to be his child, the blood he hath wrongfully shed!"

The warlock tossed the fireball high into the air. It faded ... vanished. Lightning cracked and thunder split the very air, then growled as it faded slowly away to leave another kind of space for spirits to travel through.

"Go now, my brethren. Do thou bring justice to my lady who is one with thee!"

Trees bent abruptly, seeming to bow, as, creature-like, energy melted away. Leaves were tugged from their branches in the violent rustling that ensued, and rain began to tumble from the heavens as the elements settled once more into the usual balance of natural patterns.

The warlock stood alone once more, his cloak blowing lightly in wide folds about his legs. Slowly, he lowered his staff, bringing the tip to rest in the long grass.

It was accomplished . . .

And, for the rest, Lord Robert's own soul would provide all that would be sufficient for torment.

Aye, the warlock thought, that were a wisdom he had acquired long ages before. Something that his brother had never completely understood. Conjure discreetly. Then, allow the very nature of mortal men to contrive the rest.

Merlin had been too deeply involved in mortal affairs. Likewise, Merlin had surrendered to the powers of another for love. And, now, Merlin paid the price, condemned to sleep in eternal quiescence.

But Lord Wilfred, as he had called himself for the past hundred and fifty years, practised far greater caution. He had seen the spirit people fade back into the corners of the land, slipping away into near-inseparable union with the wild things. Aye . . . thrust back by this Christian faith. Impelled to depart their tangible, human-seeming forms.

And, from his brother's folly, he had learned another discretion. He had never permitted himself to fall in love with another witch. Only involvement with a woman got of his mortal, human brethren was assurance to his safety. And, of these, only a woman gifted with that clairvoyant sight that was the rare and particular heritage from long-vanished times when men and spirits were closely bonded.

His lady had been such a one. A rare and exquisite creature, her blood had escaped dilution by the waves of human invaders that had overrun England in the course of the past thousand years. Pure . . . She had been derived from an ancient line of priests who communed with, and befriended, his own kind in a time when spirits walked among men as Gods.

The rain pattered against leaves and grass with patient, liquid steadiness.

An owl hooted softly nearby. The warlock sighed, bound his grief into tight coils inside him, and beckoned.

With a light fluttering of broad wings, the dark shadow of a large bird settled on his outstretched wrist. Wide round eyes stared curiously into his own. He settled his staff into the crook of his arm and caressed the tufts over the bird's ears.

"It is justice," he spoke softly. "Something of importance, even to these Christian mortals!"

"Whooooo . . ."

"Aye, my friend." The warlock smiled slowly, then beckoned again with his free hand.

A silver horse snorted, then stepped with fastidious care from behind nearby trees, and approached with delicate tread through the tall grass. It halted just beyond the perimeter of the fairy circle. The warlock stepped back and, with the owl on one wrist, wove a final configuration over his lady's grave.

"Peace, my love . . . ," he whispered. Then he stepped lightly across the toadstools and vaulted onto the horse's bare back, the owl's wings fluttering as it sought to retain its balance upon his arm.

Silently, the silver horse turned and cantered into the dark forest, carrying his lord back to the solitary tower that was all that remained of a once great castle . . .

Back to the infant daughter his lady had given him. Half witch . . . half human.

# TWO

An old man, whose skeletal head was grotesquely covered in yellowed, wrinkled parchment skin, emerged from the shadows to bend over her. His pitted eyes glinted amber suggestions of malice as his hands reached like gnarled talons along the sides of her swollen belly—pressing. Probing. She writhed, and he thrust lower, into that place where the portal for the babe's entry into the world lay between her thighs.

She writhed more violently, terrified by the gleam in the old man's eyes, terrified by his probing hands that were roving upward through her flesh, reaching inside her to touch her child, her precious child. . . .

She screamed, and sat up abruptly, covered in the film of a cold sweat. She stared blankly at the unperturbed darkness of her chamber for a moment, then clutched her belly possessively, feeling the child within kick vigourously against its walls.

"It . . . was a dream!" Lady Edwina De Cheiney whispered softly. But the sound of her own voice wafted through the cool bedchamber like an uncertain protest. She shivered and crossed herself and began muttering Hail Marys. Then, after a time, she huddled back down under the furs that covered her bed, curling herself tightly around her abdomen.

"Holy Mary, Mother of God . . . Let it be a son, I pray thee. Let it be a son. . . ."

It couldn't, mustn't, be anything but a son, this firstborn of her lord. In the single year of their marriage, Lady Edwina, at first enchanted by the striking looks and relative youth of her lord, had soon discovered his natural brutality. He had gotten her to bear him sons, he had told her menacingly a thousand times. He had no use for daughters. Nor had he use for women at all, save as they could serve his needs.

And his needs, Lady Edwina had likewise learned, were violent. Abrupt.

Pregnancy had relieved her temporarily of that burden. She did not care that he sought to satisfy his appetites elsewhere, upon the bodies of the serf women of his lands. Those women did not fare well either, as she understood it. Like the one that had died but two days ago of his assault. Aye, that frail little peasant maid who was purported to be wed to a certain old man living in an unknown secluded corner of the vast, rolling forests surrounding their fiefs.

Lord Robert had not killed a wench before, though he was well known to have beaten one or two. As with herself, Lady Edwina knew. But she had listened to him mutter something about that girl being a witch, his eyes slanting away from her own when the matter was brought up yester-eve.

The babe kicked again, then shifted. Lady Edwina's hand cradled her belly protectively. It felt strong, this child. Pray God it were so....

He should have left that wench alone, she thought. For it was said that the old man had been a great lord, years before ... even lord of this demesne. Likewise, it was claimed that he had been alive for a very long time. Not one soul hereabouts remembered him as a youth. But then, these Saxons were full of odd, disturbing tales and strange beliefs. Also, it was said that the girl had come from far, distant parts, not got of this region.

Mayhap she was a witch . . . ? Lady Edwina stiffened at the thought, for she had a great terror of witches. Aye—far better the girl was dead then. She clutched the Holy relic bound in leather that hung from a thong about her throat, finding reassurance in the touch of the knuckle bone of Saint Augustine.

Hovering just beyond his lady's chamber, Lord Robert felt the unfamiliar, clammy trembling of his hands, the cold sweat that crawled down his spine at each piercing scream that issued from within. At sixteen, Lady Edwina was well of an age to bear the difficulties—well old enough to give him a strong son. He went rigid at the sound of a woman's shout.

"Bear down, my lady! It comes now!" Panting sounds such as were made by a winded hound issued through the door and were abruptly rent by another, protracted, scream that seemed to take a veritable eternity to die away. Lord Robert shuddered and crossed himself, muttered a quick prayer. And heard another cry.

A thin, infant's wailing . . .

"Mother of God! Look at it!" Horrified tones came through the door. "She fainted, praise be! Poor child . . ." Unable to bear another moment, Lord Robert thrust open the door and burst into the room. The two midwives looked up, their faces pale as he strode across the rushes that covered the stone floor, ignoring his wife.

"What is it?" he growled the demand. One woman dipped a curtsey. The other shrank back from the cradle at the foot of the bed.

"A son, my lord." Lord Robert exhaled relief, then bent over the wooden cradle. And, went rigid with shock.

The babe was male beyond doubting, but . . . Its skin, and the tight curls upon its scalp were as white as unsullied snow. It screwed up its face and let out a strong cry. Lord Robert flinched as he saw its eyes. They were not blue, nor brown like his own.

They were pink. With scarlet pupils.

Lord Robert stared at it, appalled. This was his son . . . ? His heir? This—thing? Slowly, he straightened. He was sickened beyond disappointment. He turned to look at the two women who had aided his lady.

"Say no word of this to any soul, or I shall tear the skins from thy bones with mine own hands!" He snarled. "Dost thou *mark* me?"

"Aye, my lord!" The pair whispered it in unison, curtseying timidly, and withdrew yet a further two paces. Their fear was clearly apparent. Lord Robert knew they would obey him.

A groan came from the bed. Lord Robert spun about to see his lady rouse, her blue eyes opening in a face that was gaunt and wan. The hair around her brow clung, wet and lank, with sweat. Anger filled him at the sight of her, and he seized the infant from its cradle and held it up in clear view.

Lady Edwina's eyes widened as her gaze flew first to his face, then to the child. The babe mewed as Lord Robert advanced on her.

"See what thou hast wrought, woman!" he roared. "Dost thou see what thou hast wrought?" Lady Edwina went pallid with terror. "This should have been my son! What manner of demon changeling hast thou borne?" He snarled and set the babe down, none too gently, on her knees as she struggled to sit up. She flinched away, back into the pillows.

"This is no seed of mine, woman!" He growled contempt

and slapped her across one cheek, snapping her head to the side with the force of his blow. Blood appeared in the corner of her mouth. "I tell thee now. This boy of thine must become normal for me to call him my son, or to endow him mine heir! Do thou seek aid to make it so, or I will lock the pair of thee away from the eyes of men and so hide my shame!"

With that, he spun on his heel and strode from the room. The great oak door slammed behind him with violent finality.

Lady Edwina closed her eyes, face still stinging from the blow, and wilted into quietly helpless crying. The disappointment was unbearable. She had failed, and she did not wish to see how.

The infant, aware of the chill of the air about itself, and of being alone, mewed with greater persistence. The two mid-wives looked at each other, and suddenly, the elder of the pair, Meredith, turned to glare balefully at the oak door. She swung her gaze back to her apprentice, then turned it toward the naked, wailing infant. She frowned.

"My lord Robert threatens and roars. My lady Edwina weeps in fear. And I see a babe in need of care!" She snorted contempt. The younger woman gaped at her in astonishment.

"Dost thou not fear the curse upon such a child?" she ventured. Old Meredith rounded on her.

"Fool!" she hissed. "Hast thou not seen a snow-white lamb? Methinks there is little enough difference here! The babe is well enough save for his lack of colour!" Briskly, she strode to the bed, swaddled the infant, and began crooning to him as she picked him up. She glanced sharply at the other woman, who had not moved.

"See to the afterbirth!" she snapped. "Then thy lady!"

White lambs had pink eyes upon occasion, Old Meredith remembered, moving across the chamber, shifting her arms as the babe settled and gurgled. A groan from the great bed told her that the lady Edwina had finished passing the afterbirth . . . and she reached to stroke one of the infant's soft cheeks, then his brow.

Mayhap, she thought, this infant's whiteness was a blessing, rather than a curse. An omen of favour in a world of Norman darkness . . .

She moved her hand again as she drew the infant closer, and frowned. The babe did not seem to notice the passage of

her finger so close before his eyes. Again, she moved her
hand, attentive to those wide scarlet pupils.

But the infant's gaze did not waver. She made a darting
movement to see if he would flinch away. But he did not seem
to see . . . Holding the child close, she looked across the
chamber.

"Pity this child," she whispered very softly. "He is blind."

Old Meredith nursed the boy that Lord Robert angrily
named Mallory for the ill fortune he perceived in the child's
birth. Burdened by her lord's displeasure, the lady Edwina
would not have the babe she called "that Monster" near her.
And when the old woman attempted to draw her into caring by
confiding the infant's sightless condition, the lady Edwina
simply shuddered in revulsion and looked the other way.

Frail. Not yet recovered from her labour, she was tormented by her lord's renewed, intrusive assaults on her body.
And his blows—and his railing at the son she had made to be
his firstborn.

Lady Edwina sought solace in her rosary, in prayers and
fasting that grew steadily more rigourous, and even in such
discipline as nuns were wont to use for the scourging of their
flesh.

It was Old Meredith who held the infant for his baptism
two days after his birth, and attended the cursory pronouncement of his name . . . Mallory De Cheiney. And, when it was
accomplished, she watched Lord Robert's dark eyes follow
the anxiously departing priest, then flinched apprehensively as
he turned on her.

"Do thou tend this—thing!" Lord Robert growled. "Keep
him alive. And, I charge thee to tell me of any change in his
look." Old Meredith nodded. Lord Robert hesitated for a moment as his gaze flickered across the child. "I have heard that
infants may change the colour of their hair, and their eyes
. . . ," he said awkwardly. The infant cooed softly, and Lord
Robert's expression grew bitter hard once more. Old Meredith
did not dare to tell him that the child was blind.

"Aye, my lord!" she murmured.

"There is a chamber in the north tower for thy use!" Lord
Robert grated harshly. "It is my will that the child be kept
there. No other eyes save mine may see him!"

"Aye, my lord!" Old Meredith answered clearly and, dipping briefly, clutched the infant to her, turned and fled to do his bidding. She knew of the place to which he referred.

Robert De Cheiney, Earl of Wallenford, stared balefully after the departing, raw-boned old woman. Then, seeing he was alone in the tiny castle chapel, he allowed his shoulders to droop.

At thirty-four, he well knew that he was past his first youth. The younger son of a lord in Normandy, he'd endured an upbringing filled with savage reminders of his own insignificance beside his brother. The death of King Henry the First of England in 1135 had given the newly knighted Lord Robert all the excuse he could want to leave his home. Sailing to England, he had soon discovered the strife arising between the crowned and anointed King Stephen, and the late king's declared heir, his daughter Maud. Opportunity proved abundant, and the young Robert De Cheiney had carefully given his service to King Stephen. He had served well, with might and valour. He had distinguished himself. And, he had won the King's favour. Likewise, he had been given the fiefs of Wallenford and the title of earl.

Stephen's power was tenuous, and the Empress Maud determined. England endured years of bitter civil war. Lord Robert had clung to his holdings with savage will and forceful autocracy. Having achieved so much, he had no intention of being sundered from it.

But . . . He needed a son. An heir. One child was sufficient. Lord Robert well knew the problems that beset junior siblings.

Still alone in the small chapel, he passed his left hand lightly over his loins, touching the organs of manhood that were concealed beneath warm chausses and a knee-length tunic of blue wool. He frowned. He had happily bedded more than one wench in a night, and his appetites were not dulled.

His seed, he thought, was well enough. There were sufficient swarthy children resultant from his exploits among serfs. All bastards. Useless, yet bearing his stamp upon them. Nay. This unnatural white child with the vile scarlet eyes was Edwina's doing. His scowl deepened.

With what creature had she sought her secret pleasure? Or was he cuckolded by some incubus . . . ? And she, stupid woman? Always so pious and cold. Wincing. Gritting her teeth as if it pained her.

There was little warmth in his marriage bed, Lord Robert thought. But that did not concern him. He had wed to beget an heir, and he had been so careful in his choosing of the lady.

It did not occur to him to wonder if this was some fate-got punishment.

Pity . . . that was so akin to love, Old Meredith thought as she looked about the bare, circular chamber with its lofted roof and the single, narrow window set high in the outer part of the six-foot wide stone walls. Barren of both furnishings and comfort, it was a dismal place for a child . . . any child. Even this one.

Without a hearth place for a fire, the gloom was oppressive. It was of little comfort to know that the absence of light would make no difference to the tiny creature she held in her arms.

The babe began to cry, and she read his hunger.

"There, there, my sweeting." Old Meredith crooned and settled herself on the bare stone floor. She pulled a small skin filled with boiled goat's milk that she had prepared earlier, and fed the infant through a sucking hole pricked into one corner of it.

And while little Mallory fed, the old woman looked about the chamber, and thought of things she could do, items she could pilfer, to render it more habitable. Then, with a sigh of resignation, she looked down at the silver infant. Strangely, this was as close as she would ever come to having a child of her own, she knew.

Mayhap, that was sufficient reason to have given this one her devotion.

# THREE

During the darkest hours of each night, the warlock stood high upon the walk of his tower that, at such times, reached above the secretive convolutions of the vast and ancient forests thereabouts. Quietly stroking the feathers of his far-seeing friend, the warlock watched time and the world pass along their loosely ordained courses.

Likewise, he watched the web he had spun slowly draw Lord Robert De Cheiney into irreversible, silken entanglement. And, in another way, he watched the slow growth of the Earl's heir, the child that was locked away in the isolated darkness of a disused tower in Lord Robert's castle.

Different from the canny owl, the warlock's sight was wondrous with amber-hued, somnolescent power.

And, during the daylight hours, a bent old man hobbled along beside the romping exuberance of his young daughter as she explored the mysteries and enchantments of the natural things about her—the merest beginnings of the depths of his own knowledge. The old man delighted in seeing her grow, cherished her midnight hair and dark, arched brows that were a reflection of himself.

Little maiden. He grew thoughtful as he watched his child and remembered his lady. Then, he began to dress her in the chausses and tunic of a boy, bade her carry a dagger, and taught her how to use it. He undertook to teach her how to draw a bow, and the meanings and uses for sword and shield. And, on dark nights, he would summon the silver horse and set her upon it to discover the skill of riding.

A woman she would be, he resolved, but without a woman's vulnerability. Only with strength and cunningly wrought mastery of multitude skills could his Rosamund be free to give where she chose. Such was the right of her heritage.

\* \* \*

13

Lord Robert stood with his face to the wind that blew across his battlements. He leaned forward into the aperture of the crenelated parapet and clenched his fists in frustration.

Eight years. In the eight years that had passed since the boy had been born he had not got another woman with child. Any woman . . . And, least of all his lady, Edwina. His mouth tightened bitterly.

Aaah. She had trapped him more thoroughly than he had thought possible. Edwina was a mad thing. Repulsive to look upon, with the festering sores across her shoulders where she scourged herself. Gaunt from perpetual fasting, her hands ever trembled nervously as she fondled the rosary that never left their clutches. Her lips had no trace of womanly succulence, but were thin and dry, perpetually muttering one prayer after another.

It were like to rutting a piece of hollowed wood, bedding her. Hip bones that dug into his loins, her vault was dry and cold in the sunken basin of her belly. She would never conceive again. He knew that now.

Likewise, he knew that her insane, ascetic piety made it impossible for him to seek the Church's intercession to rid himself of her.

Lord Robert had sought to prove his virility elsewhere, seeking consolation with intemperate appetite among the maiden wenches of his serfs. But, strangely, since the birth of his—son, Mallory, not a single one had conceived of him either. There were no youngling bastards to grow behind those he had got before, learning the skills that were part of their bondage to the land.

Mallus, malum . . . Mallory. Portent of evil.

What manner of gelding had he become that he could no longer beget offspring? That he could not have an heir such as would suit him?

There was only that one boy that he had not looked upon since his baptism. The boy whose presence in the north tower haunted his mind. The boy whose very existence was assured only by the growing evidence that it was impossible to replace him.

"Aye. I would have done it, too!" Lord Robert muttered balefully. If Edwina had got another child—a normal child. Sin or nay, he would have left Mallory in the forest for the wolves to devour. But, the passing years made it apparent that such was not to be.

Lord Robert was keenly aware of his forty-two years. His hair was liberally streaked with the grey of an aging man. His joints ached on cold damp days. And, bitterness festered like an unhealing ulcer in the core of him.

Times were changing yet again. King Stephen's tenuous grasp on his realm was slipping, through the debility of recurrent illness. Lords such as himself, Lord Robert knew, savoured their vastly increased power, and were turning their thoughts uneasily to the virile and growing power of the young prince, Henry Plantagenet, Lord of Acquitaine, of Normandy, Maine, Anjou, and Touraine. Barely embarked upon the threshold of young manhood, Prince Henry had become a potent force indeed, for the future, as with his resources, lay before him like a meadow of unplucked flowers.

And now, he was declared to be Stephen's heir. . . .

Lord Robert scowled at his own predicament. The same could not be said of himself. And, although he held the gift of the fief of Wallenford, he well knew that the new king, for such Henry Plantagenet would assuredly be, would not be inclined to allow that gift to remain in his hands without an heir to hold it, to provide stability. . . . Lord Robert straightened and drew back from the parapet.

It was another, bitter consideration that his son's presence was well known. That foolish, younger midwife had been responsible for that. Her tongue had rattled like a pebble in an empty bowl, until he had brought its discourse to an end. Her butchered carcass had been all the testament to his will for silence regarding the boy that he had needed since. What his vassals knew, they confined to themselves. But. The knowledge was there. Another festering wound.

And the one that tended him . . . ? Lord Robert began pacing restlessly. She spoke to no one. Abruptly drawing his cloak about him, he strode to the stairwell that led from the battlements, seeking the north tower that he had avoided for so long.

Carefully, Mallory drew another thread from the rough weave of his tunic and set it on the stone floor in front of him, testing its length against the others he had extracted with delicate fingertips. He had eight. Enough to try another pattern.

He could feel the slight breeze that wafted down over him from the small window that Merry had told him was there in the wall. And his nostrils scented the damp odours that mingled with the gently falling rain beyond it. It was chilly, but he was well used to that, and sat with his bare feet tucked under the large, coarsely woven rug of heavy wool that Merry had brought him not too long ago.

He reached forward and carefully gathered the ends of his eight threads together. He knotted them, and began to develop another intricate pattern of interweaving.

It was something to do . . . Always a problem in the times of Merry's absences.

He stiffened as he heard thumping sounds beyond the arched surface Merry called the door, then frowned in surprise, for the sounds were different, not like her footsteps that shuffled a little, but abrupt. Hard. He wished it were Merry. He was lonely for her.

The thumping grew louder and had a metallic terseness as it advanced. Then, just beyond the door that Merry had told him he must never go through because something terrible would happen if he did, it stopped. Mallory set down his threads and sniffed, and listened to the rough, rasping sounds that told him the door was being opened. His nostrils flared as he caught the sudden influx of odour-laden air. Curious . . . Not like Merry at all.

These were different smells, slightly sour. Complex, and blended with the fire scent of a burning torch. Mallory knew what burning was. He had discovered the pain of touching it long ago.

He listened to the sounds of deep breathing, and, both curious and uncertain, he stood carefully and held out a hand to the empty space before him.


Lord Robert felt the skin of his face crawl across the bones beneath as he stared at the boy. Even the warm glow of the torch could not dispel such—whiteness. White as virgin snow.

Or death. Even to the hair that hung in tangled waves upon the boy's thin shoulders. And the face—it was thin, refined of feature, as was the long-fingered hand the boy held out toward him. Clothed in an oversized tunic such as serfs were wont to wear, Lord Robert marked the boy's height with abruptly indrawn breath. The hand before him groped, then wavered uncertainly. And Lord Robert found himself drawn to the eyes he was more afraid to look upon than he cared to admit. Dank moisture erupted on his brow, and a chill crawled down his spine at the pure scarlet orbs he saw before him.

Like pools of blood above an expression of innocent curiosity. Unfocused . . .

"Mother of God!" Lord Robert rasped hoarsely. Mallory cocked an ear toward the strange voice with its peculiarly unfamiliar tone, and took a careful step forward, knowing his position in the chamber that was the sum of his world, yet uncertain of the being that stood above and before him. He groped with his fingers.

"Who is there?" His higher-pitched, boy's voice was a puzzling contrast to that of the stranger.

"Lord Robert De Cheiney." The Earl spoke with slow care, then went rigid as the boy's features lit into a bright, welcoming smile. He stepped forward again, groping eagerly.

"My father!" Eagerly, warmly uttered. Lord Robert felt the blood leave his face as he stared. Tall and growing true, the boy kept his head cocked in the manner of one who listened. His fingers wavered in the air.

"Nay!" The Earl growled. "It could not be . . . ?" He shifted. The scarlet eyes did not follow him, but the boy stopped and appeared to concentrate, then pointed one blanched hand in the correct direction.

"Dost thou see me, boy?" Lord Robert demanded harshly.

"See? My lord?" Mallory frowned confusion. Merry had taught him many things, but little about the unimaginable sense of sight that his eyes were incapable of performing for him.

He felt tension, groped again, and heard the big man move.

"Do not touch me!" Lord Robert snarled brutally. Then, in growing rage: "Why have I not been told of this? My son. Pah! Blind as well. God's Blood, thou art an ill-gotten canker, boy. Thou art hideous to behold!" The boy's scarlet eyes widened horribly, and he froze. "Thou art a very sickness to the soul!" Lord Robert's tone dropped to a venomous hissing, and Mallory drew back in instinctive retreat before the force of the anger that reached toward him. "Aye! Thou doest well to shrink from me, boy!" Lord Robert strode forward as he uttered the last, caught the child by the shoulders, and shook him as he would a dog. Mallory screamed in terror, then felt himself held by one vast arm and struck by something hard and powerful. Then he was flung beyond any ability to prevent it, across space abruptly devoid of form, to collide with the hard stone wall.

Pain, and the total loss of his bearings, made him crumple to the floor. Terrified, he groped wildly to discover his whereabouts, but something large and sharp smashed into his ribs, making it impossible to even breathe.

He croaked awkwardly, and cringed as he heard the resounding slam of the door, and the thud of the bar that secured it dropping into place. Gasping convulsively, he shuddered as the reverberations slowly died away. Violent echoes that rebounded like chaos all about him. Slowly, he drew himself into a tight ball, totally shocked by the first, bruising pain of his young life.

All got from the man who was gone now. The man who had fathered him . . .

He began to cry in fear, desperate for the security of Merry's wiry, gentle arms.

"Woman. Do thou tell me. Is the boy blind?" Lord Robert snarled as his fist clutched the front of Old Meredith's gown and jerked her toward him. Her wrinkled face went ashen with fear. He shook her, heard her teeth clatter in her head. "Tell me the truth, old hag!"

"He . . . is completely . . . without . . . sight, my lord!" she got out. He jerked her again, and she flailed at the air.

"Whyfore have I not been told of this before?" he growled. An answer was barely needful, even if she were capable of giving it. Lord Robert shivered with the fury that consumed him, reached up to pound against his temples. The old woman croaked helplessly as he grasped her about the throat with both hands and shook her back and forth . . . Back and forth.

He hardly heard the snapping of her neck, or noticed that her body had gone suddenly limp until her throat began to tear in his mail-covered hands. Then, with a violently resounding curse, he flung her away. He stared for a moment at the sprawling, ragged body, and strode from the hall to seek a horse on which to exercise the rest of his spleen.

A pair of hours later, Lord Robert jerked the unfortunate animal he had chosen to a staggering halt in a glade at the top of a long, steep hill. The horse stood, legs splayed and trembling, its head between its knees, sides torn and bloodied from continual spurring, rocking back and forth in its efforts to get air into its lungs.

Covered with sweat himself, Lord Robert hardly noticed his animal's distress. He stared out across the meadows that lay in the valley before and below him, little pockets of green planting and grass in the morass of heavy forest that covered the downs. And, his castle that was a great, grey rock in the distance.

Even that faint hope—the half-formulated idea that had made him seek out his son after all this time had been dashed into useless fragments.

It had occurred to him that, hid beneath armour and helm, the boy's white skin and red eyes need not be a hindrance to the service of his father's will and interests. He could have been trained in knightly things. To fight.

But, to discover that the child was blind as well? Nay! It was easier to rear a child with but one arm or leg, than this boy who could not even see. Blindness made everything impossible—even the learning of wit and cunning.

Lord Robert swore under his breath. Those cursed scarlet eyes!

Even now they compelled him to think of things he had no wish to consider, made fear crawl like an ague along his bones—fear that was sufficient to prevent him from ridding himself of the curse the boy represented.

Lord Robert's brooding prevented him from perceiving the old man in the nearby trees who stood, leaning heavily upon a smooth and knotted staff, watching him from beneath the hood of his voluminous brown cloak. Nor was he aware of the curious gaze of the dark-eyed child that stood under the shelter of the old man's other arm.

"That is the Norman lord who foully raped and murdered thy mother," the old man murmured into the child's ear. She stiffened, looked up at him with widening eyes, then stared at Lord Robert astride his exhausted horse. She frowned, and her fist tightened about the hilt of the dagger at her waist.

"All in good time, my sweeting," the old man whispered with the softness of a rippling breeze. "All in good time . . . Be assured, he does not go unpunished." The child looked up intently into the old man's eyes. He smiled a little. "Understand this use of power. It is well to use a small manipulation, then to allow the nature of men turn it to greater purpose."

Rosamund continued to stare up at her father for a time, then returned her gaze to Earl.

"Thou was lord of all this once," she said.

"And so, I will be again," the old man murmured quietly. "It but requires an instrument."

# FOUR

The bruising pain across his shoulders and along his ribs faded
fairly rapidly. But the shock, the fear and confusion over what
had occurred did not. . . . More than ever before, Mallory
longed for Old Meredith, longed for her explanations, and for
her familiar, gentle ways.

But Merry never came.

He waited with the patience of one who was accustomed to
long periods of solitude.

Still—Merry did not come.

Some unmeasurable time later, he heard yet another patterned thumping beyond the door. He groped his way toward
it eagerly, then listened as the small, straight-edged panel in
the door, about an arm's length from the floor, rasped open.
There were clunks, and a bowl and jug were set inside. He
reached out with his hand.

"Merry . . . ?"

"Jesu!" He heard a voice exclaim. The panel slammed
shut, and footsteps scurried away in a much more rapid
rhythm, leaving him alone again.

Considerable time passed before he gave up waiting for
another sound beyond the door and began to eat the food and
drink the water that had been left for him.

Time changed its quality and became a sober, bewildering
thing, punctuated only by the footsteps that came and went at
erratic intervals, the rasping of the panel in the door that deliv-
ered food and water, and an empty excrement pot.

At first, Mallory called out Merry's name in desperate
hope. Then, gradually, he gave it up, simply listening until the
footsteps died away entirely before approaching the door.
Beyond the hope of reason, beyond any comprehension,

Merry had vanished. And he discovered slowly all the feelings of abandonment.

Mallory wandered around the confines of his circular chamber with a new attention to detail, touching the stone work of the walls, even of the floor, learning the feel and lay of every block and slab, and every crevice and cranny between.

All that remained of Merry were memories. The feel of the rough cloth of her gown over the soft places on her breast where she had invited him to huddle. The warm, yielding flesh of her arms. Her hands that stroked his hair, or washed him clean. Or guided and taught. Her gruff kindness.

And her voice that spoke to him of so many things, that had taught him to speak as well.

He thought of the knowledge that she had only begun to give him. The certainty of his name and identity. The fascinating perceptions of a vast, unfathomable world beyond the chamber that were all he knew of space. Aye—she had told him it was a world filled with many, many people. With men and women, and lords and serfs, and beasts of all kinds. And she had made of it a world incredibly lush in textures and sounds, in forms and spaces. There were so many things she had tried to describe.

She had told him, too, of something else he could not know about. Merry had explained to him that he was without sight. That he suffered a condition called blindness. The eyes that were moist, mobile orbs in his face did not function as they should. They did not function at all. And, when she had spoken of colours, of light and dark, he had only known confusion. These were words that were devoid of the tangible meaning of texture, containing suggestions of ideas of perception that were so remote as to have no significance for him at all.

Memory gradually lost its intimacy and retreated into the distance as loneliness became an agony. His solitude was absolute, introspective, confining, and as repetitive as the blocks of stone that surrounded him on all sides.

Mallory had little else. There were the two tunics that comprised the sum of his clothing, the pile of straw and the three blankets that made his bed, and the earthenware pot for his excrement.

The footsteps came and went at inconsistent intervals.

They changed the pot, and brought food and drink. Sometimes there was enough. Sometimes, there was not.

Mostly, there was silence.

And, his father—Lord Robert De Cheiney, who thundered into the chamber with complete unpredictability. Who growled and roared venomous hatred at him. His father, who was vast and hard, and powerful beyond belief. Who kicked and hit, and flung him about.

Who seemed to relish his shrieks of pain and his terror.

His father, who taught him to dread any sound of approaching feet, any opening of that terrible door. Who taught him to understand the meaning of torment.

Beyond the silence, and the interwoven stone that surrounded him, Mallory grew attentive to the hints of the vast and unknown world that lay beyond the chamber by standing beneath the high, narrow window for long periods of time. It was a world, Merry had said, that was filled with a multitude of people. Merry's world. And his father's.

He felt the thin strip of penetrating heat that wafted down to touch his skin. Sunlight, Merry had called that sensation. He felt other things. There were the drops of water called rain that tumbled from some high place far above and beyond his chamber to make a liquid roaring outside, or a softer, more patient melody of spattering sounds. He felt each drop that was thrust through the aperture of the window by an accompanying wind, and discovered the places where they congealed to trickle down the inner walls and form small cold pools on the floor.

And, when the air turned sharp and bitter cold, when he was impelled to huddle for any kind of warmth beneath his blankets in the season Merry had called winter, Mallory held out a hand to feel the soft, silent, delicate crystals of ice that melted when they touched him. He listened to the absorbent quiescence that marked their falling. Snow, Merry had said, was white like his skin, but Mallory could perceive no resemblance.

There were times, likewise, during that bitter season, when he listened to solitary, mournful calling sounds, that echoed as though from far away across a vast, poised stillness. Other such voices, from slightly different perspectives of that space, would answer. They were the voices of the wolves. Merry had told him of the fierce beasts that roamed through the unima-

ginable forests that surrounded the place in which he lived,
that walked on four legs instead of two, hunting other creatures to kill and eat. Even men. Mallory had caught the inflections of fear in her voice as she had spoken of them.

Fierce, she had said. Like his father . . . ?

But to Mallory, as he listened to the poignant echoes of
their songs, they became something else.

Lonely creatures, seeking communion with others, and, for
that, no different from himself.

Desperate for some sort of contact, Mallory would draw
his blankets about him, stand beneath the window, and howl
as they did.

He learned the inflections, the scales and variations of their
singing. He learned expression, and the subtle consolations of
release. And, not infrequently, they answered him.

There were other voices to hear when the times of rainfall
and warm air came, the season Merry had called summer.
Mallory listened with eager and relentless patience to the chir-
rups and whistles of other creatures beyond the window.
Birds, he understood. Creatures who could fly. He could not
imagine. He had no way to touch. They sounded pretty, and
small, and incredibly energetic.

Sometimes, they sounded fierce as well.

And there was a singular creature that appeared from the
spaces beyond the window, that came and perched itself from
time to time in that aperture. He learned to recognize the
whispered fluttering and delicate thud that accompanied its
arrival, and the ruffling sounds its body made that suggested it
was a soft textured creature.

It spoke to him most curiously.

"Whoooo . . . ," it said. Always, that single word, "whooo
. . . " But Mallory discovered infinite variability within the
tones of that solitary utterance. Delicate inflections that were
conversant with knowledge beyond his understanding. And,
he could feel the textures of its attention that was directed
toward him. Interest, that was intriguingly contemplative.

It seemed, somehow, a friend, and Mallory welcomed its
presence eagerly. He would move to stand beneath it, and
answer it in a like tongue. And, when it fluttered away, he
listened with unhappy hunger.

\* \* \*

Mallory had other visitors as time passed. But these were pests. Little crawling things that wandered through his scalp, and along the folds and creases of his body, they nipped and itched.

Never receiving enough water to wash them away, he gradually learned to endure their unsavoury presence. Like the grit-laden texture that came to sheath the sensitivity of his skin, and to stiffen his clothing, he learned, eventually not to notice.

Time meandered on, occasionally with intervals of startling, contradictory brevity. More often its passage was a malingering lethargy that forced the soul to probe the deepest parts of itself, to explore all the capacities for endurance and the inescapability of feelings.

Feelings, Mallory learned, that found reflective expression through the fluid grief that trickled from the corners of his eyes, filled the spaces behind his nostrils, or, from sitting with taut muscles, his arms wrapped tightly, uselessly, about himself. Such were the purposeless manifestations that did little to relieve the impossible. And, gradually, they too were abandoned.

He explored every facet of loneliness, and grew, in time, to understand it was the pain of absention from things he was not, fundamentally, made to live without. It was a pain, likewise, that was compounded by the hideous confusion of never fully understanding the nature of his needs, for, their fulfilment was a thing beyond his experience.

Terror was another passage through pain and abuse, compounded by the anticipation of the same. He heard his father's harsh voice that issued forth endless barrages of invective to the accompaniment of sour, decaying odours. To the accompaniment, also, of violent kicks, and beatings, and being hurled across space that was rendered hideously disordered.

Afterwards, there was always the relentless endurance of pain that localized itself, then slowly faded away while space found shape and balance once more. It was a cycle, and, gradually, Mallory learned to lie there, tightly curled for self-protection until it was finished and the door slammed shut once more. He learned, as well, to silence his own screams, for that seemed to slightly lessen the force of his father's blows, to send him away a little sooner.

But, from deep inside, there slowly arose another kind of

screaming. It was a violent thing of itself, a protest against the
terrible array of things his father proclaimed him to be, a deep
revulsion for things he sensed were vile, repellent.

These were utterly in contrast to the faint echoes of a remembered voice that came to him from some deep, internal
part of his mind. With profound need, he sought the redemp-
tion of listening to the illusion of Merry's voice that had told
him once, he was a good boy, a gentle lad—and fine.

Time developed another, insidious form of measurement as
the walls surrounding Mallory's existence grew gradually
smaller. The ragged tunics he wore did likewise, then rotted
and crumbled away until he had nothing beyond the failing
blankets. As Merry had told him he would, Mallory discovered that he was steadily growing.

There were other changes as well. Hair grew on new places
of his body, creating even more inaccessible homes for the
mites that infested his skin. And, the voice that had learned to
sing to the wolves with consummate skill had a new, deeper,
richer timbre.

Mallory discovered that his father, despite the overwhelm-
ing force of his brutal power, did not seem so massive as
before.

But, best of all, he had grown to be much closer to the
blessing of the window set high in the stone wall. Aye, the
window that was a portal to other, vaster, varied spaces, pure
contrast to the growing sense of restless entrapment he was
coming to feel in the chamber that contained him.

He sought it more vigourously, trying time and time again
to scale the wall, attentive to the directives of the downdrafts
of fresh air on his skin. Finally, he learned to feel his way
along the deepest grooves between the stone blocks. Then,
gripping tenaciously with fingers and toes, he found his way
upward until, at last, he was able to clutch with a single hand
through the window's deep and narrow sill.

He would draw himself up to hook a knee through the
aperture and rest there, unable to fit completely, for the window was not wide enough for the passage of more than one
limb.

Nostrils flared, he savoured the feel of the air, the sweet,
sharp, delicious scents that wafted clearly toward him, and the
differing directions and strengths of the winds that whistled
beyond. Smiling for the pleasure he felt, he listened to a new,

exquisite clarity of sounds that was not muted by the stone as it was when he stood below.

And, he would hang there as long as he was able, until pain and weakness forced him to relinquish his hold. . . .

King Stephen, never strong in any sense practicable to a monarch, was dead. The young prince, Henry Plantagenet, had, with undisputed triumph, claimed the throne of England, and with that single accomplishment, became the most powerful monarch in Christendom.

In keeping with such dominion, he had set his fist firmly upon the bridle of the realm. Uncertainties were dispelled among the lords of the land who were well familiar with the legacy of civil unrest got of Stephen's reign. Indeed, most were glad of the change, recognizing in King Henry, the second of his name, a prince of absolute authority and vigour, and, moreover, one who was given to a cunningly balanced application of discretion and a sound sense of justice.

Having spent some part of the last two years of Stephen's reign fighting for the dying monarch against his new liege lord, it was the last of these that was sufficient reason alone for Lord Robert De Cheiney to fear the new king.

He kept to his own fiefs, ruling them with the erratic tyranny that came from uncontrollable and intemperate outbursts of temper, appetites that went beyond the balance of discretion and humanity, and, increasingly, bouts of drunken melancholy.

His lady, Edwina, still lived, after a fashion. She never left her chambers, nor undertook the household duties that were the obligation of her rank. A scarecrow creature of manic devotional obsession, she was heard perpetually chanting through the door that had no need of latch or key.

For himself, Lord Robert watched the mature vigour of his forties slip away into the sagging, pendulous degeneration of his fifties. He was old, he knew. And he dreaded it, for it was another thing beyond his control.

Like the son he never quite dared to dispatch, but kicked and beat and screamed all manner of obsessive loathing at. The boy, whose life was in all ways, a curse. The boy, who grew ever taller, discarding the appearances of childhood, and who stared toward him as though he did not exist, with those hideous, scarlet eyes he was too afraid to touch.

That blood red gaze that was made the worse for the silence that accompanied it.

Surrounded, near isolated by vast forests, Lord Robert's fiefs of Wallenford were now filled with strange tales of the creature that haunted the north tower of his keep. Of red eyes that gleamed in the darkness there. And of the eerie howling that came from the same monster.

There were few who did not know of the haunting wolf cries that filtered through the stone of Wallenford keep, at times, to summon the great forest packs to prey upon livestock and run through the villages on cold, winter nights.

Or, of the ghost who flew from the north tower disguised as an owl to circle about, far beyond the reach of a well-aimed arrow.

It was terror that kept Lord Robert from killing young Mallory. Yet, it was the same terror that honed hatred into temper of damascened sharpness each time he looked upon the boy. And, it was the same distempered force that drove him repeatedly to seek out the abandoned north tower with its high, bolted chamber.

There were only illusions of satisfaction to be found in seizing Mallory's thin shoulders to fling him about, or in kicking at the boy's ribs until he gasped hideously in an effort to breathe. Or in beating him across the shoulders and back, then watching as the boy crawled blindly across the floor to huddle in a corner. Ever seeking to find an answering terror in the boy's screams. Such voice as provided a little assurance of his dominion.

But, Lord Robert found, the boy ceased to cry out. He still crawled away, and cringed, or, lay there shivering violently while Lord Robert rained blow after blow upon him. It was the absence of any outcry, and the way that Mallory stared, his eyes opened wide and gleaming strangely, that would drive Lord Robert away in the end. Blood and bitterness unfathomably combined, fraught with implicit and ominous suggestions. Like the strange tales that had begun to spread beyond Lord Robert's fiefs, beyond his abilities to control them, eventually, he knew, bound to reach the king's astute ear.

# FIVE

1160 A.D.

The air was poised to absolute stillness. Not a leaf or twig stirred by the slightest amount. Nor were birds apparent by either cry or movement. A mist hovered in the air, touched the grass with twinkling drops of moisture, and added mystery to the ancient, twisted trees that peered from its depths.

Silence permeated everything, and made the passage of the small army of knights and men, the noises of horses and armour, seem an unwelcome, even observed invasion.

"I cannot like the closeness of this forest!" Reginald De Beauvais, the young earl of Arundel, muttered under his breath as he glanced uneasily about him. It was a potent temptation to bestow the sign of the Cross upon his own breast. Fulk, Lord of Midhurst and Petworth, looked at the younger man and smiled.

"Even the trees must yield to the King's business!" he declared firmly. De Beauvais did not respond. The King's business—or Petworth's ambitions? he thought to himself. In this instance, they would appear to be much the same thing. The King had sent his lords to bring him report of the strange, un-Christian tales that were emerging from the fiefs of Wallenford, and Petworth had endeavoured to persuade the King to grant him license to take the fief, should circumstances warrant it. Lord Reginald, himself, had been given the tasks of arbiter in any matter that might arise, and, until now, it was a duty, and an honour he had been more than willing to undertake.

He glanced back at the troop of some thirty knights and one hundred well-equipped footsoldiers, and wished that the proportion of his own followers was greater.

Petworth, he had subsequently learned, had old scores to settle with Lord Robert De Cheiney, bitter resentments that dated back to the civil strife of King Stephen's time. It was a period vague in Lord Reginald's own memory, for, at twenty-two, newly come into his inheritance, and some fifteen years Petworth's junior, he could only recall the preoccupations of boyhood.

Fully aware of the older man's hardness, he kept his own counsel, and continued to let his gaze roam through the trees that seemed both to guard and to channel their passage.

He stiffened abruptly, as he caught a glimpse of flashing steel. His hand flew reflexively to the hilt of his sword. Half-masked by the mist, he distinctly saw a slim figure in chainmail and a plain, brown surcoat, face hidden beneath the nosepiece of a conical helm, astride a white horse. The figure spun its beast about and vanished. Lord Reginald breathed sharply.

"What is it, my lord?" Petworth demanded abruptly. De Beauvais looked at him, his grip still comfortably seated around the hilt of his sword.

"I fear our coming is known, my lord," he answered slowly. "I saw a knight watching our passage." Petworth nodded brief acknowledgement, his mouth tightening.

"It matters not!" he muttered roughly. The comment, and the manner of its utterance, were Lord Reginald's clearest insight into what to expect.

A sudden gust of chill air rustled the silence about them, sent leaves that were turning red and gold with early autumn brilliance, tumbling from their purchase on the branches of trees to swirl in eddies across the turf.

Then, all was still once more.

Again, Lord Reginald suppressed the urge to cross himself.


"Father! I have seen . . ." Rosamund strode across the hall of her father's tower with long, energetic strides. The old man, seated near the hearth fire, staring into the flames, raised a hand to interrupt her speech.

"Aye, my daughter. I know," he said quietly, and, reaching for the staff that never left his side, got to his feet with a brief wince. The old man's carcass he used was tiresome at times.

She stooped in front of him, slipping the helm from her head, thrusting back the mail coif to shake free her hair. Her eyes widened at the slight smile that curved his lips.

"Thou art pleased I consider?"

"Aye, child," he said softly, his eyes passing along her maturing length. "Now it begins to come to fruition."

"What . . . ?" Rosamund asked.

"Justice!" Lord Wilfred said very softly, straightening somewhat. Rosamund stared at him, well acquainted with her father's ingenious capacity for ambiguity.

"My mother's death?" she ventured, searching her father's amber eyes. He did not answer at once.

"Aye, so," he said at length, seeming to study her. Then, "Aye. Thou art near enough grown. It is time for thee to know more. Come with me!" he ordered and turned away to walk across the hall. Rosamund followed, her long black hair swinging in time with her cloak.

A black wolf puppy rose from its resting place by the fire and padded after them.

His robes sweeping the stone floor, Lord Wilfred led the way across the hall, up a spiral staircase, down a shadowed corridor that divided the chambers of the second story to a large door at the end of it.

"Here?" Rosamund breathed astonishment as Lord Wilfred opened the door to reveal another stairwell beyond. She had been forbidden even to unlatch the door that was the single access to the upper reaches of the tower where her father spent a considerable portion of his time. Lord Wilfred glanced at her.

"Aye, child. Here," he said and began climbing upwards. Rosamund followed eagerly now, and, moments later, found herself blinking purest amazement as she stepped from the worn gloom of the steps into the arched entrance of a large and magnificent hall.

Meticulously designed, tapestries woven in bright colours, and gold and silver hung against smooth walls of pure white marble. Four gleaming columns rose majestically from the black marble floor to support an intricately carven, high-vaulted ceiling, and, around one of these, a spiral staircase of elfin delicacy wound its way up to a small opening in the roof.

Between the tapestries, shields were displayed. Some round, some triangular, each was set across a pair of crossed swords, pikestaffs, or some other probing weapon. One shield, more distinctive than the rest, with its unique, crescent moon shape and emblem of green dragons entwined on a field of black, overhung the great hearth that dominated the far end of the hall. Below a mantel of marble dragons that seemed to writhe a little in the glow, a fire wove silent patterns, hints of blue and green interlacing the orange and scarlet flames. . . .

Rosamund's breath was a hissing intake of awe between her teeth.

In the center of this great hall was a large and circular table. A massive construction of intricately carven walnut, its highly polished, near-reflective surface was covered with multitude things. A great chair sat before the narrow entrance to the circular hole in its middle. A couple of others, well littered with bright cushions, were placed at the periphery. . . .

Rosamund stared, then turned her wide-eyed gaze upon her father.

"How can it be? All this?" she whispered. Lord Wilfred smiled. Shrugged.

"A little property from earlier times."

"Was thy wealth so great then . . . ?" Lord Wilfred's smile widened briefly as he shook his head.

"It is not a matter of riches, my child," he said clearly, "but of power." Her dark lashes flickered in confusion. He continued in the same, solemn tone, his voice increasingly penetrating. "My daughter, I am a warlock. I am not human, though I be kindred to men. My name in ancient times was Pendragon." He raised a hand toward the shield that overhung the hearth. Rosamund's eyes followed the direction of his pointing, then shifted back, filled with enquiry, to his face.

He flung back his cloak then. She watched him straighten —grow. She stared as his face changed, the lines and creases fading into the complexion and smoothness of a much younger man. His hair stirred as though breezes ruffled it, becoming dark and thick like her own. And his stature and form became that of a much younger, although mature man.

His staff was held by a smooth, strong hand, and his eyes gleamed canny amber perceptiveness.

"Now thou may see me as I am," he said, his voice deeply powerful.

"Sweet Jesu!" Rosamund breathed. He smiled at her awe. She licked her lips, shifted with uncertainty. "Then—what am I, my lord . . . Father?" Two questions in the same utterance.

"Thou art my child, born of a human woman of pure and ancient lineage." His answer was melodious, sure. "Thou art something of both. Part witch. Part human. And, thou art mortal in the way of humans." The last was added with a hint of regret. He stepped forward and took her hand in the powerful clasp of his own. Warm, Rosamund noticed. She stared at the masculine face that bore much resemblance to her own.

"Come, my daughter," the Pendragon spoke gently. "It is time for thee to begin to learn the skills that are thy heritage. I have given thee human things to master, and a few others, and thou hast done well. Not it is time for thee to know the rest of thy capabilities. And the governance of their use."

She allowed him to lead her through the narrow opening into the small circle at the center of the table. She began looking at all the large, vellum books that were laid upon its surface, the jewels—and the other things arranged there.

"Aye, father!" she said with sudden and intense eagerness.

The Earl of Arundel stared through the eye-slits of his helm, shifted the shield on his left arm, and drew the lance in his right hand up to couch it more securely against his thigh. His own men behind him, a mere company of ten, he waited as Lord Petworth led the main bulk of the small army down, across a meadow, through a sorry-looking village, then up, toward the ancient, rambling castle on the hill beyond.

His mouth taut, he continued to frown. It had been his wish to send a deputation to greet Lord Robert in some semblance of amicable manner, but Petworth would have none of it. Called him a boy. . .

"Haaah!" he roared suddenly, and setting spurs to his destrier, charged down the hill, his men behind him as he made to join the rest of the company. Petworth was intent to make a war of this in any case, he thought in disgust as serfs scattered left and right before his advance. But it was the King's express wish to practise diplomacy in this matter, if possible. Already, he could see Lord Robert's drawbridge being winched upward.

A minute or two later, he drew his stallion to a halt beside Petworth's restive animal.

"It is poorly done, my lord!" he declared with asperity.

Petworth glanced at him.

"And would thou, my lord, seek Wallenford's hospitality to find thyself with a dagger slitting thy full belly in the midst of the night?" he asked mildly. "Lord Robert is not a chivalrous man. He never was!"

De Beauvais could think of no response, and looked up to see a grizzled man leaning out over the parapet above the drawbridge.

"Who goes there to bring an army to my house?" A harsh, grating voice rang out.

"Petworth and Arundel, my lord. Upon the King's business," Lord Fulk bellowed answer. "We seek thy courtesy for ourselves and our men." Lord Reginald shot him a look of surprise. Still looking toward the castle, Petworth hissed under his breath, "Do see, my lord. He hath not a full garrison!" Lord Reginald's flitting gaze confirmed the mere scattering of men along the battlements.

"I am Wallenford!" the grizzled man shouted back. "What manner of king's business impels thee to my fiefs, my lords?"

"It would be better discussed over the Christian hospitality of mead and a capon, my lord!" Petworth retorted at once.

Silence followed. A suspicious hesitation. Mayhap, Petworth had the right of it, Lord Reginald thought. De Cheiney's indecision was indicative of fear, in the manner of a man who had secrets to conceal. For such rich land as he had seen hereabouts, Lord Reginald already considered that the condition of De Cheiney's serfs spoke ill of their lord.

"Thou art welcome, my lords!" Lord Robert shouted back at length. "But I do require thy forces to remain beyond my gates!" Lord Fulk laughed clearly. "Nay, my lord!" he shouted firmly. "We expect better for our service to the King's interest! Our men are due a like courtesy. Else . . . ?" The threat in the last word was beyond any mistaking.

Again, they waited in silence.

"So be it!" The churlish, furious voice came back to them. A moment later, the drawbridge began its slow, noisy descent. Petworth raised an arm to signal his men, and set spurs to his warhorse. After a brief meeting of the eyes with Sir Geoffrey, who flanked him, Arundel did likewise. . . .

Within minutes, Lord Reginald found himself experiencing a deep sense of appalled shock. He brought his stallion to a halt well in the middle of the inner bailey of the castle, and passed his lance and shield to his squire.

Everywhere, there was slovenliness and disorder. Refuse that competed with disrepair. He dismounted, relinquishing his stallion's bridle to his squire, and, unlacing his helm, held that out as well. He turned to stare then at the dishevelled, sullen-faced, burly old man who stood glaring at them from the steps that led to the main entrance to the keep. De Beauvais found Petworth's eyes and knew a moment of shared feeling that understood the grim lines of the older man's face.

Allowing Lord Fulk to move ahead of him into the keep, he recognized in himself the anger of a contentious lord at the sight of a fine demesne being allowed to fall into ruin.

But why . . . ? That was the puzzlement of it.

He directed a more penetrating look in De Cheiney's direction, seeing the wine stains that made vertical splotches on what had once been a magnificent blue robe. The florid complexion—unhealthy, intemperate.

Lord Robert's manner remained warily belligerent as he escorted the two lords, with their knights flanking them, into the heart of the castle. The lesser fighting men were left outside to tend the horses and themselves, and De Beauvais was glad of the others behind him as he stared about him with ever-increasing distaste.

It had been a magnificent construction once, this castle. It could be again, he thought, frowning as he assessed structure. It should be now.

But the rushes that covered the floor of the great hall were stale and damp and sour, filled with the accumulated refuse of years, it seemed. And the furnishings were likewise uncared for. Soiled. Unkempt . . .

Lord Reginald did not demur when Lord Fulk quietly insisted that a guard of their own men stand watch outside the chambers to which they were escorted.

Even those rooms were despoiled by musty odours and cobwebs.

Lord Robert made uncertain efforts to be cordial during the evening meal that began a short time later, but his hands trembled visibly, and his gaze kept flitting uneasily about, passing from man to man across the company about him. He looked, Lord Reginald decided, like a man nearing the point of some total collapse of the wits.

He ate sporadically. Drank steadily and consistently.

"I had hoped, my lord," Fulk of Petworth deliberately undertook directed conversation, "to give thy good lady our courtesy. But she is not present, it seems." A little surprised at this ploy from one known to be exceeding forthright, De Beauvais sat back to observe. Lord Robert's response was equally curious. He shifted abruptly, then glared.

"Nay, my lord. Lady Edwina keeps to her chambers. She is

ill!" he half growled. There was no mistaking the purposeful intensity of Lord Fulk's gaze.

"It were a pity . . . ," he murmured with peculiar smoothness. Lord Robert leaned toward him abruptly.

"Do thou tell me the nature of thy duty to the King, my lord, that brings thee to storm my house!" he demanded. Lord Reginald chose that moment to intervene.

"His Majesty," he said with quiet authority, "who is attentive to all the matters of his jurisprudence, and who establishes justice and solid prosperity for all his vassals, has much concern for the tales of witchcraft and other such unnatural things that have come to him from this part of his Christian realm." Now, Lord Robert's dark eyes were focused as they stared at the Earl of Arundel.

"Witchcraft . . . ? My lord," he rasped yet Lord Reginald could tell from De Cheiney's eyes this came as no surprise. "What other things . . . ?" De Beauvais exchanged a glance with Petworth, and continued.

"Vile tales, my lord, of wolves that hunt serfs unchecked." He gestured with one hand. "Demons and the like. His Majesty is concerned for the disposition and ruling of this fief, for, in all matters, he considers the future, my lord. It is not certain that thou hast got an heir . . . ?" he added suddenly. "Though, there are rumours that it is so."

Lord Robert's florid complexion became a mottled and ugly dark hue. He looked away and snarled incoherently into his wine goblet. His hands, Lord Reginald noted, trembled even more. He sought and found Lord Fulk's gaze. Petworth nodded slightly and settled back into his chair, turning the conversation to his favorite pasttime of hawking.

Wallenford had not answered. And, Lord Reginald knew, their departure from this castle was far from imminent.

"My lord!" An urgent whisper, roused him, and Arundel catapulted himself from his bed and dived for his sword just as the knight before him completed his entrance into the chamber.

"Aye, Sir Geoffrey?" He found clarity and his voice in the same instant.

"Treachery, my lord!" The other man grated. De Cheiney attempts to dispatch our company this night. They fight now. In the bailey!" Petworth had known, Lord Reginald thought, glad that he had been cautious enough not to discard all his clothing. He lunged for his hauberk and began to arm himself. The older knight moved quickly to aid him.

Within moments, the pair was rushing toward the fray, now clearly audible within the castle walls. Lord Reginald shouted his battle cry as he lunged toward the first of the foe, and Lord Fulk, jerking his sword from a corpse, spun toward him.

"See to De Cheiney!" He roared at the younger man, and De Beauvais, with another shout to his men, veered toward the great hall.

The battle proved to be more of a farcical rout than any true and deadly enterprise, for the Earl of Wallenford reeled drunkenly about the hall, brandishing his sword with but a parody of the skill that had been his in his youth. His men, hearing their lord spew forth shrieks and curses, were yet reluctant to loose their lives to the King's servants, and yielded readily with each opportunity that presented itself.

Soon, peace was restored. Robert De Cheiney, tightly bound, hung between two angry knights, and the rest were meekly submissive. Servants reappeared from their hiding places and crept nervously forth to watch and to wait.

"Robert De Cheiney! I declare thee unfit for the entitlement and gift thou hold of the King!" Petworth roared angrily at the shaking old man. "Moreover, I consider thee a fool, and worse, to attempt such treason as thou hast wrought this night upon the King's person through the body of his true vassals sent to serve his interests!" Lord Fulk set his hands upon his hips and glared his contempt at the bound man.

"Let it be know to all," Petworth continued with clarion resonance, "that I . . . Fulk, Lord of Petworth and Midhurst, do claim the fiefs of the Earl of Wallenford to hold for the King. And I do declare thee, Robert De Cheiney, no longer lord of the same, but prisoner to the King's justice!" De Beauvais' brows tightened. Neatly accomplished, he thought. Lord Fulk had achieved his wish—and De Cheiney had played, even with crude simplicity, into his hands.

"I am the King's good servant!" Lord Robert shrieked.

"That King is long dead!" Lord Fulk spat at him, then waved a hand. "Take him away! Chain him in the dungeons, such as I presume there must be!"

Striding toward Petworth, Lord Reginald did not glance toward Lord Robert as they dragged him away, but listened, rather, as Lord Fulk barked orders to soldiers, servants and the like.

It was a point of concern, Lord Reginald thought carefully, that, unless, as rumour suggested, Lord Robert did indeed have an heir to whom this fief could legitimately be given, his own lands of Arundel would well nigh be surrounded with this addition to Petworth's other holdings. He signalled for Sir Geoffrey to come to him.

"My lord . . ." He sat himself before Lord Fulk. "I will undertake to search the rest of the keep." The older man nodded approval.

"Mother of God!" Lord Reginald whispered as, his hand still frozen to the latch of the door, he stared across the chamber the woman servant had told him belonged to Lady Edwina De Cheiney.

"Mea culpa . . . Mea culpa . . ." The same chant he had heard in muted tones through the door, hoarsely repetitive, rasped from the throat of—aye, a naked woman kneeling on the hard stone, wielding the hooked scourge of religious discipline with savage pleasure upon her own back. It was pure horror.

He shivered, repelled. Blood dripped down along the bumps of her spine, slid across ribs that were skeletal. Flat, wrinkled breasts flopped loosely in time with the motion of her arms, tangled brown hair hung in wisps about a wild-eyed face distorted by the throes of an orgy of self-induced pain.

"Mea culpa . . . mea culpa . . . ," she continued to chant, seemingly unaware of his presence. Lord Reginald swallowed against the bile that rose in his throat, and paled as he jerked from the chamber, slamming the door behind him.

"My lord . . . ?" It was Sir Geoffrey. Lord Reginald looked at him.

"This is a place of madness!" he breathed fervently. Sir Geoffrey did not reply.

# SIX

Seated beside Lord Fulk on the dais of the great hall, Lord Reginald felt as though he had aged a year in the few days that had passed since he had found the lady Edwina in her chamber. Entirely mad. Beyond reason or care, they had left her there for the present. Lord Robert resided in chains within his own dungeons, securely removed from the sight of all, and, where it could be seen with increasing clarity, he long deserved to be.

Petworth had assumed control with absolute and undisputed authority, reinforced by the aggressive discipline of his small army.

The rest was chaos.

Common folk and other vassals of the fief had stared at them with terror, slipping away if they could. They were now only just beginning to emerge as it became apparent that the nature of Lord Fulk's rule would be vastly different from that of their own lord.

Now, in the latter part of a long day spent holding court in the great hall of the old castle, Lord Reginald directed a look of respect toward the older man as Petworth sighed grimly and took brief respite in rubbing his hand against his brows.

"Aaaah, Sweet Jesu!" Lord Fulk murmured as he glanced about the hall, at the timid, yet increasingly hopeful folk that were assembled before him. "This business sickens me!" He inhaled deeply and straightened in his chair.

"Aye, so!" Lord Reginald muttered fervent agreement. Petworth shot him an assessing look that was not without approval, and nodded to the old man who was currently being questioned.

That had been the sum of the day. Relentless questions alternating with reluctant answers containing information pried through the application of honest justice from reticent lips. Lord Reginald shifted to continue his attention. The tales were grim.

The evidence of grotesque mismanagement that was so apparent everywhere was embellished by such reports as had been coaxed from a succession of timid folk. But there was worse. Serfs spoke hesitantly of the rape, even beating, of their womenfolk for the lord's pleasure. Of starvation where there should have been none. And, as with the discourse of the aged man before them now, of murders committed for no other reason than Lord Robert's fits of unbridled temper.

Lord Reginald stiffened abruptly as he listened. The old man's sister Meredith, the village midwife who had attended Lady Edwina's birthing some years before, had been found with her neck snapped like a pullet in the corner of the great hall one day.

"Dost thou say Lady Edwina gave birth?" De Beauvais demanded as Lord Fulk leaned forward. The old serf before him flinched visibly and glanced about him.

"Aye, my lord. Some fifteen years past, it were."

"To what?" The peasant cringed. "Tell me. Dost thou know?"

"My lord . . . There was talk of a son . . . But it were never seen. I think it was dead soon after, my lord . . . But Old Meredith was ever at the castle, here, my lord, in the north tower . . . until she were found that day."

"Hmmm!" Lord Fulk grunted as an apprehensive murmur rippled through the crowd. The north tower? Lord Reginald frowned.

"It began then, my lord," the old man offered with fractionally greater confidence.

"What?"

"The curse, my lord."

"So? We are come to it at last!" Lord Fulk commented, then vigourously began to address the matter of the strange tales that were the reason for their presence.

And, strange they were. A discoordinate collection of fancy and terror sprung from a common root seated in the north tower. Lord Reginald was puzzled. He had been given to understand that part of the keep was abandoned.

Yet, food was taken to the tower to placate the red-eyed demon that was harboured there. And for those impelled to such duty, to speak of it was a death sentence administered by Lord Robert himself.

Lord Robert was the only one to go there and return unscathed.

"Mad...!" Lord Reginald breathed. Petworth glanced at him, then made a coaxing gesture to the servant who now stood before them.

"Nay, my lords... It were God's truth." That frightened individual protested. And there were witnesses enough to testify that the demon turned into an owl upon occasion. And there were none who had not heard the wolf calls that summoned the packs of those fierce and dreaded tyrants of the forest down upon the villages in the midst of each winter....

"Go! Leave us!" Lord Fulk waved them away and sat back, his face drawn and stern as he turned to meet the equally firm face of Lord Reginald.

"Mother of God!" De Beauvais murmured. "This place is an asylum of madness!" Petworth's gaze did not waver.

"I cannot dispute it! " he said grimly after a moment, then straightened to pass his gaze across the company of some thirty knights and others of his own that remained in the hall. "The matter of the north tower must be resolved!" he announced clearly. "This fief cannot be put to rights with such intemperate tales distorting the wits of the people! Find me a priest."

The gathering of knights shifted restlessly. A battlefield contained familiar hazards, but, to a man, they all had another mode of respect for the supernatural.

Feeling challenged, Lord Reginald stood.

"Who will come with me?" he barked, his question ringing clearly through the hall. "I will dispose of this nonsensical myth!" He stared at them all, and his own ten, challenged to pride, stepped forward.

De Beauvais glanced at Lord Fulk, who simply nodded, then turned, and strode from the hall, his men grouped closely behind him.

Mallory huddled on the rotten mound that had, once, been straw bedding. His mouth was parched, his tongue felt like the texture of stone, and his stomach rumbled painfully with hunger. The chamber stank with the unrelieved rancidity of excrement.

He shivered with a chill that came as much from his need for food as from his near nakedness. The single remaining piece of cloth that was bound about his hips provided no protection from the pervasive damp cold air.

It had been a long time since they had come with food and water. Much, much longer than usual. He had groped his way to the door once, tried to push his hand through the panel, but it was latched somehow. He had given up and crawled back to his usual place, still stiff and sore from his last beating by his father.

Mallory stiffened abruptly and cocked his head, hearing sounds. Nay, not the patterned regularity of one set of footsteps, but erratic, overlapping ryhthms that suggested many. Different—confusing.

He listened to the approach that came along the acoustically tangible space beyond his door, then shifted the catch the sound of voices. There were several. Partly muffled, and with differing ranges.

"What lies above this?" he heard someone ask. More footsteps, that passed by and seemed to rise, fading away to reappear moments later.

"There is naught, my lord, save a way to the battlements." He heard an intake of air.

"Then, good sirs, let us discover what lies behind this door!" Mallory drew his legs under him and sat upright, listening to the scraping of the thing that barred that dreaded door, the squeaking that invariably accompanied its opening. Again, there were footsteps. Just a few, that stopped abruptly. He sniffed, smelling smoke, and heard several rasping intakes of breath as though there were suprise. He flinched, uncertain.

"Soooo! This is the demon of the north tower, my lord!" There was a lilt to the deep voice, and an accompanying snort. "'Tis a youngling!" Mallory could not perceive his father's presence, and turned carefully toward the voices.

"Mother of God!" Astonishment. "Look, thou. It hath red eyes!" Mallory heard the slow appalled horror, and shrank back against the stone wall behind him.

"Red eyes or nay, my lord," another voice was brusquely matter-of-fact. "It is most evidently, a creature to be pitied!"

Lord Reginald met the meaningful and determined look of Sir Geoffrey, then stepped closer, lowering his torch and bending a little to peer into the scarlet depths of the wide, unfocused eyes before him.

He saw a thin, young-seeming man of light complexion and hair, though it was hard to be certain for the layer of grey filth that covered him.

Half starved. Unclean beyond bearing. Yet, not appearing to be diseased. Lord Reginald straightened, his mouth tightening as he turned to stare meaningfully at Sir Geoffrey.

"I am compelled to wonder what pitiful victim of De Cheiney's we have discovered now, Sir Geoffrey!" he said in a hard voice. The knight did not blink. "I charge thee to bring him out of this hole and tend to him that this, too, may be resolved!" De Beauvais strode from the stinking place.

"Very good, my lord!" Sir Geoffrey murmured, then signalled to his men to take the huddled boy.

Mallory shrank away in fear as hands touched him, then clutched at his arms. So many . . . He gasped and shuddered as they pulled him to his feet and bore him forward in the direction of the hated door. Then, incredibly, he was through it, veering suddenly. Then down . . . His feet scrambled upon a surface that fell away in layers, and he cried out once. Then he was swept forward once more, trying to walk with the bodies that surrounded and held him, through more space than he had ever experienced.

Directions changed. The ground tumbled away again . . . all impossibly confusing. Then, from some point ahead, he sensed more space, filled with a considerable volume of noise. Voices, other sounds, that swept toward him until he was surrounded.

Then, those holding him halted abruptly and let him go. Mallory flung out his hands for balance and fell with a gasp to find beneath him a surface that was much like the old straw of his bed. He jerked himself up to sit propped on his elbows, and turned his head, trying to sort directions for the voices and other sounds that bombarded him, catching undertones of surprise . . .

"What is this, Lord Reginald?" A hard, deep voice spoke from some distance away.

"This, I consider, is the demon of the north tower, my lord!" The voice he had heard once before responded acidly. "So much for devils! But there are mad folk aplenty here!" Mallory pulled himself to his knees and stretched out a hand, groping toward that second voice, unable to quell his instinctive shivering. Mutterings passed like a breeze around him, and he straightened warily. He sniffed. Feet shuffled. Things clattered and clunked. He stood and groped about him with hands that found naught save air, then took a tentative step toward the dominant voices on legs that were weakened from hunger. He stopped as feet came toward him.

"Mother of God!" he heard the voice called Lord Reginald just before him. "He is blind!" Something touched his cheek, and Mallory flinched away.

"And, little more than a boy, besides." The voice belonging to the other "my lord" responded more slowly. "Jesu! He stinks! I vow, I have never seen so much vermin!" Again, Mallory groped, then drew his hands back toward himself as laughter echoed about him.

He flinched again as a hand settled gently on his shoulder, and heard the voice that was part of it.

"Dost thou have a name, lad?" Mallory swallowed. He had heard Merry use such a tone an eternity ago, he remembered. Kind.

"Sir Geoffrey, do take this boy and clean him. Find clothing and food for him." Lord Reginald's voice had a softer edge this time. "From the look of him, he hath much need of care!"

Once more hands seized him, though somewhat more gently this time, and Mallory found himself impelled again across strange and unfamiliar spaces confused by abrupt, unpredictable, changes in direction and sudden shifts in the level of the ground that caused him to trip, or painfully jab his toes.

"Be thou easy, lad!" a gruff voice said near his ear. "There is naught to harm thee here." But Mallory could not be reassured and stood rigid with fear, sniffing the air, and trying to assimilate the other noises about him. He flinched violently as another voice sounded.

"What hast thou got here, Sir Geoffrey?"

"A prisoner of Lord Robert's, Broderick. Do thou help me with him?" A chuckle followed. Then.

"Aye, I will!"

Mallory gasped and hunched over as hands tore away the rag about his loins. He heard sloshing sounds, and cried out as cold water slammed against his head, poured down along his body.

"Nay, lad. Be still!" the gruff voice ordered. But Mallory flailed wildly and tried to jerk away as the hands grasped him,

held him and, again, poured water over him. He tried to raise
his arms to protect his head, but the hands were everywhere,
probing, scrubbing at him until his skin shrieked protest. He
huddled down as even his hair was attacked. His face, too,
and ears. The hands were strong and relentless, and it was
terrible.

Like his father...

Finally the hands fell away. Then another mass of water
doused him. He choked and spat, and lay there in the cold
puddle shivering convulsively. His skin felt raw, strange, and
the bruised places where his father had last kicked him stung.

"The lad hath skin as fair as a maid!" some voice commented.

"And hair of a like silver to match!" The gruff, Sir Geoffrey voice added. A hand grasped him and pulled him up to
stand. "It is done, boy," the same voice told him, not unkindly. Mallory felt his body being enveloped in something
heavy and warm and dry. He blinked and groped, glad to hold
the thick cloth against him, and shook his head to clear his
face of the water that trickled down from his hair.

"Mother of God! Look at his eyes!" the voice called Broderick rasped out. "They are as red as Satan's! And the rest of
him so white. What manner of unnatural creature is he?" Mallory flinched, remembering his father's curses, but a hand
seized his arm firmly and pulled him to walk with uncertain
steps across the ground.

"Come with me, lad," Sir Geoffrey said quietly. "I will
find food and clothing for thee...."

"Food?" Mallory whispered, his stomach clenching at the
thought. The hand upon him tightened briefly, not ungently.

"Aye, lad. Food."

It was unbelievable pleasure, Mallory found some time
later, to sit upon the ground in another place, exploring the
sensations of a skin that did not crawl or itch, and was infinitely more explicit in its sense of touch. And there was
more beside. The unfamiliar warmth of soft chausses on his
legs, flexible shoes, a thick tunic and a warm, long cloak to
draw about himself. And, best of all was the ecstasy of a belly
filled to bursting with foods more flavourful than he had ever
conceived possible.

Thirst had also been slaked, by water that was sweet upon
the tongue, and by a frothy, tart brew that Sir Geoffrey called

mead. Mallory felt his own lips curve in response to this incredible satisfaction. He held out a hand to the fire that crackled and popped to one side of him, welcoming its radiant heat, and listened to other, muted, yet continuous sounds that came from across the chamber. Some kind of activity, connected with the man whose presence he felt there. His smile widened a little. He had not thought it were possible to know such well-being, and he could not fear Sir Geoffrey for bringing him to this.

"Is this the world. . .?" he asked.

The knight, sitting on a chest, attending to the maintenance of his arms, looked up, startled by the question, and by the open curiosity on the youth's lean white face.

"Aye, lad. So it is," he responded carefully, then, struck by another thought, asked, "How long were thou in that tower from which we brought thee?" The boy's face sobered.

"Since I was born," he said slowly.

"Sweet Jesu!" Sir Geoffrey breathed as the full significance of the statement imbedded itself. Little wonder, he thought, that the boy was bleached to a dead man's hue. Pity rose like a pain, for he had likewise seen the great bruises that appeared with the removal of years of encrusted filth.

"Tell me, boy," he asked gently. "Dost thou have a name?"

"I am Mallory De Cheiney." The response were immediate. Sir Geoffrey exhaled in a long, low whistle, and the boy cocked his head, his expression at once curious.

"Who is thy father, lad?" He was impelled to ask.

"Robert De Cheiney, Earl of Wallenford." Mallory answered as he understood, as he had learned from Merry in a past now remote.

"Mother of God!" he heard the knight whisper. "But this is a pretty coil!" He did not understand at all.

Sir Geoffrey resheathed the sword he had been sharpening, and stood. So, he thought, this strange, white-skinned, white-haired, red-eyed, blind boy was the heir to the fiefs of Wallenford. The elusive and suggestive rumours were true after all. He frowned, recalling Lord Reginald's muttered comments on the matter of Petworth's desire to acquire the fief. And, the boy sat before him with the quiet patience of one unaccustomed to either movement or conversation, entirely vulnerable. "Is this the world?" What manner of question was that? He stepped forward and reached for the boy's hand.

"Do thou come with me, my lord," he said roughly. Mallory got to his feet with much greater confidence than before and allowed the knight to lead him along another strange and twisted course, his free hand held out before him.

Mallory felt surprise as he recognized the large place of noise and many voices again, and sensed, likewise, that attention was fixed upon him as Sir Geoffrey led him across the rustling floor. Conversations became muted. Savoury odours filled the air, and he detected sounds that made him think of eating.

The knight's hand drew him closer to one such center of sound, then dropped its grasp on his arm. Mallory stood very still, stiffening slowly as uncertainty returned, as space became an undefined void.

Lord Fulk directed a brief and questioning look at Lord Reginald, then leaned forward to look at the nervous boy with unnatural pallor and thick white hair that fell in waves to near his waist.

"Vastly improved," he murmured. "Boy, tell me thy name?" Mallory shifted his head a little to focus on the voice before him.

"I am Mallory De Cheiney," he said. A sudden rustling swept around him, accompanied by tangled mutterings. Then there was absolute silence.

"Who got thee?" the same voice asked.

"I do not understand. . . . " Mallory felt confusion.

"Who fathered thee?" It was more briskly asked. "Who mothered thee?"

"My father," Mallory's voice dropped a little, "is Lord Robert De Cheiney, Earl of Wallenford, My mother. . ." He frowned as he remembered that which Merry told him he must never forget. "Is . . . Lady Edwina De Cheiney."

Again, flurried whisperings passed around him. Petworth met Lord Reginald's stern look as the younger lord leaned forward.

"Lord Mallory," he asked with careful courtesy. "How long hast thou been in the north tower?" Mallory understood. His brows flickered at the change of voice. Aye. It was the one called Lord Reginald.

"Since I was born . . . my lord." During the brief pause that followed, Lord Reginald allowed his face to reveal the combination of outrage and pity he felt.

"Thy age?" he asked.

"I do not understand." Mallory caught the word "simpleton" amid the mutterings around him.

"How many years hast thou?" Lord Reginald rephrased the question.

"I do not know . . . my lord." Mallory said quietly, feeling confusion, and a strange, ignorant helplessness.

"So," Lord Petworth said slowly as Lord Reginald sat back in his chair. "The heir to Wallenford is a simple blind boy!" Lord Reginald shot him a dark look.

"Aye. But he is the heir!" he retorted with clear emphasis.

"Apparently!" Petworth shrugged with declining interest and reached for his wine cup as one of the large hunting dogs in the hall padded up to the pale boy before them.

Mallory heard the differently cadenced, lighter footfall approaching. He cocked his head toward it, heard panting sounds, and sniffed a strange, rancid odour. Carefully, he held out a hand toward the sounds. Something wet and supple flicked across the back of it, then he heard a low, wary growl. Startled, he dropped to his knees and held out both hands as he recognized that this was another kind of creature from men. It growled again, more clearly, as his fingers found the thick, coarse pelt that covered a form he could not have imagined. Four legs . . . And he smiled recognition. Aye. It was a wolf friend.

He put back his head and howled a slow song of loneliness.

The panting stopped, and the creature settled beside him to howl its response.

Some crossed themselves. Lord Petworth sat in grim and frigid silence. Lord Reginald's face paled to an ashen hue. And, as the last echoes of the howling died away he got to his feet and faced Lord Fulk.

"Ghosts and devils, my lord?" he said harshly. "The tales of this fief are little to be wondered at! It is a mad place, and every soul within it, lunatic, or possessed!"

"Aye, my lord. Just so!" Lord Fulk said coldly, his narrowed gaze still fixed upon the blind boy who knelt in the midst of them, stroking the savage mastiff. "There is no fit lord for this demesne, and, for that, I do claim it for the King's interest!"

Lord Reginald looked at him without answering. Aye, he thought. Petworth was welcome to it. For himself, he was eager to make the departure he had intended two days hence. He strode from the great hall.

Sir Geoffrey, still standing near the boy, watched the groping hands that explored the great hunting dog. His mouth tightened in hard pity for the loneliness that was apparent to him. For the years of imprisonment, and for the helpless deformity of blindness. He bent to gently touch young Mallory's arm.

"Come with me, my lord," he said very softly. The boy rose. Sir Geoffrey took his arm and led him away. It was clear enough to him that the lad would find no friends in his own house.

# SEVEN

For all the intense and, hereto, unresolvable desire with which he had longed to know the world, Mallory now found himself overwhelmed by it. His confusion was near continual in the perpetual barrage of unknown and unpredictable things that bombarded his senses.

Space was filled with unexpected barriers, and the ground changed texture and level with equal unreliability. He tripped and fell often in his efforts to find his way about, and there was only the reassurance of the man called Sir Geoffrey, who brought him food and mead, and guided him to sleep in a soft, dry place, who quietly proffered information in his gruff voice, and who was not reluctant to touch Mallory's outstretched hand.

He began to understand that the myriad other people in this maze of stone and space were not so willing for a like contact. Nor did they have his own difficulties in getting about. Their footsteps were assured, and sometimes useful to follow.

And, when he fell, he learned to recognize the chuckles that were directed toward him, began to understand the mocking intonations that underlay the addressing of him as "my lord."

At first, he asked questions, encouraged by Sir Geoffrey. But then, he grew silent, for, with others, his questions were not welcomed.

Only the great wolf creatures in the vast space of the great hall greeted him without reservation, and welcomed his touch with wagging tails and long wet tongues.

Mallory sat in rigid and attentive silence through the grim and bewildering process of his father's trial. He flinched at each easily recognized shriek or roar that came from Lord Robert, always at the same, unknowable distance from him. He cringed as well, at the venomous accusations of witchcraft

and sorcerous misdeeds that his father's hoarse, loud voice
hurled in his direction, blame for wrongs he did not understand at all.

There was only the reassurance of Sir Geoffrey's hand
upon his shoulder, and the quietly murmured,

"Pay no heed, lad. He raves. . . ."

And then, there was the strange, howling terror that followed Lord Petworth's summary order that Robert De
Cheiney be put to death.

Puzzled, he likewise flinched at the higher pitched, sing-
song, disconnected cries of one addressed as Lady Edwina.
His mother, who was ordered to be removed to a convent to be
cared for until her demise. She was mad, Lord Petworth declared. His father was mad.

And himself . . . ? Was he mad as well?

Sir Geoffrey vanished abruptly. Nor did he reappear. Mallory discovered that there was no one who would help him get
about. No one who would show him how to find food and
water, or where to sleep.

Leery of the falls that punished his explorations, Mallory
groped his way about in an effort to find some manner of
order in the spaces and structure of the world about him. He
struggled constantly with confusion. And, at first, eagerly
stretched out a hand toward the other people that moved to
within a reasonable proximity. Then, he learned not to reach
toward them punished by their increasingly apparent scorn,
fear, or distaste for him.

It was a new and bitter pain to find himself so isolated
within the midst of so much abundance.

Nor, did he understand that his presence was tolerable only
for the confidence his helplessness instilled.

Only the wolf creatures, the dogs, as they were called,
seemed willing to seek him out. To touch. And, in the same
manner as the dogs, he learned to scent out, to grope for
scraps that were flung from the great tables of feasting men
and women in the great hall each evening. Likewise, increasingly reluctant to leave the friendly company of the dogs, he
found a corner to huddle in when all went quiet, his sleep
becoming a tenuous and apprehensive thing.

Sometimes, he would sit and quietly sing the wolf songs
that talked of feelings he could not otherwise express. The

dogs understood. Sometimes, they came to sit nearby and howl as well.

Gradually, space acquired order, definition that was a combination of direction and form. Memory made it possible to find his way within the few parts of the castle that he explored. Gradually, as well, he learned from listening to the conversations of men. He began to understand much more of human language and meaning, the embellishment and significance of variable tonal inflections, and the expression of emotions.

And more . . . Mallory gradually discovered something of the business of daily life, the ranks and duties of men all ruled by the decisive leadership of Lord Fulk of Petworth, who had dominion over the kingdom in which he groped about.

Mallory discovered the entry way that led to places unconfined by stone. He learned to feel the undiverted flow of the wind against his face, his body, the ground that was unpredictably dry, or hard, or wet soft and clinging, and the air that varied in temperature, and was, not infrequently, filled with the tumbling drops of rainfall.

He listened to other creature sounds. There were the frenetic, piercing cackles of elusive fowl. The grunts of other, bare-skinned, slightly hairy beasts called hogs, and the whinnied calls and snorts, the sharp clopping rhythms of the great beasts called horses.

He groped his way through myriad new textures. Dust, and mud. Great stacks of straw, or sweet-smelling hay. Other things—a hot place where fire roared and metal clanged and men worked.

He found, as well, the place where the horses stood when they were not in use. Vast and quiet, he found a common bond with them, discovering a kindred sensitivity to sound and touch. He wondered at the men who rode upon their backs to be carried through, he suspected, even greater spaces. And, one day, he attempted to do the same.

Muscles of unimaginable strength rippled under him, against his legs, and Mallory smiled at the feel of the warm, shaggy body.

"What doest thou there, boy?" a voice demanded angrily. Mallory flinched, and at once clutched the long hair that came from the horse's neck. Another voice laughed.

"Dost thou not see, Wulf? It is plain enough! This mad lordling would ride my lord's war stallion!"

" 'Tis impertinence!" the first voice gritted. Mallory cried out as hands jerked him from the animal and flung him through the air to land with a hard thud against the ground.

Something struck him in the ribs, and Mallory curled up in pure instinct.

"Get out of here, thou mad thing!" The voice was another sort of blow. Again, a foot thudded into him, and Mallory groped, then began to crawl away. "Leave the horses be. They are not for the likes of thee!" Another blow . . . and Mallory scurried away from the kicks, uncaring of direction. He picked himself up, feeling the mud beneath his hands and knees, and ran across an open space until he collided violently with stone. Winded, he gasped and crumpled to lie against some unknown wall, hearing the voices that pursued him, that gathered into a populous and venomously angry force about him.

"Vile and unnatural thing!"

"A pox on thee!" He held out a hand and turned his face toward them.

"Beware, Wulf. His eyes! He may send the plague upon thee!" Something foul smelling and slimy hit the side of his head.

"Aye, so. The lord should have rid us of him as well!" There was a bellowing of multiple agreement, and another piece of refuse struck his left leg. Mallory collected himself, and stood, reflexively setting his hands before his face.

"Let us rid ourselves of him then!"

"Aye! He is a curse upon us." More debris pelted him, and Mallory shifted to grope along the wall. Something hard struck him. A stone—like the shouts of contempt, of loathing. It was like his father all over again.

Mallory groped his way along the wall, seeking only retreat from the unbearable deluge of verbal and literal refuse. Pain welled up in him, and he screamed with violent, incoherent protest as the wall fell away from his hand. It was a corner—and he dropped to his knees to crawl uncaring around it into whatever space lay beyond.

As quickly and violently as it had begun, the bombardment ceased. He could not know that his own agonized reaction had appeased them by revealing his terror. Mallory huddled against the wall, feeling the rain that fell from the air to touch, then penetrate his clothing. It muffled other noises into muted unrecognizability as well.

"Why . . . ?" he whispered to the cold stone beside him. "I do no harm . . . Surely, I do no harm . . . ?" He gave up trying to move and hunched further to bury his head in his arms. Breath came in uneven, painful gasps of feeling. Futile, for there were none to help.

After a time, as the rain seeped through his clothing with cold insistence, Mallory recovered himself somewhat. He straightened and groped along the wall again. Direction, space, had become entirely unknown, and he knew he was lost. He could not perceive how to find his way back to the shelter of the great hall, to food, and the friendship of the dogs. Not knowing what else to do, he continued, allowing the wall with its bewildering shifts in direction, to guide him until—his foot touched a different texture. He bent, and explored with his fingertips, puzzled by the wooden beams. He groped further to discover that this new ground fell away suddenly to one side of him. And, below, he heard the sounds of water.

He straightened to listen, entirely at a loss, then stiffened at the sound of an approaching horse. He froze, then heard the impatient bark of a man's voice from the animal's back.

An instant later, the beast thudded past him with over-whelming force, and a foot struck his shoulder.

"Get out of the way!" The order was unneccessary as Mallory found himself catapulted aside. He clawed at the air and fell forward on the wooden ground, his head and shoulder over the precipitous edge. He gasped, and picked himself up, then crawled forward, keeping his hands in front of him until they sank into mud. Then he stood, and tried to understand where he had come to.

Fulk, Lord of Petworth, drew rein abruptly, and swung himself from his palfrey, relinquishing it to the care of a groomsman. Then, adjusting the hood of his cloak, he swung about to stare at the drawbridge with his mouth drawn in a taut line.

Mallory De Cheiney continued to grope his way like a blind calf, across the drawbridge, then, after a hesitation, onto the trail that led away from the castle. Lord Fulk's eyes gleamed. Aye. Let the boy be lost, he thought. It were better so. The wolves would find him soon enough. Finish him. The last of the cursed De Cheineys would be dispatched from the world. His expression grew briefly grimmer as he thought of his sister. Lady Edwina deserved some compensation for the madness her lord and son had driven her to.

He turned and strode briskly toward the keep. In a fairly short period of time, he knew, he would be Earl of Wallenford as well as Lord of Petworth and Midhurst.

Mallory wandered on through the rain that continued to fall all about him, smothering other sounds. Now chilled and beginning to shiver, his brittle cold hands searched for the barriers that normally barred and directed his way, his feet stumbled across ground that had become remarkably irregular.

But, there were no barriers. And the ground seemed to fall steadily away before him, then, after a time, to rise again. The muddy track he pursued faded into a new kind of footing, a soft ground that was covered in a thick layer of the long-stemmed, upstanding plants that smelled much like the fodder horses ate.

Mallory paused and shivered violently, pulled his cloak tighter about him, and continued in silence. He understood the futility of calling for aid. He tripped over something that scratched at his legs and fell into what felt like a tangle of twigs such as were used to start the hearth fire in the great hall. After a brief struggle, he picked himself up, took a few more, tentative steps, and stopped, his head cocked to listen.

Above and before him he heard unfamiliar rustling sounds. And creakings. Dense . . . extending far away . . . He stepped forward, his hand out before him, and touched something rough and unyielding. He stopped, puzzled, and explored the erratic, abrasive textures of a tall, unevenly round column. He felt the quality of the rain change as larger drops splattered down from above.

Uncertain as to how he knew, Mallory sensed that the great thing before him lived. Very slowly, he shifted away from it and took more cautious steps. He found another, rough column. Then another.

Now, the rustling noises surrounded him, moved above his head. The wind whistled, and rain tumbled differently from the air

The columns increased in number, and Mallory began to discover their remarkable individuality. No two were alike, in girth, or texture, or straightness. Some even branched out, splaying upward into the rustling sounds overhead.

After a long time, Mallory found another, very large column where the rain did not seem to descend with so much force. He knelt slowly in the grass at the base of it, and wrapping himself as tightly as possible into his cloak, he huddled into the small amount of shelter it provided.

Terror and bewildered helplessness drove him to violent shivering as much as did the drenching cold. He bowed his head and hunkered over. He had no idea what else to do, where else to attempt to go. And so, he stayed there.

After a long time, the wind died away. Mallory discovered that his body told him more about the duration of his stay under the rustling column than anything else. His stomach snarled with hunger. And he was exhausted.

Still, he did not leave. Space had become chaos, and he heard no human noises at all.

But, as the rustling sounds died away, the air grew still, and the rain gradually ceased falling, he found other things to listen to. Space extended itself. Sometimes, he detected a sequence of scurrying sounds, or the occasional chirrup of a bird. Random drops of water fell heavily as though the rain had been caught and held by something overhead.

Then, far away, he heard a clear and familiar call. Mallory stiffened alertly. Again. And he pulled to his knees and howled his answer. Friends.

Another voice answered, echoing through space in melancholy communion, and Mallory began to sing as the wolves did. Mayhap, he hoped of a sudden, they would find him.

He howled exquisitely poised scales and welcomed the reply that was closer this time. Then, he fell abruptly silent as he heard another kind of stealthy rustling. Padding footsteps passed close by. There were heavy familiar panting sounds. He smiled and held out his hand. Something growled low in its throat. Another creature did likewise, and another. Mallory held out both hands and made the friendly wuff sound he had learned from the dogs, then wondered why they did not come closer.

He started as he heard a louder growl, then a menacing snarl. Of a sudden, he knew these were not like his friends of the hall. He stood up and pressed his back against the tree, and listened as they circled about him with low, appraising snarls, their appetite apparent now. These were the wolves that Merry had told him about, that he had heard others speak of. The wolves of the great forest that did not fear to eat human meat.

He shuddered helplessly.

# EIGHT

"Get thee hence!" A deep voice boomed resonant thunder nearby, and Mallory cringed in startled terror. In an instant, the beasts closing about him ceased their growls and snarls, and began to whine humility. He flinched as he heard them pad away, making soft, shuffling footfalls that vanished rapidly. Then, his nostrils flared as he sensed another unknown presence, and felt the clear impression of power that was coming from some place close by.

"The wolves will not harm thee now," the same voice rumbled through the air, though with gentler inflections. Mallory clung to the tree, his body shaking with reaction. Then,

"Aaah . . . !" he cried out as something fluttered down to land in the sod beside him. He jerked away and lost his footing, fell.

"Whooo . . . !" it spoke, and Mallory twisted toward the sheer astonishment of that voice. Reached out, though tentatively, and touched soft, layered covering. Feathers. Such as he had learned to recognize. "Whooo . . ." it said again as if pleased.

"My friend told me of thy presence here, Mallory De Cheiney." The deep voice rumbled toward him again. Mallory shifted to focus his ear.

"Thou know my name?" he ventured. The presence chuckled softly.

"Aye, lad. I do!" Mallory licked his lips, half afraid to ask.

"Who?" he ventured.

"I am Lord Wilfred of Wodensweir," the warlock said, seeing how the boy stiffened further at the title. He had not fared well in the hands of lords. "I am no foe of thine, young Mallory," he said with clear gentleness. "But thy friend, rather." His amber eyes traveled along the thin, bedraggled frame of the silver youth, and his mouth hardened in pity got of his knowledge of the truth in other things. "Do thou come with me," he said, "and I shall bring thee to comfort and safety."

Mallory clambered to his feet and stood, one hand outstretched, but he did not otherwise move. He had little reason for trust, and few expectations of human kind. Fire gleamed in the depths of the warlock's eyes, for so he had contrived it to be. The large bird flapped upwards, then fluttered away into the night, and Mallory cocking his head, followed the sounds of its departure.

"Whoooo . . . ," it murmured once more.

"Do thou come to me now, lad," the deep voice spoke again. Mallory swallowed, took a step, then another, his brows flickering in puzzlement as the power feeling grew stronger. Then another step, and his outstretched fingers were seized with irrefutable strength. He tried to pull back, but the other hand tugged steadily, and his arm seemed to wrench from its socket as he was drawn suddenly into the air. He flailed wildly.

"Be still!" the deep voice said, and then he found himself held within the embrace of a pair of strong arms and drawn to sit half across the back of a horse. "All will be well." The voice was intent on reassurance, as something warm and soft enveloped him.

Then, there was motion. The horse snorted, and made a smooth, buoyantly fluid rhythm as it rushed through the air into the anonymous space beyond—Mallory surrendered.

"What is that?" Rosamund demanded baldly as her father strode into the hall, a large, half-shrouded, indeterminately elongated bundle sprawled in his arms. He directed a look at her, but did not break stride, passing across the tower hall toward the steps that led to the upper regions.

"Mallory De Cheiney," he said, then, before Rosamund could respond. "Do thou bring water for bathing. And food. He hath much need of both!"

"De Cheiney . . . ?" Rosamund began, but her father had already disappeared. She strode after him, taking the stairs two at a time. "But . . . ?"

"This is the son," Lord Wilfred's answer came back at once. "The father is dead!" he continued, striding forward, sweeping down the corridor to veer abruptly, thrusting his way into a little used chamber.

"But they are our foes!" Rosamund called out in indignation as she ran after him, then stopped just inside the door to the chamber. The warlock did not answer, but moved straight to the large, four-posted bed near the center of the room, and bent to lay his burden down upon it. Rosamund scowled and set her fists upon her hips. "They are our foes!" she hissed fiercely. "They raped and murdered my mother who was thy lady!" The warlock looked up to face her.

"For all he bears the name, this De Cheiney is not thine enemy!" he said sternly. One hand moved swiftly, pointing to the hearth place across the chamber, and instantly, a fire burned upon the logs set within it. Then he reached to draw aside the smothering folds of tattered material that covered the human form beneath. Rosamund glowered outrage and confusion, and, again, opened her mouth. But the warlock cut her off. "He is mine, Rosamund," he said quietly. "He is as I have made him, for I wrought changes in him before the time of his birth." She stared. He beckoned. "Look, thou. Do thou not see the white skin and hair that are beyond human purity?" Reluctantly, she moved toward the bed and looked down at the thin, grimy face, at long, snowy, and tangled hair. "He hath not the use of his eyes, my daughter. He is blind!" She looked up to meet her father's gaze.

"But . . . ?"

"Know, likewise, that this boy, this Mallory De Cheiney, hath been mine own instrument of vengeance upon his sire. His very life and blind condition have wrought Lord Robert's destruction in the manner that I wished." Rosamund's expression lost the last traces of anger as she sought to understand.

"He is a De Cheiney for all of that!" She tried, aware of her own ignorance of specifics.

"By name. Yet, he is not as his sire. He hath not the same unbridled lusts or distempered passions. Nay, Rosamund, know that this boy hath been his father's own chief victim."

"Why hast thou brought him here, then?"

The warlock smiled slowly and touched the white brow of the unconscious youth.

"His purpose is not yet fulfilled," he said softly. "Go now, as I bade thee, and fetch that which I instructed thee to bring that I may tend the lad before the sleeping spell I put upon him completes its course!" Rosamund frowned as she spun on her heel and strode away.

\* \* \*

Mallory stirred into astonished awareness. Shifted. Never had he felt such softness as that on which he lay, nor yet, such liquid-seeming smoothness as that which covered his lower body. He felt his eyelids open, and moved his fingertips to touch the wonder of the materials that surrounded him. Silken furs and . . .

"Aaah. Thou art awake at last!" Mallory recognized a woman's voice in the different timbre of the declaration.

"Aye . . ." he whispered hesitantly and sat up cautiously, discovering that he was devoid of his precious clothes.

"I have food for thee," the woman's voice sounded briskly. His stomach lurched and clenched at the mere mention of food, and he felt something settle on the covers that lay across his legs. He sniffed, then groped carefully, discovering a tray from which emanated savoury odours. His hands trembled as his fingers found soft bread, roasted meat, a goblet of milk, and a pair of apples.

He ate with savage hunger, Rosamund noted. But, it was not surprising for he looked more like a starved white cubling than anything else. She glanced toward her father, now comfortably reclined in a large chair near the fire. His smile revealed him to be lightly amused, the fingers of one hand idly toying with the fur at the nape of the young black wolf by his feet. Her own stern face revealed her doubts.

Mallory stiffened when she removed the tray, cocking his head to follow her movements. Then he sat very still, hearing something else as the young wolf got up from its place by Lord Wilfred's feet, stretched, and padded to the bed. Mallory turned toward the panting sounds that were at once familiar. He groped and found rough fur as the wolf pup raised itself on its hind legs and sniffed at him. Rosamund stared in surprise, for she had always found the pup to be remote. Mallory smiled as the young pup jumped onto the bed and began licking at him, its whole body wiggling in time with the enthusiastic thumping of its tail. He leaned forward to embrace the animal.

Rosamund looked at her father, but his smile had widened.

"The wolf is thine, my lord Mallory," he said quietly. Rosamund stared, and the young man in the bed froze in astonishment, recognizing the voice of the one called Lord Wilfred. But . . . ?

"How so?" he asked hesitantly. The warlock stood and moved slowly toward the bed.

"He hath chosen thee. The creatures of my domain are free to choose their own lords," he said with deep calm. "Do rest now, lad, and know thou hast naught to fear here. This chamber is for thy use, as is all it contains. And, there will be much more for thee beside."

Mallory poised in absolute stillness, even to the hand that lay along the wolf's supple back, as it settled down beside him.

"Why?" he whispered after a moment. "I am blind—Mayhap, I am mad . . ." The deep voice that came from that strangely palpable presence chuckled a little.

"Mad thou art not, my lord Mallory!" The answer came with smooth, even tangible assurance. "As to the blindness, 'tis of little consequence, for there are realms to perceive that may not be viewed with eyes. Thou wilt understand in time, as I will reveal to thee. Come, daughter!" The last was more firmly uttered, and Mallory listened to the pair of footsteps that signalled the woman's disappearance, the fading of presence that was accompanied by only a whispered rustling.

He sat still for a long time, feeling the wolfling doze beside him. He heard the crackling hearth fire from some distance away, and felt the shadows of its warmth as exhaustion seeped down through the core of him like another ague of chill. Finally, he sank back into the embrace of the softness all about him. For the moment, nothing could have greater importance.

And, in the hall below, the warlock settled into the great chair he commonly used. He sipped wine from a jewel-encrusted goblet, and extracted a crystal sphere from the pouch at his waist. He nestled it into the palm of one hand, and stared into it, watching the boy in the chamber above— and the daughter who ate in silence at the table behind him. He smiled at the wary resentment he saw in her.

It was as a dream entirely apart from all he knew of life, to explore and feel the comforts that now surrounded him, and filled his waking hours. Mallory wondered at the abundance of smooth-textured, finely made garments that he was given for clothing, at the delectable choices of food that were always available to him. And, at the quiet courtesy that Lord Wilfred consistently offered him.

He felt the aches and bruises fade from his flesh, and found a sweetly welcomed pleasure in the growing energy and well-being of his body as flesh began to cover his bones.

There was pleasure also, in the friendship of the young wolf that rarely left his side. And Mallory learned new confidence in Lord Wilfred's deep and wondrous voice that spoke to him with frequent and unceasing patience.

He listened to the wisdom that taught him new ways to utilize his hands and ears, and how to develop further that tactile sense of space that was the means by which he learned his way, firstly about the chamber in which he dwelt, then other places. The corridors and steps of the tower. The great hall that was below.

He listened eagerly to the voice that talked to him of the forest world that lay beyond the tower, a voice ingeniously able to describe in terms of the sensations and perceptions that were available to him, without adding the confusion of meaningless light and colour and remote shapes that he could not understand. And he began to practise the suggestion that he learn to feel and utilize the knowledge in the movements of the young wolf as it padded along beside him.

Space began to acquire balance and form, to have order and design—began, despite its convoluted vastness, to be negotiable. Mallory began to understand those other qualities of his hearing and touch that informed him beyond the overt meanings of sounds and silences, about the shapes of the spaces through which he moved.

His confidence grew with his vigour as he learned to place his trust in Lord Wilfred, feeling the beneficence that flowed toward him through the strangely palpable force of presence that accompanied that deep-voiced man. Through the reliability of the truths that Lord Wilfred told him, Mallory gradually lost the hesitancy of fear, and the perpetual expectation of punishment that was, so far, his lot with men.

But, Lord Wilfred's daughter, the lady Rosamund, was another matter. Mallory always stiffened in her presence, attentive to the edged courtesy, the brusqueness that marked her addresses to him. He felt the anger, that was somehow instigated by his presence, that qualified her speech and actions. She did not have her father's smooth, and timeless patience. She was a volatile brew of tempestuous feelings, like the roaring of the hearth fire, or the winds that howled bitterly around the tower. Her walking made bold sounds across the stone, and she was fierce. But, Mallory came to understand, unlike his own father's unrestrained belligerence, the lady Rosamund's ferocity was tightly restrained on a leash of self-control.

Such attributes brought him to know a great awe of her. Yet, for the sum of his new life, he was well content in the growing peace within him and the safety of Lord Wilfred's generosity. But, as with all things, that, too, changed.

"Now, my young lord Mallory," Lord Wilfred's voice broke across the serenity of the leisurely consumption of the evening meal in the great hall, "it is time for thee to undertake to learn those things that will make a man of thee!" Mallory set down the sweet bread he had been about to bite into to listen. He heard a grunt from Lady Rosamund. Lord Wilfred continued. "There are skills that are essential for life in the world of men. Thou must learn the same. How to hunt. How to run, and ride a horse. How to wield sword and lance, and to have all the skills of war."

"My lord . . . ?" Mallory breathed. Rosamund abandoned her own meal to stare her surprise at her father.

"My daughter," Lord Wilfred said firmly, "shall teach thee all that is needful!" Mallory swallowed. Rosamund's eyes widened further, then narrowed as she began to glower at her sire.

"But Lord Mallory is as helpless as a babe!" she voiced her contempt. Lord Wilfred smiled.

"He is not a vessel to be molded by my teaching alone, daughter. He is a man, and must come to his own pride in the same!" Rosamund shot a look of acute dislike toward the death-pale youth who sat among them with such obviously simpleton acceptance. De Cheiney—who occupied so much of her father's time of late.

"Thou wilt do this, Rosamund," Lord Wilfred said very softly. She scowled the more fiercely for the knowledge that she would obey. He addressed Mallory. "Let not my daughter's temper dismay thee, Lord Mallory! She is a warrior of profound ability, and fierce in such things, as I have taught her to be!"

"Aye, my lord." Mallory's response reflected the unqualified obedience of his newfound trust. Rosamund's lips curled in even greater contempt.

Mallory soon learned the full scope of Rosamund's fearsome temper. She goaded him at every opportunity as she impelled him to the confusion of mastering unknown things.

"Puling boy!" she sneered. "Cripple!" And, "De Cheiney pig!"

She made him run beside her through the uneven and unpredictable terrain of the forest that surrounded the tower. Run, until his lungs heaved to bursting. Run, despite the relentless tripping and bruising falls that attended his efforts. And when he fell, she snarled at him and goaded him to rise and try again.

She hit out at him, taunting him into an effort to do the same to her, yet, ever jumping lightly out of reach as he groped about in an effort to do likewise. She put the sharp steel of sword and dagger into his hands, and ordered him to strike using the targets of her voice, and the shield she carried, prodding, pricking at him with her own weapons, even nicking to draw forth the blood beneath his skin, until, in sheer self-defense, he was forced to exert all effort to counter her blows.

And she put him on the back of the silver horse, then set the animal to gallop away with him, veering sharply between the trees that wove the forest together into myriad twisting paths.

Those falls were the hardest. Mallory was catapulted through the air to slam into the ground so hard as to jar the wind from his body. And there were always new aches and bruises that tormented him for days.

Rosamund, whose insults were threaded with cords of instruction to attend. He listened, still obedient to Lord Wilfred's wish, and ignored the rest.

Then, he began to learn how to cling to the horse, to feel the warnings of movements just to come in the clenching of the muscles against his backside and between his legs, to feel and flow with the abrupt and bewildering changes of direction and speed. And, of a sudden, it seemed that the shattering falls occurred less often.

But Rosamund would get astride the horse and make him run beside the pair of them until he reeled, then fell to lie still from exhaustion—lungs heaving as he listened to more of the relentless barrage of insults she hurled at him.

And, finally, he began to feel angry in return.

It was enough to impel him to pick himself up no matter how he longed for reprieve, to begin it all again.

"Weakling! Pah! I do declare thou art a feeble maiden fit

for naught save to sit and broider garments!" Mallory clenched his teeth and kept his bitter learned silence.

Then she put a longbow in his hand, taught him how to string it, set an arrow, and shoot toward some elusive, barely audible target. And, she added the weight of chain-mail hauberk and leggings to his body, then began it all again.

She thrust him, fully clothed, into fast-moving streams of tugging, swirling water, and laughed scornfully at his struggles.

"Thou hast the look of a drowning rat!" she sneered as he choked and floundered, struggled to find the bank where he could crawl out and retch out the water he had swallowed, then she pushed him back in again.

She made him run through the heavy, treacherous mud of autumn and spring, and, in winter, pelted him with hard snowballs as he floundered through deep drifts, skidded across icy places, and in summer brought him to reel with heat, his flesh sheathed in sweat.

She set him upon the horse with shield and lance to make him charge at objects that, when they were struck, sent forceful pain reverberating through his body and hurled him out of the saddle, until he learned to grip and bend, to take the blows, and cleave to the saddle.

Likewise, she taunted him to find his own food and mocked the voracious appetite he had developed. She laughed when he clothed himself incorrectly, with a garment slipped on backwards, inside out. She called him a fool, and much, much worse.

Of the warlock's presence, there was very little. Lord Wilfred kept to himself, slipping quietly aside to watch them in his own way. He was well pleased in what he saw, in the strange and intimate weaving of hate and respect and trust that developed between his daughter and the young man who was, after a fashion . . . his son. It was a relationship that was becoming complex, an intricately interwoven balance of every emotional element. A bond—he smiled—of far greater power than either of them knew.

Time, the warlock understood, brings all things to fruition.

In many respects, Mallory was unaware of the changes that were occurring in him. He had become, in truth, a young man. Taller now than Rosamund by more than a head, his body had filled out from the scarecrow proportions it had revealed when Lord Wilfred had brought him to the tower. Now he was sleek and hard, muscular and strong. His white skin gleamed with the pristine combination of cleanliness and good health. His hair, now trimmed to shoulder length, sparkled silver in the sunlight.

His face had lost the gaunt, wraith-like appearance of his boyhood, and had changed to combine refinement and masculine symmetry. His nose was straight with flaring, flexible nostrils. His jaw was grown square and strong. His lips curved neatly with peculiarly mobile sensitivity, and his eyes gleamed with the red fire of new courage and self-control, and aimed boldly into the darkness of his inability to see.

He walked with confidence, the great black wolf, now long full-grown, a monstrous beast ever at his side. For without being aware of the consequences of relentless struggle, Mallory had learned to feel the world about him. He had learned to hear and identify myriad sounds with ears of uncanny keenness, to scent other particularities with a clarity that bloodhounds could well desire.

And he had learned to sense densities and spaces around him through skin and fingertips capable of incredible tactile sensitivity.

Mallory De Cheiney had moved beyond any need of sight.

# NINE

1165 A.D.

"Whyfore dost thou continue to press this match upon me?" Reginald De Beauvais glared exasperation at his diminutive mother. "I want none of it! I have no wish to bind myself to Lord Fulk's daughter!" The Dowager Countess looked steadily back at the son who did not, even slightly, intimidate her. She shrugged.

"It is sound politics," she pursued firmly. "The Earl of Wallenford stands high in the King's favour for the peace and prosperity he hath brought to his fiefs, and such an alliance would be beneficial!"

"Pah!" Lord Reginald snorted. "He does no more than any good lord to his duty!" he said with asperity. "I do not wish to ally myself with Lord Fulk's ambitions, for I consider that he casts his eye upon my fiefs! Why else would he wish to wed me to his daughter and declare me son?" The Countess made a discarding shrug with one shoulder.

"'Tis a match that would strengthen Arundel...," she began.

"Would it so?" Lord Reginald countered at once. "Or, dost thou forget the ease with which he dispatched the De Cheineys?"

"But they were mad. Possessed of demons!"

"Mayhap. But, were I wed to the lady Julia, and were my life to be lost—do thou think upon how neatly Arundel would tumble into his hand! And none could contest his claim!" Her eyes widened, making her face seem youthful in contrast to the truth of her forty-three years.

"Never so!" she began. He nodded vehemently.

"Aye. There is talk!" he said. "Nay, lady mother, my safety lies along another course. I know that Lord Fulk's heir is to wed Sussex's daughter, and by that alone, his demesne becomes unwonted vast. I will not add to his power. An accident is not so difficult to manage. It has happened before!"

"But, De Cheiney's heir was mad! Lord Fulk did attend to him." Lady Arundel probed slowly. Lord Reginald shook his head.

"On that, I have thought long and hard, and am come to be convinced otherwise. The boy was blind, and his flesh bleached to the hue of a white horse. But mad? I know only that he was imprisoned by his sire from infancy and subject to the unending abuse of the same. I do consider that it was strange care that permitted him to wander so as to be consumed by wolves." She kept silent as he paused.

"Nay, Mother," Lord Reginald went on more softly. "I will have no part of Wallenford's schemes, nor will I be bound to his fiefs in any way, for, despite his rule, the tales still come from that place of mysterious things, of magical creatures in the forests thereabouts. It is a strange fief, Wallenford."

"And ancient," Lady Arundel offered in a like tone. Then, she sighed. "I do but consider thou art no longer in thy first youth. It is time to be about the begetting of an heir!" Lord Reginald shook his head.

"Twenty-seven is hardly dotage, Mother!" he retorted.

Mallory cocked his head to listen as he lowered the bow. He heard the animal cry out, flounder, then tumble to the accompaniment of the rustling of disrupted undergrowth, to lie unmoving some distance ahead and a little to his left. Rosamund's fingers clawed at his arm to drag him forward, and the wolf, pacing against his leg, told him by its movements, the nature of the ground before him.

"It was a good strike. An instant kill!" Mallory did not comment on his surprise at this unqualified praise, but floundered after her, then knelt, sniffed, when she stopped, to grope with his fingertips. Blood odours—and his fingertips touched the warm hide of the dead deer.

Tracing his fingers along it, he felt the textures of its stillness, and his own disappointment as its size revealed it to have been but little more than half grown. He found the place behind its front leg where his arrow had penetrated to pierce its heart, then he stood abruptly and stepped back.

"This is thy kill," Rosamund said roughly. "And, therefore, it falls to thee to do the butchering of it!" He heard her move, compacting herself beside the venison, her dagger slipping from its sheath with a light hiss. Mallory continued to stand very still, caught up in the realization that he had never actually killed anything before, feeling the strangely sickened sensation in his middle that was expression of his distaste for it. It was no easement at all to know that the venison was to be eaten.

"Do thou help me then, and cease standing about like a useless dolt!" he heard Rosamund's annoyance clearly. "Or do thou fear to bloody thy dainty fingers?" she added with a sneer. Mallory frowned as temper flared within him. His muscles tightened and he turned abruptly away.

"Puling boy!" he heard her snarl. The wolf beside him whined eagerly, welcoming the scents of blood and raw meat as Rosamund's blade slit open the animal's belly. Mallory's nostrils quivered as he smelled it, too.

Something slimy hot and vile-smelling struck the side of his head and shoulder. The wolf snapped at it as it slithered down his body to the earth beneath his feet.

"Thou art fit for naught save the liver, Mallory!" he recognized Rosamund's eternal contempt. His fists clenched and he turned back in her direction.

"Enough!" he roared. Rosamund, completely taken aback, stared at him in blank astonishment. Mallory never raged or shouted.

"Then, do thou help me!" she demanded again, watching as the frown between his silver brows deepened. "Be a man!" she added, "and not so delicate in thy sensibilities!"

"I am a man!" Mallory roared, again, surprising her. "I am not a monster who takes pleasure in the destruction of a creature that would have, in no way, harmed me! It was a pretty thing. And alive! As thou art. As I am. Have some respect for that!" In an instant, he turned and strode away, one hand held before him, the other holding his longbow. The wolf, half of the liver consumed, the other half in its jaws, padded inevitably at his side.

Crouched beside the carcass with her dagger still poised, in her hand, Rosamund stared after him in undiminished amazement. Only after he had completely disappeared did she return to the rest of the butchering that awaited her.

She frowned as she finished disembowelling the animal. Respect for each and every living thing in the forest had always been of profound importance. Ever since her memory had begun, it was an essential part of her life with her father. But—her eyes narrowed thoughtfully, but, her habit of baiting

Mallory? Aye. Had gone beyond such consideration. Had become, she was startled to recognize, purely a habit that would employ any means to goad.

Another thing that left her feeling peculiarly disoriented came from Mallory himself. Of a sudden, he had seemed so large as he stood there roaring at her. So powerful. And, it seemed that he had been no taller than herself until—aye—now. And more, she realized. He had walked away from her with sure-footed grace, his need for the guidance of the wolf, entirely transparent. He had not stumbled, or, flailingly groped with his arms.

Mallory De Cheiney, Rosamund realized with deeper shock, had become something different.

Shouldering the carcass, she rose to her feet and began to walk back to the tower by herself, her features composed into an uneasy frown.

That evening as they lingered over the meal of fruit and meat, and the bread that she had taught Mallory to make, Rosamund found herself watching him again. Found herself, strangely, biting back the taunts and insults that collected like creatures beneath her tongue.

Mallory kept a white ear turned in her direction, and, once or twice, she saw a puzzled frown cross his face. He said nothing, and she noticed that he carefully avoided eating any of the venison he had killed, supping on nuts and apples and bread instead. Even then, she did not voice the scathing comment that moved against her lips. And, when the meal had concluded, she continued to watch as Mallory got to his feet, bowed with unerring accuracy toward herself and Lord Wilfred, then left the hall to disappear up the steps that led to his chamber.

Rosamund scowled as her father's gaze followed Mallory's departure, seeing the satisfied half-smile that lurked about the corners of his mouth.

"Thou art greatly pleased by something, my lord!" she commented sourly. Lord Wilfred continued to cradle his wine goblet between gnarled old hands, but his eyes found and locked with hers.

"Mallory begins to be a man, my daughter!" he said softly.

"Pah!" she muttered.

"Nay, child. I caution thee. He is not the same boy thou hast ruled with such wilful tyranny these past five years!"

"Hmmmph!" Rosamund grunted belligerently, frowning more deeply. Lord Wilifred shook his head.

"Consider, Rosamund," he continued. "He does whatsoever thou set him to do. Nor does he complain for all thou hast cost him uncountable pricks and bruises and tumbles, but strives with wonderful persistence to meet any challenge that thou choose to require of him." Rosamund stared warily at her father. Lord Wilfred leaned back in his seat. "Thou hast tormented him with his blindness, and all manner of attendant difficulties. And now, he hath come to rule the same," he finished quietly.

"Dost thou favour him—this De Cheiney—so well then?" she asked after some moments of silence. The warlock rose to his feet, his look changing a little, much in the manner of a reflection on a pool of water when a ripple passes across it.

"Should I not?" he said softly. "I could have contrived no better for a son."

"A son?" Rosamund was dumbfounded. "His father murdered my mother, and thou call him, son? Thou cannot think to favour him so!" She half-rose from her seat, but the warlock grew taller, straightened, shifting his form into its more youthful interpretation. His amber eyes gleamed sternly as they met her own.

"Know now, as thou hast not been permitted before, Rosamund, that we of the Fairie are most fastidious in our begetting!" His voice deepened to reflect the tones and promise of distant thunder. "Thou, my daughter, art a blend of my blood and thy mother's humanity. Thou art the child of both my heart and my loins, and all that I contrive is to favour thy interests. Do thou remember that!

"I am the last High Warlock, the last of my kind endowed with full powers. And, I am old. I grow weary." With that, he turned and strode away toward the steps that led to the upper regions of the tower. Just before he disappeared, he spun about and faced her again.

"I have noted," he said with glee, his eyes glinting mischief, "how many times in the course of these past months Mallory hath been well able to best thee in thy contests of arms! Yet, he hath chosen not to do so!" His chuckle fluttered across the hall for some time after he had vanished.

Rosamund clenched her fists and glowered outrage. Mallory could not best her! Nay! He could not . . .? Yet she knew better than to refute her father. Nay. The very thought that he could condescend to allow her to win.

She seized the wine flagon and strode from the hall herself. A moment later, she paused outside Mallory's door to point at it, directing it to open in one of the simple little spells she had learned from her father. Then, she passed a hand over the wine, chilling it to near ice, and strode into the chamber.

Mallory stood on the far side of the room, near the fire, washing himself. Rosamund sucked in her breath, for he was stark naked, such as she had never seen him before. He turned his head toward her.

"My lady?" he enquired softly. Rosamund swallowed, her anger jolted by the excruciating awareness of other things.

His white skin gleamed with wonderful continuity. And he was sleek and muscular, broad shouldered, flat bellied—narrow hipped. . . .

Fine hairs sparkled against the surface of his thighs and forearms with the delicacy of silver cobwebs, and the accoutrements of manhood jutted with unselfconscious arrogance at his loins.

Her stomach lurched. He was beautiful—fey.

"My lady?" Mallory asked again, moving to face her, his silver locks sparkling in the firelight as he shifted, one hand reaching out toward her.

Fury seized her again, with greater power for this new awareness that had pounced upon her senses. How dare he . . . ! She strode forward.

"I brought wine for thee!" she said coldly.

"My thanks . . . Aaaaah!" Mallory's body went rigid as the icy wine splattered across him, trickled down to give a peculiar pink discolouration to his pristine skin.

"Think thou to best me at arms?" Rosamund snarled. "Look to thyself on the morrow, De Cheiney! I have not even begun to show thee how to fight!" She spun about and strode from the chamber, the door obediently slamming behind her.

Mallory stood there, entirely dumbfounded. What had he done to cause such distempered virulence in her? For this went beyond the familiar levels of her normal railing.

The wine began to dry, sticking unpleasantly to his skin. Whyfore did she hate him so? He turned back to wash himself all over again. The unhampered sensitivity of his skin had become extremely important to him.

He shook his head, still puzzled.

"Why dost thou not guard me from this witch?" he asked the wolf that lay panting nearby. He heard the animal swallow, the change in its breathing that meant it was grinning at him. "Nay—" he smiled ruefully. "I cannot hate the lady Rosamund either!" he whispered softly.

Mallory had barely begun to draw his own blade when Rosamund's sword slammed against his ribs, fortunately shielded by the heavy mail he wore.

"Look to thyself!" she snarled. "I am thy foe, not thy teacher this time!" Startled, Mallory raised his shield in instinctive response, listened to the sounds of her feet, the hiss of her blade, and the changes in the air that marked specifics of its passage.

Steel rang against steel as his blade countered hers. Then again, and he caught the force of one blow across the triangular surface of his shield. Again, he stopped her weapon with the fingertip of his. Again, and her fury was as venom in the air. Why, he wondered, was her rage so great . . . ?

She broke through his guard to nick his thigh just below the short hauberk. He felt blood and leaped back as he countered her next blow.

"Aye! Do thou retreat, De Cheiney!" she growled. "I will have thy blood for gravy on my meat this night! Thou do well to fear me!" He ducked as he heard the hiss of her sword sweep toward his shoulders, and caught it on his own, deflecting the blow that could have well nigh beheaded him.

Suddenly, he had borne enough. He lunged forward, swinging the end of his shield toward her, catching her somewhere in the middle, and heard a thud as she went sprawling. He dropped his own weapons in the same instant he heard her sword hit the turf, and pounced to find her body and hold it down.

Teeth bit into his wrist. He jerked away. Hands clawed at his face as she squirmed and writhed under him, immensely strong.

"Get off me, oaf!"

"Be thou still!" Mallory roared, his temper fully roused at last. Her fist slammed against his jaw. "Enough, I tell thee!"

He managed to catch her wrists and pinned them back as he flattened himself on top of her to feel her gasping under his greater weight.

She writhed and struggled, and he panted, seeking to re-cover his control.

"Enough, Rosamund!" he said more gently. "I am weary of this ceaseless and ill-tempered goading of thine! I do not wish to fight thee!"

"Aye!" she spat into his cheek. "Thou art squeamish as I saw with the deer yesterday . . . ! Get off me, dolt!"

"Nay!" Mallory shouted back. He shifted as she squirmed with renewed violence and rolled her onto her belly, bringing her wrists behind her to anchor them with one hand. Rosamund screeched and kicked, her temper more inflamed than ever. Then, panting with effort, Mallory hauled her to her feet, and, thrusting her along in front of him, made his way toward the large, spring-fed pool near the tower. "This time . . . ," he vowed breathlessly, "I will cool thy fury!"

Rosamund shrieked again, and struggled violently enough to almost break free. Mallory wrapped his other arm around her body, which was smaller than he had expected, then grunted as her heel connected with his shin to send pain shooting up his leg. He listened to Wolf padding ahead to show the way and felt across the uneven ground—down a slope toward the sounds of water. Then . . .

"Nay! Pig! Whoreson! Bas—tarrddd!" Rosamund screeched as he flung her forward and heard a great splashing. Spluttering sounds . . . Mallory grinned and quickly peeled off the short mail hauberk he wore and plunged recklessly down the last of the bank toward the din. He caught her.

"Naa . . ." He pushed her under, his fingers tangling in the long hair he had never touched before. She thrashed and kicked, and Mallory ignored the blows that bludgeoned his belly and ribs as she came up for air. He pushed her down again.

"So it will be," he shouted at her, "until thy temper is damped, my lady!"

"Pig! Cur! I hate . . ." Again, he submerged her. She spluttered and choked when she came up for air this time.

"Is it enough?" he asked. Her fist caught him across the jaw again, and with his fingers still caught in her hair, he pushed her down, held her there, only hauling her up as he felt her weaken.

This time, she stood more quietly in the water that came to both their waists and coughed violently. Mallory stood very still, waiting. Her dagger caught him unawares as it raked along his ribs, just missed slipping in between them. He caught her wrist and pried the weapon loose, flinging it far onto the bank behind him.

"Witch!" he roared. It was the first invective he had ever used to her. "Be still!" He ducked her head under the water again, and, when he hauled her up this time, he could feel that her strength was gone. She made strangled, choking noises and doubled over weakly, hardly able to breathe.

"Rosamund . . . ?" Suddenly anxious, Mallory picked her up, finding her surprisingly light for so much strength, turned, and climbed out onto the bank. He laid her down in the long grass. She rolled away from him, still hunched and choking painfully. "Rosamund . . . ?" The anxiety in his voice got no response from her. He groped and found her body, abruptly aware of feeling a form that had not been apparent to him before.

There were curves and softness, and swelling protrusions on either side of the place where her heart pounded against her ribs. He felt a sudden startling and unfamiliar hunger to touch, to know. His fingers found the laces of her hauberk and undid them. She did not resist, as he pulled the steel garment away from her and discarded it, but lay there, breathing heavily.

His fingers found her wet, long hair, her face—acknowledged the silken feel of her skin.

"Don't touch me!" she said sullenly, erupting into another fit of coughing. Mallory turned her onto her back and leaned over her.

"Rosamund. I am not thy foe," he said with all the earnest intensity he felt. "Hear me. I fight because thy father wishes it. I bear thy insults and thy scorn for my love of thy father as well. I do all that thou wish of me because it is thy father's wish, not because it is mine own." He heard her silence. Felt the attention that was, at last, focused differently on him. He sighed deeply, awkwardly. "Thy father, Lord Wilfred, hath given me my life. He brought me here to dwell in the midst of so much. He hath been kind to me. He teaches me of things I could not have known, bound as I were, in stone. And he hath brought me to know other things—a content, a joy in life that I had not known possible." Again, he breathed deeply.

"How could it be, my lady Rosamund, that I could ever think to bring harm to my lord's daughter?" He heard her breathing ease, felt her probing silence. "I do not understand why it is that thou art impelled to hate me so?" He spoke the last of it.

Rosamund felt his weight half across her, and remembered the gleaming white form she had seen the night before.

"Thy father raped and murdered my mother." She told him that which was known only by herself and Lord Wilfred. Mallory stiffened, his face changing a little, and her gaze slid down his throat to the open lacings at the front of his tunic, to the skin beneath.

"I am not my father," Mallory said quietly, after a moment. "All I ever knew of him was pain as well. Kicks, and beatings, and curses worse than thou are wont to bestow!" He smiled faintly. Rosamund swallowed, impelled to recall the tattered, skeletal boy he had once been. She could not answer. His fingertips found her face and traced along the side of her jaw, over her eyes, across the furled neatness of one ear, then along the tingling sensitivity of her lips. His smile widened.

"In all this time, I have not known the look of thee," he murmured softly, huskily. Rosamund felt something twist through her, and the tightening of her breasts that accompanied a sudden, heightened awareness of the differences between them. Suddenly, she did not want to move, to get away.

Mallory's breathing deepened strangely as touching her did things inside him, sweet-feeling things, at the base of his belly. His face tightened into a new sobriety.

"Thou art soft to feel, my lady," he heard himself murmur. "Unlike thy will that is more familiar to me!"

"I am strong!" Rosamund muttered defiance. His smile returned.

"Aye. Thou art that!" he acknowledged, his fingers moving lower to find her breast. Her breath came in a rapid gasp at the sensation his touch invoked, her eyes watched the astonishment of his face, the growing intensity, and she felt an urge to reach up and pull him closer.

"Sooo . . . ," he breathed. "A woman is different in more than voice and size!" Mallory felt an exquisite spasming in his loins as he found the peak of her breast and felt it harden against his hand. "Beautiful!" he rasped hoarsely, and leaned closer to touch his mouth to hers, shuddering for the pleasure of it.

* * *

This was delicious beyond belief, Rosamund thought with her own astonishment, abandoning any interest in resisting him to wind her arms about his neck, her fingers through the silver softness of his hair.

Aye. He was sweet to feel as well, she acknowledged as he moaned a little, his breathing quickening. Mallory shivered with the fire that was building in his loins, with the pleasure of her breasts that thrust up against his ribs, and he opened his mouth and tasted her with his tongue.

He moved his lips along her jaw, to her ear, across her throat. Aye. It was an unbearable sweetness, and—suddenly he knew their garments were in the way. He sat up abruptly to unbuckle his belt, and peeled off the wet tunic that clung to skin that starved to feel so much more. Boots and chausses were likewise discarded and he reached to do the same to her, savouring the warm summer breeze that blew over them both to gently rustle the leaves above.

Then he bent to her again. Rosamund moaned and closed her eyes as his hands moved closer, stripping away the last of her attire while his mouth found her breasts. His hands . . . She arched and twisted, and felt herself open to the fingers that moved much lower, and set piercing flames of delight to shiver through her belly.

"Aaaah, Rosamund!" she heard him murmur, and welcomed the encompassing, sleek warmth of his body as he moved over her, between her thighs.

"Mallory . . . !" She clawed fiercely at him, anger surrendered to unbearable hunger. Then he slipped inside and began to move. Breath that groaned as muscles moved hard beneath silken skin, all caught in the rhythm that swept them both away.

It was purest magic. And Mallory cried out as utter pleasure prickled through his body, exploded into waves that shimmered. He heard her cry out as well, clenched so perfectly about him, then felt himself slip down toward a new and exquisite peace such as he had not known before.

He rolled onto his side, drawing the wonder of her now pliant form against him, gladly burying his face against the lush mass of her hair, and breathed the sweet-scented sensuality of her into nostrils that welcomed.

"Aaah, Rosamund . . . ," he whispered again, his fingers tracing along the smooth line of her hips to find a breast again.

"Thou are beautiful! Now, I think I understand why it has been so hard for thee to rouse anger in me. Something within me—must have known. Must have known . . . !"

Rosamund stared upwards, watching the leaves of the great oak above them ruffle and flutter in the breeze. Still surprised and bewildered by so much feeling, she explored the sense of contentment that was its result. Mallory's body against her own was pleasantly warm and large and smooth, as though he belonged there. . . . Belonged?

Could it be that this were what she had sought? The reason for her baiting of him? Or the reason for her father's wily smiles? She frowned a little, struggling, for she was unused to being gentle, save with the silver horse. She shifted in the circle of Mallory's arms, and stroked his hair, touched the strong line of his jaw where the bruises she had inflicted earlier were beginning to show.

She watched his smile. His eyes closed, his face was remarkably happy and young. And he shivered delicately under her touch as her fingers traced lower to explore the firm column of his throat, across the broad hard muscles of his chest, to the soft part of his belly and the quiescent member below. Her fingers closed around the soft skin that sheathed it, and it stirred and hardened. He gasped and arched a little. Of a sudden, Rosamund grinned.

"Thou art mine, Mallory!" she told him fiercely. He groaned.

"Aye, my lady. That I am!" His head tossed and he gasped. "Do to me as thou wilt!" She rolled on top of him as though mounting a stallion.

"I will!" she said, and Mallory, reaching for her, laughed pure joy.

# TEN

Mallory felt the strange acuity of self-conciousness with Lord Wilfred's presence at the evening meal. Rosamund was likewise different. Tamed by the passion they had discovered together through the afternoon hours of a warm summer day, she sat beside him, as she never had before, willingly sharing her meat, her cup. Yet, for all the peculiarity of it, he felt serene, content, until their appetites were appeased and Lord Wilfred rose.

Mallory heard the movement, then stiffened a little, feeling power shimmer through the air with greater tangibility than he had become accustomed to.

"My lord Mallory. Daughter. Do thou come with me. The time is come for revelations and gifts." Puzzled, yet obedient, Mallory stood up. He felt Rosamund's fingers on his arm and allowed her to guide him forward.

The sensation of power grew in intensity with each footstep as they followed Lord Wilfred, and Mallory realized that the old man was leading them out of the tower, then around one side of it, to the place where Rosamund often left the silver horse.

"Wait here, my children." The warlock's voice seemed deeper, more potent. "Firstly, my gifts to thee, Lord Mallory." Rosamund watched with widening eyes as her father flung back the folds of his cloak, held out his staff, and uttered a strange and eerie call that flew through the night.

Once more, he cried out. And, from the shadows of the trees that surrounded the moonlit patch of turf on which they stood, a dark wraith appeared. It snorted like a horse and grew substantial, becoming a creature of monstrous proportions.

Rosamund stared and Mallory held out a curious hand toward the creature's presence as the stallion undertook its final form. Powerful muscles rippled beneath a coat of myriad shifting blues. Strong legs ended in neatly gleaming, black hooves, and it was endowed with a mane and tail of great thickness and length.

"Young Mallory," the warlock spoke." I make a gift for thee in this, a warhorse fit to carry the lord thou wilt become!" Rosamund gasped a little, and the stallion, its dark eyes catching the moonlight into canny reflection, shook its head and blew loudly through wide nostrils. Mallory, with sober expression, stepped forward to greet, he sensed, this new friend. His fingers found the velvet muzzle, and laced through the heavy mane that tumbled about the horse's neck. He felt the stallion's beauty. Then his fingers stilled as the warlock spoke again.

"Likewise, to Lord Mallory who must move into the world of men, I make another gift. I give thee the friendship of a creature whose sight is more cunning than that of any human soul!" The warlock raised his staff toward the heavens and uttered another, piercing call that echoed with mournful poignancy through the air. "Lord Mallory," he said then, "do thou hold out thy left arm."

Mallory obeyed, and fluttering sounds came from above as another wraith appeared and took form, drawing in mighty wings to land on Mallory's arm and grip it with fearsome talons. An eagle with midnight plumage and fierce golden eyes settled itself, glanced at the warlock, then at Rosamund, and blinked slowly in acknowledgement of Mallory's exploring touch.

It was with wonder that Mallory listened to the warlock's next words, his free hand moving between the two creatures.

"Know thou, my lord," Lord Wilfred spoke quietly, "that this bird will never need the hood or jesses such as are needed to control a common wild falcon. Nor will this stallion need to feel the tug of curb, or the goading of spurs to bear thee. Do thou apply that which thou hast learned with the black wolf, and guide these creatures with conversations of thy will. They will heed thee. More, they will guard thee." Mallory began to nod acquiescence. "Now," Lord Wilfred said suddenly. "It is time for other things! Come."

Mallory felt the great bird depart his arm as he turned to follow the faint sound of Lord Wilfred's departing footsteps and the shifting aura of power. He heard Rosamund tread lightly a little behind him as they traversed the familiar path that led back to the interior of the tower. Then they were inside, and he followed across the hall, up familiar steps and along the corridor he knew, to a door that was previously unknown to him. Mallory felt a curious wonder as he climbed up another strange winding flight of steps that he had not known existed. Then he stepped into a considerable space where Lord Wilfred's power seemed to diffuse, to flow and change, to move as though dancing.

Mallory stood very still in the hall, wonder becoming amazement. He held out his hand, his fingers spread to touch, awed to perceive through the rhythms of that flowing power, the form of a great hall with smooth stone walls and high vaulted ceiling, upreaching columns, and the central focus of what seemed to be a great round table that spiralled before him. He heard Lord Wilfred move toward it—and Rosamund, who moved with her father.

What manner of strange place was this? Mallory wondered. For it seemed to lack that true sense of stable densities and substance that were so quietly familiar below, in the rest of the world such as he knew it. Energy reverberated here.

He took a careful step forward.

"Just so, my lord Mallory." Even the depths of Lord Wilfred's voice were illusory of a sudden. "Thy blindness gives thee another, differently astute sight. This hall is but an illusion, a memory conjured from another time to ease my desire for an environment that is comfortable to me."

"But, Father . . . ?" Rosamund's voice revealed confusion. "It is real . . . I have touched . . ."

"That is the witch blood in thee, my daughter. Reality is a flexible medium. It is unconstrained by the limitations that mortal men are impelled to dwell within. So it is that the Fairie are not governed by the same restraints as men. Aye, lad, do thou come to me, for I have other things to reveal to thee," he added, and Mallory stepped toward him with greater confidence, his attention fixed upon the contradictory nature of the floor beneath his lightly booted feet. Substance and fluid both. His fingers found the smooth, fine-grained surface of the table and he stopped.

Lord Wilfred's voice softened to potent melody as he spoke.

"Do thou, my children, attend most carefully to that which I now reveal to thee, for, it is from these things that thou may come to understand my purposes, and thine own heritage.

"To begin it, do thou know me as I am, for I am the last High Warlock. I am the Pendragon! And I am old. I am older than thou may imagine." Shadows slipped into the tones of his voice, shades of knowledge, textures that were a reflection of the stamina of time.

"I, mayhap more than any other of my kind, have watched the destiny of humankind that hath brought them to occupy all the corners of the earth, their numbers growing as they became distinct from all other of the creatures that dwell in the forests and upon the plains, learning through the use of their hands and the contriving of tools, to undertake dominion over the world.

"We, of the Fairie, were lords of the earth once. And, being creatures that are kindred to men, although not the same, the Fairie once dwelt in harmony with humans when they dwelt as other creatures. And, in those ancient, forgotten times we were revered as Gods for our powers. Men sought our aid and intercession increasingly as they learned to mold the world after the fashion of their capabilities, as they saw our palaces, and began to understand something of our powers.

"Likewise, the minds of men learned to be aware of things beyond the realm of their mortal existence, such understanding as brought them to know that death was not a finite matter." The warlock settled himself into the great chair at the mouth of the round table. Rosamund stared solemnly at him, seeing fully the entirety of his age. And more—a weariness . . .

"We of the Fairie came to understand the disposition of men, and the unfolding of destiny. Then there occurred great strife among us. Some feared the impending dominion of humankind and sought to destroy this creature that was fated to replace us as tangible entities in the world. Some, myself among them, in compliance with the path of fate, befriended men, and favoured them. And so, the wars that diminished the Fairie were brought as well, into the hands of men who had learned a great appetite for power.

"War! Humankind hath revealed a great proclivity for it," the warlock sighed. "Aaah . . . Those were the dark times. Invasions shook the world. Fire and famine spread, and scavengers, as men learned the full meaning of seizing power for themselves. Still, the numbers of the Fairie diminished, and to men, who had trusted once, was borne a great fear of the greater powers of such as sought to destroy them. They turned against us, and thrust us back by silence, and denial.

"I, the Pendragon, was Lord High Warlock of this realm in alliance with my brother, who was called Merlin. We were the last of the entire and purely bred of our kind. The only ones remaining to endure with full and intact powers, for, as they faded, many of the Fairie begot sons and daughters of mortal form and thereby diffused their purity. So it is with thee, my daughter.

"And, during an age when destruction seemed to have reached its height, when there was little else beyond war and pillage, I undertook the guise, for a time, of one known as Uther Pendragon. I did beget a son who was called Arthur. My brother undertook to be his teacher and his counselor. Arthur came to be a mighty king. He brought unity to this realm, and gathered about him men of high purpose to accomplish it. Aye. They were pretty times.

"But doomed by mortality! Arthur is long dead. And Merlin sleeps forever. So—I will, at last be doing in the not too distant future. My age weighs upon me, not in the manner of the fading flesh of men, but for all that which I have seen. Each conjuring draws from me some little part of my strength, and my will to replenishment is gone. I have a great desire to rest awhile. To sleep with the spirits."

"Thou wilt die, my father?" Rosamund asked in a husky, strangled voice. Mallory stood very still, feeling—feeling . . .

"It is not a conclusion, daughter, such as is known to men," the warlock said softly. "Now, we must attend to other matters." His voice gained power again. Stillness stirred to brew and swirl with vigour. "Rosamund. Thou art my child, and thou art the true lady of Wodensweir, for I was lord of the same in the guise of Lord Wilfred until a hundred years ago. When the Normans came they called the fief Wallenford and seemed to take it from me to the rule of one of their own." He smiled. "They did not know.

"And so, I have dwelt in this tower, in these forests, well content to my peace. And, when thy mother's body was pillaged, and she was killed of it, I did conjure vengeance!" Mallory stiffened, then froze as he felt the warlock's voice shift, like a pointing finger, toward him. "Aye, my lord Mallory. I did torment thy father through his lusts and ambitions and so destroyed him. More. I tampered with the seed in thy mother's womb. It is from my hand thou art blind of eye and different of colouration than other men."

"Mother of God!" Mallory rasped, feeling himself tremble

as he thought of all he had endured. "Why...? What harm have I wrought...?" he whispered.

"Hear me out." The warlock spoke sternly. "Were thy father's seed to have remained in thy mother's womb, then, thou would have been made to be a man as thy father, his sins brought to another perpetuation. I did something else. I changed thee. More—I made of thee, mine own son. My son, got of my contriving and of me. For that, thou was brought to learn through another course." Mallory gasped incoherent pain and hunched his shoulders. All those years of suffering. The bruises and the loneliness. The crawling pests and hunger. The rest of it.

"Why...?" he managed.

"As I have removed from thee such as was normal human sight to bring thee to another different and clearer vision, so, too, I have forged the depth of thee upon the anvil of pain. Aye. I have watched over thee. As with my other son, Arthur, who was impelled to learn through the years of his boyhood, so, too, thou were made to do the same. My sons are not got to be children in the ways of power, but rather to have the wisdom of understanding all its consequences." The warlock's voice softened again. "For," he added, "my sons are got to be great lords among men!" Silence trembled. Energy poised alertly.

"I am humbled!" Mallory said very softly after a time.

"He is thy son?" Rosamund's voice reflected her shock as her gaze moved from the warlock's face to Mallory's white one, then back again.

"He is my son. Yet, he is not thy brother of blood," the warlock told her. "Wodensweir, or Wallenford as it is now called, is thine inheritance, and Lord Mallory's as well.

"In but a short time, I will send thee forth to win the same for thyselves and for the children that shalt be got of thee. But," he turned to Mallory, "I do give thee another inheritance from me, my lord Mallory. Thou shalt never more use the name De Cheiney. Thou shalt call thyself before the world, Pendragon!

"Thou shall bear my shield of dragons as Arthur did before thee. Thou shalt wear mine own armour, and my colours that have been given to no other. Thou shalt bear the weapons I will give thee. Thou wilt ride upon the back of mine own war stallion. The eagle and the wolf shall accompany thee, and Rosamund shall as well, be thine.

"It is for thee to go forth into the world of men to win back thy rightful fiefs and entitlements of the King's will. And it is for all this, that I have prepared thee." The warlock reached into the pouch at his waist and drew forth the crystal sphere, held it out to Mallory's hand until his fingers closed about it. "Instead of vision, I bequeath thee this. Hold it in thy palm and search its surface with thy fingers. Thou will have no need of any other eye." He breathed deeply. "And, it is my final decree that thou be lord to my daughter's lady. It is for thee to husband her, to guard and keep her!"

Rosamund's eyes were enormous as she searched her father's face. Her features tightened and her fists clenched as she thought of afternoon sweetness that had abruptly become bitter.

"Thou hast plotted all this from the first!" she said harshly. The warlock's amber eyes glinted knowingly.

"So I have, child," he said mildly.

"I am so much baggage to be given away! And to this blind—boy! Am I not to be asked if I wish to wed?" Rosamund raged her knowledge at having been completely, cunningly managed. "It were ill done of thee, sire!" she snarled. Mallory winced. The warlock chuckled.

"Be still, witchling!" he ordered. "I greatly fear, Mallory Pendragon, that my daughter will be the most onerous of the burdens I have placed upon thee!" he commented. Mallory smiled briefly but did not respond, and Rosamund seethed in a fury that was the more potent for its silence.

The blue stallion was a wonder to ride, uncanny in its knowledge and wise in all the ways of battle. The eagle perched itself upon Mallory's helm, or on one armoured shoulder, and, when it soared the air far above, he learned to listen to the meanings of its eerie cries. And, ever faithful, the wolf ran at his side, both guardian and guiding friend.

Mallory spent much time alone then. With the crystal sphere in his hands, his fingers passed across the surface of the globe to feel the exact dimensions of all manner of things about him, their densities and structure, their textures and spatial dimensions, all details of the world about him that went beyond the spectrum of sound.

Was this, he wondered, what it meant to see . . . ?

Likewise, he spent much time in arduous thought. Rosamund had become aloof and sullen, remote and cold toward him, and Mallory discovered a new and different loneliness inside. He longed to touch her again, to laugh with her, and to know her warrior's ferocity was softened into passion exquisitely shared.

He loved her.

# ELEVEN

1166 A.D.

"What manner of knight rides with but the attendance of one, and such beasts as those?" Lord Reginald De Beauvais squinted against the brilliance of an early spring morning sun as he tried to study the small party riding in leisurely fashion up the long hill that led to his castle.

"I know not, my lord." Beside him, Sir Geoffrey spoke slowly. "But it is a strange sight, nonetheless."

"A mercenary?" Lord Reginald frowned as he muttered it. "Nay..." Only a lord of considerable wealth would be riding a monstrous warhorse of that calibre, or could mount his squire upon such a tall, pretty beast as the white horse that danced beside it. But then, a great lord was not likely to be without other escort...? He leaned forward over the parapet to peer more intently at the strange emblem mounted on the unknown knight's helm and saw a great wing extend briefly as the usually colored horse plunged into a small gully. Aye, it was a live bird, he realized—an eagle.

Likewise, a huge black wolf trotted tamely beside the knight's horse, its jaws open, tongue lolling in the manner of a dog.

Lord Reginald and Sir Geoffrey exchanged glances and went back to watching, staring at the shield the knight wore upon his left arm.

"I do not know the insignia, my lord," Sir Geoffrey muttered as they saw green dragons entwined upon a field of black, noted the peculiar, half-moon shape of the shield, and were able to see the knight's surcoat of green with black dragons upon it.

"Nor I!" Lord Reginald said briskly, "likewise, 'tis a curious exchange of colours." He pushed away from the parapet. "Let us resolve this mystery, then!" Bellowing orders, he strode along the battlements, then ran lightly down a flight of steps that led to the great court below.

The blue horse snorted challenge as it clattered across the drawbridge and swept under the portcullis, its black tail streaming behind it like a banner. It was a roan, Lord Reginald noted with wonder, but a roan of marvellously unique colouration. The stallion came to a halt and De Beauvais noted the squire who drew his own silver mount to a halt beside the knight. Arrogant, he thought, and felt a sudden jolt at the remarkable beauty of the boy's face, at the sight of enormous dark eyes veiled by lashes of improbable length that travelled over the keep, along the walls, then met his own— coolly, briefly.

"I seek the lord of this demesne, the Earl of Arundel." A quiet voice echoed from beneath the concealment of the knight's helm. Lord Reginald collected himself, eyeing the eagle that rode upon the crest.

"I am he. I am Arundel, good sir," he responded with proper courtesy. "Who is it that seeks the hospitality of my house?" The knight did not answer, but slung his unusual shield across his saddle bow, lowered his unadorned lance and held out an arm. The great black eagle hopped down to grip one gauntleted wrist, and the wolf beside him studied Lord Reginald with predatory interest. De Beauvais frowned his unease, his lips tightening in reaction to the lack of response to his courtesy. The knight dismounted with easy grace, and his squire did likewise, a slighter figure than his lord.

"My lord." Finally, answer came from the anonymity of that casque helm. "I am the rightful lord of Wallenford." Lord Reginald stiffened. "And, I do solicit thy aid to petition the King for the just return of my fiefs!" Politely uttered, but intriguingly audacious, Lord Reginald acknowledged beyond his first astonishment, well aware that Wallenford now belonged, by the King's gift, to Lord Fulk of Petworth.

"I know the Earl of Wallenford, and am puzzled as to who else might make a claim upon his stewardship, sir knight!" he said with a dry edge to his voice.

"I am not yet a knight, good my lord! But I am in truth, the heir to that demesne!" This was said with quiet assurance as one hand went to the laces of the helm. "I am Pendragon, my lord. Once known to thee by the name of Mallory De Cheiney!" The knight drew the casque away and thrust back the mail coif beneath. Lord Reginald stared in dumbfounded astonishment at white skin of gleaming purity, at hair that sparkled lush silver, and eyes that gleamed like fresh, twin pools of blood in the morning light.

"Mother of God! De Cheiney!" he whispered, recalling a pallid grey, timid, and skeletal boy that howled in madness like a wolf. This tall and dignified, unlikely young man could not be the same, yet? "It cannot be?" But, a gently amused smile curved the lips of that strong and perfect face. The white head cocked a little in the manner of one who listens, and the red eyes did not fix their gaze.

"I have taken my adoptive father's name, my lord, there being greater honour in it! I am Mallory Pendragon now!" The quietly assured reply seemed to emphasize Lord Reginald's exclamation. Aye, he was entirely blind as well, De Beauvais realized with an additional shock. As that other had been. He swallowed, recalling his manners.

"My lord," he said with even more careful courtesy. "I bid thee welcome to my house! It is time for the breaking of the fast. Do thou take my arm, good sir." But the blind man shook his head and smiled.

"I have aid to find my way," he said gently, touching the wolf that flanked him. "I would see to the comfort of my horses?"

"Thy squire will tend to them, surely, my lord?" De Beauvais responded in surprise, catching the resentful gleam of dark eyes as he glanced toward the boy.

"So be it," Mallory Pendragon responded pleasantly. He moved his wrist upward and the black eagle hopped onto the pommel of the blue stallion's saddle. Again, Lord Reginald caught the expression of the boy as he moved to take the bridles of both animals. Insulted fury. He turned and began to walk up the steps that led into the keep, the lord—Pendragon following with unerring accuracy. Pendragon? It struck him then, that the name had a vaguely familiar, eerie ring to it, such as should recall sorceries and ancient legends.

"Thy squire appears discontent in his duty, my lord," he noted aloud. To his surprise, the other grinned a little.

"His disposition is such as prefers the giving of command!" Lord Mallory responded without apparent discomfiture. Lord Reginald frowned, well aware of his own preference for proper order. But, he acknowledged, there was assuredly little of the usual about Lord Mallory to begin with.

*       *       *

"Whyfore, my lord," De Beauvais asked a short time later over the breaking of the morning fast, "hast thou come to me before presenting thy petition to the King?"

"For a twofold reason, my lord." Lord Mallory's face was quietly intent. "Thou were the one who removed me from the imprisonment my father, Robert De Cheiney, had made of my life, and, secondly, by that, thou art the truest witness to my birth and blood." His head cocked a little, he added softly, "Aye. I do recall, also, one of thy knights who was disposed to treat me with good charity." Lord Reginald sipped light ale, and watched the other man neatly find part of the cold roasted fowl upon his trencher.

"There would be few to contest the truth of that," he agreed cautiously.

"When I am knight, there will be none can contest the gauntlet I will cast before Lord Fulk and his heir!" Mallory Pendragon said with calm deliberation. Lord Reginald's eyebrows rose and he exhaled sharply. This was a blind man . . . !

"Thou intend to challenge the Earl . . . ?" he began.

"And, his heir." Again, that certainty.

"To battle for Wallenford . . . ?"

The silver head inclined agreeably.

"It is the best way, my lord, for that fief is entailed by the right of more than one lord, and thus it would be the simplest manner of resolution! There is another whose claim upon the demesne of Wallenford is even greater than mine own."

"Who is that?" De Beauvais got out, still struggling with the impossible as he tried to understand how a blind man could prevail in battle, even hope . . .

"The lady Rosamund of Wodensweir. Her father held the fief by right and descent since long before the coming of the Conquerer."

Lord Reginald shook his head.

"Mother of God!" he breathed. Then: "Do thou seek to serve thine own interest, or to champion this lady?"

Mallory Pendragon cocked his head a little and smiled. "Both, my lord. The lady is betrothed to me!" he said.

Lord Reginald stared at his unusal guest for some moments in dumbfounded silence. The other continued his meal with a calm that seemed, somehow, absurd.

"Thou cannot think to fight Lord Fulk and his son . . . ?" Lord Reginald tried carefully at last.

"Because I am blind?" Lord Mallory finished it for him.

De Beauvais shifted with discomfiture as the other man smiled ruefully. "Having no understanding of the meanings and— losses of such condition, my lord, I am not confined by the same!" Lord Reginald felt heat seep up his neck to touch his ears. Lord Mallory cocked his head and turned a little, listening, seemingly aware of the presence of others in the hall, servants and the like. His expression became puzzled.

"Mayhap, good my lord," he asked softly, feeling the wary curiosity about him, remembering mockery, loathing, and fear. "Thou may resolve a matter for me. Is my countenance so fearful that it must hinder the ease of any human soul about me?" The gently curious, rather bewildered courtesy of the query had an excruciating effect, Lord Reginald acknowledged as he cleared his throat.

"Thou art, in God's truth, a comely man!" he managed. "Save—thou hast hair and skin of unusual whiteness. And thy eyes—are scarlet-hued as blood, not the blue, or brown, or green as with other men!" Lord Mallory shifted a little, his expression thoughtful.

"I had not thought," he said softly, "that I differed in form. Colour . . . It is hard for me to understand colour, my lord. It is a series of distinctions without sound or texture." Said without rancour, Lord Reginald felt the ineptness of any answer, and fell silent. His feelings were mixed, heightened as he watched the white-hued man, ruled chiefly by a sudden acknowledgement that this man, this lord, had inexplicably contrived to capture his respect.

He sipped again from his cup, and thought that he desired to see Mallory Pendragon succeed in his endeavour, doomed as it was, to failure.

"I will aid thee as best I may, my lord," he heard himself say. Lord Pendragon poised for a moment, then smiled.

"I am fortunate," he said simply.

The southerly, evening breeze blew the scent of wildflowers from the meadows beyond the castle walls. Lord Reginald stood alone with his preoccupations upon the battlements, seeking the silence that was needful as the sun began to slip down behind the trees to the west. A mantle of dark shadows had begun, likewise, to stretch forth from the east. He heard footsteps, and turned to see Sir Geoffrey's well-lined face.

Sir Geoffrey—who had stewarded his own boyhood, had

served his father, and now himself. Sir Geoffrey, who had been reluctant to leave that boy then called Mallory De Cheiney.

"Strange circumstances make this day," Lord Reginald said in invitation. The knight moved closer, shifted his shoulders as though they were stiff, and leaned upon the parapet.

"Aye, my lord," he said. "I have never liked that we left the boy to Lord Fulk." He was ever direct, De Beauvais knew. "I am glad to see him well!" It had been a sore disputation between them, Lord Reginald remembered. Sir Geoffrey had been icily remote for days.

"It seems," he said carefully, "that he was found by one lord Pendragon rather than by wolves, as are common known!"

"One wolf, at any rate, my lord!" Sir Geoffrey surprised him with the sally. "That beast that goes so tamely at his side, is a very monster of its kind!" Lord Reginald frowned.

"Aye . . . ," he said slowly. "It is that, and other things, that trouble me. I am torn between doubts of fancy and that which I see, for it seems to me there are qualities of magic—strange powers, about this Lord Mallory. His eyes . . ." Sir Geoffrey snorted dismissal.

"White cats, or lambs, or horses and dogs do upon occasion have that same distinction, yet, save for enfeebled sight, I have not found them to be otherwise different! I find none of the Devil's handiwork here!" His tone changed to deliberation. "Indeed, my lord, I perceive sound advantage to thee in aiding him to recover Wallenford!"

"He is blind, Sir Geoffrey. He cannot hope but to commit suicide should he undertake to battle Lord Fulk." Lord Reginald expressed his doubts.

"In God's hands!" The knight offered incongruous piety. Lord Reginald frowned as he shot the other man a sharp look.

"Ever my conscience!" he said tersely. Sir Geoffrey grinned and shrugged as he turned to inhale deeply of the sweet fresh air.

"'Tis a pretty maid that squires Lord Mallory!" he said dryly. "Uncommon arrogant, though!" Lord Reginald stared, entirely diverted.

"What maid?" he demanded. Sir Geoffrey gave him a sardonic look.

"My lord! For all the women thou hast tumbled with such

abandon, surely, I cannot conceive thou did not recognize this one?"

Lord Reginald did not reply, but kept his astonishment to himself.

"Squire, indeed!" Rosamund hissed, stepping forward to punch Mallory with all her strength in the belly. Caught with his tunic pulled halfway over his head, he let out an "oof" of surprise. "Shall I sleep with the beasts as well—my lord?" She sneered as he whisked the garment off. He grinned.

"There is, I think, a pallet for thee by the fire!" he offered. "Or . . . !"

"Aye! Or . . . ! Do thou think to soften me so? Thou hast won my father's favour. He sends thee forth to fight my battle, to claim my fiefs of Wallenford. Pah! I do not need thy aid, for I am better able than thee to claim what is mine by rights! Nor, do I need thy guardianship." Her voice lowered to purest venom. "All this because I am born his daughter, rather than his son! It is vilest injustice!" Mallory found the bed and sat down on it with a sigh, hearing her stamp about.

"So it must be in the world, Rosamund," he tried carefully.

"Then it is an unreasoning world!" she flared again. "Who hath taught thee what thou know of arms, I wonder? Who hath made of thee a man!" Half sneered. "And this is my reward for such labour? Nay, it will not serve! It does not serve that thou art to be my lord, or that thou art to, aye, how it seems to appear, to fight for me!"

"Mayhap, to die of the same effort!" Mallory pointed out more firmly. He felt thoroughly wearied by her relentless coldness, her sullenness to him. He heard her stop pacing at that. "Aye, Rosamund, I think thou hast not thought upon that. I may not succeed in this undertaking, to the cost of my life!" He had her attention for the moment, he felt it in her silence. He leaned forward.

"For myself," he pursued, "I would be well content to dwell in thy father's tower, and to know the friendship of the forest. I wish to live peaceably. For whatever skill of arms I possess, I do not find joy in the same. That, too, I have learned from thy tutelage!

"Should thou ride forth alone to claim the King's justice for thyself, for thou art a woman and will ever be so, it is most like the King would make thee his ward. Then it would be his choice to bestow thee upon some other unsuspecting lord as baggage and wife with thy demesne as dower!"

"Never . . . !" Rosamund breathed.

"He hath the power to do it!" Mallory pointed out reasonably. "Even to make of thee his mistress, should he choose!" He sighed deeply. "And, should thou wear armour, and conjure spells to aid thee? Think upon what would befall thee then. Thou would be condemned a witch. And, Wallenford would be lost to thee in any case!" She did not answer, and Mallory softened his tone.

"Thy father hath contrived wisely on thy behalf, as I have come to understand this winter past. He hath set the burden of magic on my shoulders. I am blind, and, I am given to know, strange of appearance, and it is fitting. . . . Likewise, my claim to Wallenford and the King's justice is more immediate than thine. Lord Fulk sought my death and committed a grievous wrong thereby. That alone requires the King to give me attention. Thy circumstance is more disputable. And," he stressed, "should I fail in this, thou wilt not die of it!

"All this thy father hath wrought for thee, Rosamund. Not for me who are born the son of his power, not the child of his body!"

Silence lingered between them, and Mallory could almost hear the movements of her mind.

"What is thy gain in this, then?" she asked warily, at length. He smiled, shrugged.

"An honourable name," he said quietly.

"That seems little reward for so much risk! There is more, I know it!"

"It contents me to serve thy interests and thy safety," he said with the same quiet tone.

"Hmmmmph!" Her comment faded into uneasy silence.

"Thy father knows thee well, Rosamund," he spoke carefully. "Why else would he choose a man who honours thy warrior spirit, and is well content to walk beside thee. One who will not set thee behind him."

"As thou hast done," she cut across his words. "I, who play squire to thy knight. Pah! Enough of this!" She turned away, missing the disappointment that flickered like a sigh across his face.

Mallory listened to Rosamund's movements as she settled herself for the night without uttering further comment. He had thought to offer her the bed, but, no doubt, that would have served as another opportunity for her to rail at him with some nonsensical thing about her weakness.

He finished undressing, and, extracting the crystal globe from the leather pouch at his belt, tucked himself between linen sheeting and soft furs. If she wished the bed, she was welcome to share it, he thought!

He held the sphere in his palm, and listened to Rosamund's breathing waft like whispers across the chamber. He passed his thumb gently over the smooth, warm surface of the globe and thought of her. Felt each reclining curve of her form, and smiled to himself at the new value in the magic of the warlock's gift.

Touch, that stirred his desire for her. He probed past the textures of the clothing she had refused to remove, and savoured the blending of memory and magic as he felt the silken warmth of her skin. Those soft and velvet places . . . He felt himself harden, felt her stir as he found those sensitive places he had known once before.

He smiled a little as he heard the soft, ruffling sound of the covers on her pallet, and almost groaned as he throbbed hungrily.

"Mallory. . .?" She sounded breathless, and enraged. "Stop it!" she hissed then. Mallory grinned with delight and cradled the crystal next to him, well content to bear the dissatisfied ache of his loins now.

She would have to come to him, of course. But, he had found another way to touch her senses, her needs.

Nor, he knew, would he resist the urge to use it.

# TWELVE

Sir Ranulf of Wallenford, on the verge of loosing the jesses of his falcon, stiffened abruptly as something else in the treeline ahead caught his eye. He brought his walking horse to a halt and squinted, raising a hand to shield his eyes from the glare of the brilliant sunlight.

"Sweet Jesu!" he heard his father exclaim behind him, and was forced to tighten his grip on the suddenly nervous animal beneath him.

"What is it?" he asked, staring at eyes, a row of them, some twenty pairs or more that gleamed yellow, coldly watching from a point near the crest of the hill.

"Wolves!" Lord Fulk half-shouted angrily. "Each year they grow bolder, and now they plague my fiefs in summertime as well. In God's name, it is not natural!" His horse under control, Sir Ranulf looked at his father.

"In other forests, I have heard that wolves only appear during the time of winter famine. Even then, they are easily dissuaded, being for the most part, hunted down. But here, it hath never been the same."

"Those are not ordinary wolves, I am convinced on it!" Lord Fulk glowered. Then, in a more wary tone: "I begin to think these are not natural forests either!" He glanced back at the great sprawling castle that had been his primary seat of residence for the past six years. "Even that stone is filled with ghosts," he muttered, half to himself. Sir Ranulf frowned surprise.

No one had ever found mad young De Cheiney's remains. But then, with the wolves such as those that haunted the forests of Wallenford, it had not been expected that they should.

"My lord. Look yonder!" Sir Ranulf pointed suddenly, his gaze diverted from the eyes that melted away, a pair at a time, to a place high on the hill some two hundred yards from where the wolves had been, where a stooped figure stood, leaning on a staff.

"It is the old man . . . ," Lord Fulk muttered. Sir Ranulf looked at his sire in some confusion. As was common among firstborn sons, he had spent much of his young life being fostered in another house, being trained for the knighthood he had finally won, under the guidance of another lord. Now, considered fully a man, he had recently returned home to take his place with the inheritance that would, in the years to come, fall to him. "Why have the wolves not killed that soul, I wonder?"

"Who is that old man, my lord?" Sir Ranulf asked, watching as the figure walked without faltering, down the hill toward the darkest part of the treeline.

"I am not certain, Ranulf." He listened to his father's answer. "There are tales among the serfs, who say that he was lord of this fief once, before the coming of King William Conquerer. Lord Wilfred—of, aye. Wodensweir, it were called then." Sir Ranulf stared.

"But that is impossible, sire!" Ranulf protested at once. "That was a hundred years past." He looked back toward the horizon. But the old man had vanished. Lord Fulk frowned deeply.

"Accursed, impenetrable forest!" he muttered. "I will seek to change the King's will, and though it take an army, I will have this forest felled. Every last tree of it!" The Earl swung his horse about and rode for the keep.

Still puzzled, and with great sobriety, Sir Ranulf followed, his interest in the day's hawking gone.

Staring at the back of his father's grizzled head, he began to think of the madness that had overtaken the last lords of this fief, the De Cheineys. Aware of a deep, internal sensation of caution, he crossed himself in the habit of one who was convieniently devout.

"The forests of Wallenford are vast, sire." Sir Ranulf attempted to broach the practical aspects of a disturbing subject some time later. "Surely, thou do not seriously consider the clearing of so much land . . . ?"

Lord Fulk looked at him sharply. "I can, and I will!" he replied harshly. "The wolves have grown in number for all my efforts to hunt them out. The forest, likewise, grows toward the fields, encroaches on crops and the common land used for pasturing livestock, for all we attempt to hold it at bay." He shook his head. Sighed slowly. "Nay, Ranulf, even the serfs hereabouts have come to fear their own shadows. When a crow flies overhead, they cower and cross themselves. When an owl is seen, there is talk of doom! There are too many legends and tales of curses and sorcery here. It is like a subtle pestilence, and I see no other recourse but this—to exorcise the cause.

"King Henry may well favour the preservation of the great forests of this realm to the sustenance of game. He may well delight in the pleasure of the hunt! But, on this fief, all those who enjoy such useful and pleasurable occupation meet with accidents. A broken limb, a lamed horse. Some manner of disaster. 'Tis unfailing." Ranulf did not interrupt the brief silence that followed. Instead, he saw weariness in his father.

"Of late, there hath been increasing talk of the curse of De Cheiney's mad, lost son. I do not credit it, but it is said that his spirit roams with the wolves, and that his red eyes are seen amid their yellow ones. It is not forgot that he howled with the wolves when he was imprisoned in the north tower, and it is now believed that he was the cause for his mother's madness and his father's ungoverned fits and rages.

"I have fought it for six years. I have seen the fruitfulness of the land become diminished by this fear of curses among the common folk. It is a rich fief! The land is good!" His tone revealed frustration now. "And it is time to bring these matters to the King's ear that we may cleanse this place of demons!" He gave his son a long look, seeing much resemblance to himself in the long, waving brown hair, and the strong face set above a muscular body. He leaned forward.

"And I will seek out the old man!" he went on. "He shall be burned for the witch he is! And we shall be rid of the last of it, for all these evils are befallen since Robert De Cheiney took and killed the woman of that old man!"

"Never say so?" Sir Ranulf stared his surprise.

"Why else do I keep thy mother and sister at Petworth? I dare not bring them here."

Sir Ranulf nodded. He could understand his father's caution in that. And he knew his father's wish to wed fifteen-year-old Julia to the Earl of Arundel, and get a grasp upon those lands. Ambitious himself, Sir Ranulf was inclined to applaud his father's plans, and he had applied himself to a like securing of power since childhood. The throne was secure, and civil discord ended. King Henry was young. Sir Ranulf had little reason to think his expectations could not be achieved.

His own betrothal to the daughter of the Earl of Sussex was another step along that path. More, Sussex's heir was but a child, a boy of eight not yet ready to be a squire, and it had been arranged that the boy should come to Wallenford for his training. He frowned.

If accidents hereabouts were commonplace? He looked at his father with cool blue eyes and a determined jaw.

"It is a matter to be brought to the King's ear with some discretion," he said slowly. Lord Fulk nodded slightly. They understood each other.

Even sorceries and curses were of practicable use, as long as they did not get out of control. And, were his sire to bring Wallenford to heel, then there could be much gain from such achievement in the eyes of Holy Church. King Henry's piety had become as reknown as his ceaseless travels.

"Thy attire puts me to shame, my lord!" De Beauvais commented lightly as he eyed Mallory's clothing with something of wonder. Truly, he thought, the Pendragon was an uncommon wealthy man to clothe himself in the manner of a prince. Marten's fur collared his cloak of finely woven, dark blue. Jeweled gold brooches pinned the cloak to shoulders covered by a tunic of scarlet linen and a richly broidered surcoat of the same blue. Boots of scarlet leather came to mid-calf on legs covered by chausses of black. His belt was intricately woven and laced with gold, carrying an ornate dagger and a purse of blue leather that appeared to be well filled.

Mallory was puzzled by the remark. "I but use what I am given by my father," he said.

"Thy father must be a great man, then?" Lord Reginald probed. Mallory smiled at that.

"He hath considerable means at his command," he said agreeably. Devoid of specifics, it was a neat evasion, Lord Reginald recognized at once. He changed the subject.

"The King is now holding court at Winchester, my lord. Should thou ride to seek His Majesty, I will offer to go there with thee. I have thought much upon thy claim to Wallenford, for it is a matter of great interest to me. Lord Fulk, the present earl, casts his eyes upon mine own fiefs, and I am not at all reluctant to see his growing power brought to heel!"

"My father informed me that thy lands adjoin with Wallenford." Lord Mallory frowned a little. "I consider that the Lord of Petworth hath sufficient endowment to content him!"

"He is ambitious," Lord Reginald said flatly.

"To what end, my lord?" the Pendragon enquired, cocking his head a little. It was disconcerting to converse with a man whose eyes never focused, Lord Reginald thought. "Power is naught save obligation. In this matter, I do but seek to accomplish my father's will. To secure justice with my lady's inheritance and mine own, for Wallenford will never bear other than its rightful lords!"

Lord Reginald frowned uneasily at the eerie promise of that last, and thought of the tales he had heard of late. Reports had been brought to him of the wolves that had grown in number and ferocity until none wished to set foot in those dark forests. Of the game that abounded there, but could not seem to be hunted, of nervous, superstition laden serfs. It was as though the lands of Wallenford were cursed.

"It is not a fief I should wish to hold, my lord!" he said. Lord Mallory smiled, his fingers stroking the top of the black wolf's head with uncanny delicacy—the sinister black wolf that never left his side, that watched other men distrustfully.

"Nor are thou meant to, my lord!" he replied at once. "Nay, only one endowed with right and proper knowledge may suit the tasks that Wallenford imposes!" Again, Lord Reginald was filled with peculiar unease. Yet, as he glanced at the wolf and watched the blind man, he wondered at the equally disconcerting conviction that he was secure in all that had begun to brew about him.

"I am given to understand, my lord," he ventured cautiously, glad for the solitude of the battlements that isolated them, "that the name of Pendragon was given to King Arthur's sire. An old name, got of legend?" Again, Lord Mallory smiled.

"Uther Pendragon. Aye, that is so," he said, shifting his face to feel the breeze that swept across the wall.

"I am impelled to wonder how thou art come to possess such a name?" Lord Reginald pursued.

"My adoptive—nay, know him for truth, my father—is the same Pendragon, my lord." Quietly answered, and Lord Reginald's face opened in surprise.

"But that is not possible. Arthur and the rest are dead these six hundred years and more . . . !" Lord Mallory's smile widened.

"True, for Arthur was a man, and mortal, my lord. But the lord Uther Pendragon is not, but rather, is of the same kind as his brother Merlin!" Lord Reginald swallowed. Frowned fiercely.

"Merlin was a wizard. And long gone . . ." he began.

"He sleeps, aye. Under enchantment, and the Lord Pendragon is the last of his kind in the realm. Know this, my lord, for thy clear understanding. Wallenford is his. And I must claim it for the daughter of his loins, the lady Rosamund of Wodensweir. As to mine own claim," he went on, "that is sprung from two sources. The gift of Wallenford was made to the man who may be considered my natural sire, Robert De Cheiney, and is mine, therefore. More, the greater right of holdings belongs to my true father, Lord Pendragon." His tone softened, and Lord Reginald stared. "My father is old, beyond imagining. He is wearied as one who bears the weight of ages, and seeks to rest. And it is his wish to see his children recover their inheritance and undertake to live in the world of men."

"Witches . . . ?" Lord Reginald grated, crossing himself. "Thou talk of sorceries and the like as if they are commonplace things, my lord!" The white face before him sobered, and he thought he saw fire in the scarlet eyes.

"There is naught to fear, my lord. We are folk akin to thee," he said with the same quiet assurance. "As my father hath taught me to know, much of the knowledge and skills of men were bequeathed to them in past times through the teachings of the Fairie. That is why, in part, thou, and the rest of thy kind, are no longer one with the beasts, and why mankind hath dominion over the world!"

"Mother of God, this is heresy!" Lord Reginald breathed, terrified of the implications he perceived. "Where is God in all of this?"

"God, my lord?" The Pendragon was briefly puzzled. "As He hath always been, God is the Creator! Of the earth, and men, and of the Fairie who were lords of the earth before men!" Lord Reginald poised to stare at the other man in uncertain fascination. Man . . . ? That, aye—unnatural purity of colouration.

"Art thou a warlock, then?" he asked. Lord Mallory's expression grew thoughtful.

"I seem to be a man," he said slowly. "As thou."

"Thou hast powers . . . ," Lord Reginald began.

"I have not discovered them, then, my lord!" The Pendragon smiled a little. "Nay, my lord. I have only the gifts of sensing that come with my blindness. I have keen hearing. I touch and feel. I am not dazzled by this thing called light, nor by colour, and, therefore, there is naught to stand between myself and the perceptions of truth in other men.

"I feel thy mistrust, my lord. Thine uncertainties. I do but request thy aid and testimony for the man I am, not for the rest." His tone softened further. "I seek justice, my lord of

Arundel. Not malice. And, I am given to understand, the King is a wise and just prince. I am content to do his will."

Lord Reginald exhaled violently. It was a peculiar coil, he thought. Yet, for the rest, he could not mistrust the last that Lord Mallory had spoken. He, too, was capable of recognizing honesty.

"So be it," he murmured slowly. Then: "I pose thee another question, my lord. I am troubled, for should the matter be brought to battle with Wallenford and his son for thy right, as such disputes are oft resolved, then—how will thou accomplish it?"

Lord Mallory grinned. "I am not without skill at arms, my lord!" he said.

Perhaps, Lord Reginald thought in the few days that followed, it was those qualities he discovered in the Pendragon that impelled him to form an increased liking and respect for the blind man. Lord Mallory was given to a quiet demeanor, and yet, revealed great depth of courage. More, he bore the wary suspicion, the aloof treatment of other folk, without resentment, or malice of any sort, but rather, with a relentless and generous courtesy.

Sir Geoffrey, from the first, aligned himself with Lord Pendragon, and his friendship was warmly received. It was the knight's example that brought others, gradually, to follow suit. His manner devoid of arrogance, it was apparent that Lord Mallory harboured an honest liking for people.

Strange, Lord Reginald thought once, in view of the bitterness of his childhood. Or, were these spells of another sort . . . ?

Likewise, Lord Reginald found himself increasingly fascinated by the remarkable tolerance Lord Mallory demonstrated toward his supposed squire. Hot tempered, vacillating between a surly, resentful obedience to the Pendragon, and a cautious curiosity about everything else, the "boy" kept to himself for the most part. It was ironical as well, that, save for himself, no one had observed that which Sir Geoffrey had so easily seen—that the squire was not a boy, but a woman. Moreover, a woman of striking beauty, with a lithely curving, athletic body.

Lord Reginald found himself increasingly drawn to gaze at her enormous dark eyes and their lashess of wonderful richness, at crisply arched brows, the fine features, and the suggestions of dark hair concealed beneath the hood of the jerkin

she wore. She had a mouth that curved like an artfully designed bow. Red lips that were a natural invitation to kissing.

Why, he wondered, not without envy, did Lord Mallory
disguise his wench as a boy when they slept together at night
in the bedchamber accorded them, doubtless enjoying many
delightful frolics?

Intrigued, as much from appetites that he was not accustomed to denying, Lord Reginald wondered with increasing
fascination if the woman's irate sullenness toward Lord Mallory offered the promise of her interest in other dalliance.

On the fifth morning after Lord Mallory's arrival, Lord
Reginald managed to find her alone in the stable of the bailey.
He watched for a moment as she brushed the silver horse, and
realized that he had not learned her name.

Rosamund sensed a presence, and paused in her strokes to
look at the Earl's pleasant face before resuming her task.

"My lord?" she asked in cool, formal tones. Lord Reginald's lips curved in fleeting humour as he perceived the need
for flanking maneuvers.

"I am brought to realize, that I am not yet informed as to
the name of Lord Pendragon's squire," he said pleasantly.

"Robert, my lord," she said gruffly, using the first name to
come to mind.

"Robert . . .?" Lord Reginald mused, stepping closer.
"Robert of where?"

"Robert of—Anglesford!" she invented hurriedly.

"Hmmmm. I do not know that house. But, thou art highborn, it must be presumed, to serve as squire!" Rosamund
brushed at the animal with something more than her usual
vigour. "How old art thou, lad?"

"Fifteen, my lord!" She attempted to pick an ambiguous
age, wishing the Earl would depart. But the Earl seemed dis-
inclined to do so, and propped himself comfortably by the
manger.

"How is it that thou squire a lord who is not yet a knight
himself? That is most curious to me." Lord Reginald reached
to stroke the silver horse's neck.

"So it were arranged by my father!" Rosamund growled
something akin to the truth, yet could not entirely veil her
displeasure.

"Thy manner suggests thou hast little liking for thy lord,"
De Beauvais tried to control the flickering corners of his

mouth, "which would make thee seem rare in something more than name!"

She shrugged.

"I consider Lord Mallory to be an uncommonly tolerant man," Lord Reginald pursued mildly. She shot him a look fit for killing, and, unable to help himself, he chuckled. "And, Robert is a strange name for a woman, mistress!"

Rosamund faced him at once, her eyes wide, expression fierce.

"How...?" she began. Oddly, Lord Reginald felt his ears grow warm.

"It is apparent!" he managed, abandoning credit to Sir Geoffrey. "Besides, thou art beautiful beyond the possible for men!" he added in an effort to salvage.

"Oh!"

It worked, he thought.

"Do I misunderstand thy dislike for thy lord, mistress?" he asked with gentle concern, the chase begun. "Art thou ill used? I will not have any guest in my house suffer ill from another." Rosamund flushed this time.

"Nay!" she said flatly.

"Yet, I think it is not fitting for a woman to perform a man's labour?" Lord Reginald pursued. She shrugged.

"These beasts will not allow other hands to tend them, my lord!" He gave her a more penetrating look.

"Men's garments on a maid so fair!" he coaxed. "And the name of Robert? Ah, mistress, it suits thee ill! Do thou tell me thy true name?"

"It can be of no concern to thee, my lord!" she retorted, though with some discomfiture. Lord Reginald shifted a little closer.

"As I am agreed to give aid to thy lord, mistress, thy name is of concern to me!" She gave him an uncertain look, seeing friendliness and warmth.

"I am Rosamund of Wodensweir!" she said after a few moments of silence. Lord Reginald's eyes widened in surprise.

"Then thou art Lord Mallory's betrothed!" he breathed. "My lady!"

Rosamund scowled. "Betrothed? Is that what thou have been given to think, my lord?" All of Rosamund's resentments boiled to the brim, and overflowed.

"'Tis untrue?" Lord Reginald felt confusion in the face of her sudden, even vengeful vehemence. "Or, is the match so much misliked by thee, my lady?" Marriages were made for reasons beyond the likings of men and women, he knew, even as he expected for himself. She turned back to the silver horse.

"Nay, my lord," she said quietly, and Lord Reginald felt consternation. He tried further.

"I am troubled to discover a lady of such high birth, as thou art, serving as a squire. I would prefer, for mine own repute and thine was to see thee honoured as my guest, my lady!" She stopped brushing the horse and swung about to face him again, looking at him with a great deal more kindness.

"It is gallant for thee to so declare, my lord!" Rosamund said softly, aware that he was looking at her in a way that Mallory could never do. Lord Reginald shifted as he stared into her dark eyes, wondered for a moment, if he were drowning. "I would be glad to accept, my lord," she added, and smiled at the feel of her own power.

"I will have a chamber prepared for thee, my lady, and such woman's garb as thou may require. My lady mother will attend to it," Lord Reginald told her, feeling decidedly mesmerized by new qualities to her uncommon beauty.

"That would please me well, my lord!" Rosamund said with regal gentleness. The Earl bowed and left her, and she turned back to the horse, stroking its neck and grinning to herself, her eyes glinting with mischief.

"Mayhap Mallory will not have it all his own way!" she murmured to the beast. "Mayhap I have other options and may yet choose my course!" The animal flicked its ears. For this night, at least, she thought, she would be rid of Mallory's distant seductions, and the torments of passion that intruded into her sleep as he caressed the crystal sphere her father had given him.

# THIRTEEN

Aye, she looked very well, Rosamund decided, studying herself in piecemeal fashion with the small brass mirror she had added to her pack. Attired in her own gown of forest green velvet with borders of gold dragons sewn along hem, sleeves, and throat, set over a chemise of scarlet silk, she had added an intricate girdle of gold and scarlet, and had braided ribbons of the same into her waist-length black hair.

Lady Arundel had been generous, offering her clothing as well as the chamber, kind in her woman's submissive way— irritating for the same.

Rosamund frowned as she wondered if she were expected to adopt a like manner toward whomsoever became her lord. Toward Mallory?

And Mallory had changed of late, had become a creature of quiet unmovability and determination. She felt uncertain as well as angry for the dominion her father had given him, for he had become serious of demeanor, offering her but a particle of the good-natured humour he extended toward others. It was as though he misliked this match as much as she.

His tricks were equally intolerable, for now he sought to tame her with mere passion. She—the Pendragon's daughter, a witch, at least partly, in her own right, was not some meek creature to bend to the cajoling of a mere man.

With great dignity, Rosamund swept from the chamber and made her way down to the great hall where the evening meal was shortly to begin. She paused at the entrance, and looked about at the company there, then began to smile a little at the awed looks and murmurings that came from the knights and other men gathering at the tables in the hall. Best of all was Mallory's slightly puzzled expression.

To her delight, Lord Reginald's face bore a stricken look. Like an eager boy, he lunged to his feet, strode toward her, and bowed.

"My lady Rosamund! My house is honoured before the presence of thy beauty!" Rosamund smiled and held out her hand in clear invitation for him to escort her.

"Thou art gallant, good my lord!" She said with dulcet clarity, glancing toward Mallory who stood unmoving upon the dais, his face sober, undecipherable.

Nor did Mallory comment when she took her place moments later, in the vacant chair between him and Lord Reginald. He simply reseated himself, and, as the meal began, became preoccupied with eating. Annoyed, Rosamund turned to Lord Reginald who was clearly eager to gain her attention. From there, she found herself exploring a role she had never practised before. Demure, flirting lightly, she experimented with her effect on the young earl, discovering in the eagerness of his manner and the warmth of his eyes, evidence of his growing fascination, the extent of this new power.

And, Mallory did not even seem to notice. Rosamund seethed fury beneath her smiles.

"Thou . . . my son, behaved as a besotted mooncalf!" Lady Arundel said in a scathing tone as she paced restlessly before Lord Reginald. "What canst thou be thinking of? The lady is bespoken, and it was ill-mannered of her to toy with thee as she did before her betrothed!" Lord Reginald flushed, feeling like a small child caught dipping his fingers into his mother's jewel casket. He scowled.

"The lady Rosamund is displeased in the match her father has arranged, and Lord Mallory does not seem to be content in the same!" he protested without thinking. Lady Arundel looked at him in disgust.

"That is of little import!" she snorted. "It remains, however, an unchivalrous folly in thee to be so obvious!" He turned away, to pace himself.

"I consider, my lady mother, that if the lady Rosamund's father is intent upon recovering the fief of Wallenford, he may consider my suit as a worthy alternative to this arrangement! Arundel lies alongside Wallenford. It would be a good match!" Lady Arundel stared at him, and Lord Reginald supressed an urge to flinch.

"It cannot be, thou art serious?" She breathed astonishment.

"Aye. I am!" De Beauvais retorted, well aware that he sounded more defensive than he might have wished.

"Reginald!" she said in the same tone she had used when he was a small boy. "Wallenford is already given to Lord Fulk. It is doubtful that the King will move to change that for this lady's claim. And, who is there that knows of the House of Pendragon? I think the King will not act upon such a fantasy as that!

"Lord Mallory has some legitimate argument, for he is De Cheiney's son, and was understood to be dead. He will have the King's ear. Not thee! Thou hast become befuddled by this witless passion I see in thee! Do thou recover thy sense, and cool thy loins upon some serving wench to set thy head to rights!"

Lord Reginald stood very still, heat flooding his face. But she had not yet finished. "I thought thee a man, not some gawking boy to be led into folly! Lord Fulk will not be over-eager to relinquish that which was bestowed upon him, and I understand and condone this reasoning that gives thee to aid Lord Pendragon in his petition to the King! But this other? I think thou dishonour thy guest by so much obvious attention on his lady! I had thought thee wise enough to, at least, if she is willing, practise discretion . . . !"

"Mother!" Lord Reginald exclaimed, dumbfounded by her suggestion. She shrugged.

"Thy father and I were not close. We were content to amicable dealing, save in the begetting of thee, and the others I miscarried. We were discreet. No one knew. So it is in the world!"

"But I thought . . . ?" Lord Reginald floundered. Her gaze upon him remained unwaveringly powerful in so diminutive a woman.

"Thy thoughts were the result of that discretion!" she said abruptly. Sighed. "For the rest, we both were given to good sense, and some manner of friendship! But—it seems to be the nature of men to think with their loins rather than their minds!" she finished crisply. Lord Reginald found a chair and sat down heavily. He felt like an idiot boy. And he did not look up from staring at his hands as she left him to his rest. It was some time before he raised his head, and when he did, his expression was filled with uncertain consternation.

The lady Rosamund was, indeed, uncommon fair in both face and form. But, beyond that—she was so vibrantly— alive.

And, he acknowledged painfully, she had snared him more easily than a huntsman could catch a rabbit.

Mallory sighed as he rolled onto his back. He listened to the crackling of the hearth fire, and the wolf breathing nearby. It was of little use to be angry. Yet, that was how he felt. Rosamund had taken the bridle and run as she chose this night, which made matters infinitely more complex.

And she had wound Lord Reginald's pleasant disposition around her finger as though he were a defenseless grass snake. He felt a fleeting pity for all that the Earl could not know of her.

For himself, Mallory acknowledged a powerful urge to repeat that which he had done once before. To fight and wrestle with her, to pin her down and show her, once and for all, who her lord truly was. Mayhap, he sighed, it would come to that. This stubborn jealousy got of the favour her father had shown him. Favour . . . ? Could she not see the burden that had been placed upon his shoulders, and give a little kindness for that? Foolish question. He knew her too well.

And, whyfore, with him, could she not accept her womanhood? Understand the freedoms that were got of it, so different from his own? Mallory shifted uneasily as his thoughts turned to that time that lay before them, when he must set his petition before the King, when he would request knighthood of the King's own hand for the righting of multitude wrongs.

He had listened with stoic control to the murmurings that seemed to accompany his presence, to the words of "witch" and "warlock" and "Satan," that had been ill-concealed by vocal undertones. He had heeded the Pendragon's advise and had practised patience, and courtesy. Offered kindliness . . .

Nor had he anticipated the awful pull of memories he had thought become remote, nor the protests that welled up inside to be denied expression. He had kept silent and had begun to find threads of friendship interlacing the discomfiture his presence generated.

It was another, subtler form, perhaps, but just as potent— this new experience of loneliness.

He longed for the forest, for the creatures to whom his blindness and other peculiarities were irrelevant. And, for Rosamund—for Rosamund to say again, triumphantly,

"Thou art mine!" And, aye, to pleasure her, to drown again in the joy of her . . . Mallory reached slowly and found the

head of the wolf close by him. He fondled an ear in the manner the animal most favoured, and listened to its responsive
panting.

Intelligent, the creatures of the forest. And elegant, for the
simplicity with which they lived and endured. Not for them
the peculiarities of human avarice, or the convoluted savagery
of human passions.

It was Sir Geoffrey who led the way upon his great, raw-
boned destrier. Lord Mallory rode quietly just behind him and
Lord Reginald. Lady Rosamund, again attired in the garb of
squire, rode third, just ahead of the three other knights chosen
for guard to the party.

Lord Reginald had been reluctant to take more men, pre-
ferring to leave his holdings fully garrisoned, pending the outcome of this enterprise.

Lord Pendragon had been quiet and remote for the two
days preceding their departure from Arundel Castle. Lady
Rosamund had been both vivacious and charming, a seductive
combination of ferocity and innocence. Lord Reginald shifted
in his saddle, feeling unease, as he let his eyes wander to the
lady who had been the chief preoccupation of both his mind
and time for the two days past. She flashed him a light smile.

Abruptly, Lord Mallory brought his blue stallion to a halt.

"Nay, Sir Geoffrey. Do not go so far along that path. There
is a shorter distance to travel, I perceive!" The knight swung
his horse about.

"How so, my lord?"

"If Winchester is to the north and west, as thou hast said
. . . So." Mallory pointed with unerring accuracy, utilizing the
feel of the sun upon his face, and his knowledge of the time of
day.

"Aye, my lord?" Sir Geoffrey commented respectfully.

"Why dost thou seek a longer route than to pass across the
land as the eagle may fly?"

"To go that way is to pass through Wallenford lands, my
lord. I had not thought it wise." Mallory smiled.

"We are but a small party, I grant, Sir Geoffrey. But Lord
Fulk may not discover us if we stay in the forest!"

Hearing unsettled murmurs behind him, Lord Reginald
nudged his horse forward, and voiced his own puzzlement.

"I cannot conceive he would not know . . . ," he began.

Lord Mallory turned an ear toward him. "The wolves are

abroad, my lord. They guard the forest until the return of their lord," he said. Lord Reginald and Sir Geoffrey exchanged meaningful glances.

"I have heard of those same wolves, my lord," Sir Geoffrey said uneasily.

"Lord Mallory is right!" Rosamund interrupted crisply. "This way, we may save two days or more upon our journey! Come. I will lead the way!" With that, she put spurs to her horse's ribs and cantered away from them, down the hill to plunge into the dense forest below. Lord Mallory grinned.

"Where my lady goes, I follow!" he declared cheerfully as his stallion plunged and bolted in pursuit of the silver horse, the eagle erupting from its perch to take flight, climbing high overhead.

Lord Reginald locked gazes with Sir Geoffrey, as wary comments were exchanged behind them. But the older man shrugged and grinned as well, and set off likewise. Frowning, Lord Reginald felt trapped as he put spurs to his own beast, well aware of being bested by a woman's fearlessness.

The trees closed about them with a somber, almost anticipatory embrace that was entirely devoid of welcome, embued, rather, with a petulant moodiness. Lord Reginald remembered another time when he had ridden through the forests of Wallenford. The mists and silence—the feeling of witchcraft, and how he had sensed being watched. Aye—that fleeting glimpse of a figure on a white horse. His eyes widened as he looked ahead to Lady Rosamund. It had been her! He was suddenly convinced of it. The very same, in chain-mail, in the guise of a man!

With an excruciating jolt, Lord Reginald felt his fascinated passion tempered by wary suspicion. Aye. She knew the forest, he realized, she knew it very well.

Even Lord Mallory did not touch the reins upon his stallion's neck, but was content to let the beast choose its own way, as if the animal knew. . . . Could it be, Lord Reginald wondered, that these two had lived in this forest all this time?

Rosamund let her horse walk as it picked its way up another tree-covered, heavily thicketed hill. Mallory's stallion kept its place close beside her, and she glanced back a little to see an expression of comfortable relaxation on Mallory's white face as he cocked his head, listening to the sounds about him. A slight smile curved his lips.

"This is home," he said softly.

"Aye. It is that," she conceded, then glanced back further to watch Lord Reginald some distance behind her. His face reflected an alienated tension that suddenly made her think the past days at Arundel had been more dream than reality. She offered him a smile.

Mallory took the lead then, attentive to the barely audible cries of the eagle he had sent aloft to soar above the trees. He let the stallion pick its way, trusting the beast to know his mind, and listened to the wolf that padded a little ahead. He heard the movements of myriad creatures about them, pausing to observe their passage—and of Rosamund, who slipped back to ride beside Lord Reginald. Mallory felt the fading of his own slight smile.

A horse whinnied sharply in terror. Others stamped and pulled against the ropes that held them tethered. Mallory, hearing the noises through the mists of light sleep, roused abruptly and sat up. He reached to touch the wolf that stood beside him with alertness, but felt no tension in its frame.

He stood and found his sword. Heard the crackling of the fire that had been built in the middle of the clearing where they had chosen to camp for the night. Someone came up beside him.

"What is wrong?" Mallory asked. Lord Reginald, sword in hand, scanned the surrounding trees, his face paling at the gleaming of so many pairs of menacing golden eyes. He crossed himself and looked at Sir Geoffrey, who, with the other three, sought to control the horses by bringing them closer to the fire. Only the Pendragon's blue stallion continued to graze as though unperturbed.

"What is it?" Mallory repeated more loudly. The Earl spun around, seeing the eyes all around them.

"Wolves!" he said tersely. "Mother of God, never have I thought to see so many! My lady Rosamund, do thou mount thy horse for safety." Mallory heard the low, penetrating growl that came from all about.

"My lord! Sirs!" he shouted. "Be thou still! Set down thy weapons, for thou shall not do battle with the guardians and survive!" Rosamund, who had not moved, stared in surprise at the blind man, unaccustomed to such tone from him. Lord Reginald and the rest froze, their faces paling further at the fire in the blind man's eyes, scarlet reflection of those about them. Menace of purest intent that waited, poised and eager in the darkness.

"This is mad, my lord, to wait until . . . ," Lord Reginald began a violent retort.

"Be still!" Mallory roared. "The wolves have rightly come. Thou art not a part of these woods!" With that, he resheathed his sword, and strode briskly toward the edge of the trees beyond the fire, his white hands held out, and the black wolf beside him.

Entirely taken aback by the order that still rang in their ears, Lord Reginald and his knights remained rooted to the ground, able to do little more than stare as Lord Pendragon stopped. He flung back his white head, loosing a low, eerie call. Gentle sounding, almost mournful, it beckoned. . . .

Those watching shuddered as the cry was answered by a hundred like voices. They drew back, together, fists tightening about their weapons as the eyes in the darkness moved— came together—and materialized into grey dark shadows that slipped from the undergrowth toward Lord Mallory's outstretched hands.

He knelt then, head up, unseeing, and murmured softly as the wolves gathered about him. Monstrous large, shaggy, irrefutably fierce with their great jaws open, they grinned at him like so many tame dogs, each one in turn seeking to touch a white hand with a wet nose.

"Mother of God!" Lord Reginald found voice enough to rasp at last. Rosamund stood frowning. Where, she wondered, had Mallory learned this trick of her father's? How much power did he have now? She had never been able to commune with the wolves like that.

"These woods are cursed!" Sir Geoffrey muttered, meeting his lord's eye. Lord Mallory, still kneeling in the midst of the grey gathering that settled to lay down all about him, cocked his head and stood.

"Nay, good sir knight," he called out clearly. "It is not a matter of curses, but rather that these woods are the last, true, natural place left in this realm." He turned to face them, walking toward them through the mass of grey bodies. "Herein is all that remains of the times before the great floods came to tear this kingdom from the mass of land that makes the continent to the east. All that remains of the world that was in the time of the Fairie, before men were given dominion over the earth and disturbed the balances between hunter and hunted and the rest."

"Well and truly spoken, my son!" A deep voice rumbled subdued thunder from the darkness of the trees. Again, Lord Reginald and the rest, compelled by instinct, froze once more as they stared with ashen faces at the tall, shadowed figure that strode forward, first appearing to be some manner of two-headed beast until the firelight caught his form to reveal the owl that rode upon one shoulder.

The bird took flight to move the short distance to Lord Mallory's outstretched arm. Tall and proud and dark, the warlock stood in the middle of the clearing, his amber eyes gleaming at the frightened mortals.

"Father!" Rosamund said, and flew to his embrace.

"My lord!" Lord Mallory's tone were equally pleased. The warlock smiled a little, his considering gaze still intent upon Lord Reginald, caught in the throes of a strong urge to retreat.

"Art thou so much afraid, my lord of Arundel, to expect threat or harm before friendship or beneficence?" The warlock's voice was a melodiously rumbling inquiry. "I am given to consider that is inconsistent with the teachings of thy Christian Faith."

Lord Reginald swallowed. Any reminder of the Church seemed incongruous in the extreme. He found his voice.

"My lord . . . ?" he began unevenly. Then, more firmly: "Thou art the one called Pendragon?" The warlock inclined his head with regal grace.

"I am the same. Once known as Uther Pendragon. And, for the past hundred years and more, as Lord Wilfred of Wodensweir." His response was agreeable. "I know thee, my lord of Arundel, and inform thee accordingly. I am the true lord of this demesne. Lord Mallory is mine heir. And his sons shall be his." Rosamund pulled away from her father's arm, face paling, her fists clenching as she began to glower furiously.

"It is never so! I am thy true child!" But her voice died away under the warlock's knowing stare. She turned and looked at Lord Reginald, and felt the flush that crept up her neck.

"Child of my body!" The warlock intoned with peculiar somberness. "Not of my mind. Thou art intemperate, daughter!" Rosamund stood in frigid silence, numbed by this bitter chastisement such as she had never known from him before.

Lord Reginald, his gaze flitting from the lady to the one she called father, stepped forward a pace.

"Thou art a warlock...?" He half-asked, half-accused. Pendragon's eyes gleamed slight amusement.

"As my son has told thee!" he answered courteously, turning at once to the quiescent wolves. He held out one hand in the manner of a priest bestowing a benediction.

"Go in peace, my children," he murmured to them, and, one by one, the wolves got to their feet and padded away to vanish into the night. Lord Reginald heard accompanying sighs of tenuous relief from Sir Geoffrey and the rest, as the warlock turned toward Lord Mallory.

"I have brought thee a final gift, my son," the warlock said and flung back the concealing folds of his cloak. He drew a sword from the scabbard at his left flank and held it out, hilt first, toward the blind man. The owl took flight. The broad, long steel blade shimmered brilliantly and the hilt and guard were composed of golden dragons. Mallory's white hand groped, then found the sword and took it. His face filled with wonder.

"This is no ordinary weapon, my lord," he said softly.

"Nay, it is not," the warlock answered. "This is the sword Excalibur, that I gave to my other son. Do thou bring to its use, the same honour that his name of Arthur did bestow upon it!" Lord Mallory knelt then and bowed his head, his hands on the sword that glittered before him.

"So, I will endeavour, my lord!" he intoned solemnly. The knights and their lord, all watching, were silent, caught by their understanding of ceremony.

"For the good of the realm, do thou serve thy King with honour, and pride, and generosity, as befits the last Prince of the Fairie!" The warlock's command shivered through the trees.

"So, I will endeavour, my lord!" Again, Lord Mallory intoned his vow. The warlock then raised his hand to the air, and a staff of wonderfully gnarled wood flew from nowhere into his grasp. He pointed the tip toward Lord Mallory, still kneeling before him, and with it described circles and incomprehensible symbols above the silver head.

He uttered an incantation. Lightning cracked the darkness asunder. Thunder brought the earth to shudder. And Mallory did not move. The warlock's voice echoed like a tempest, eerie and powerful in the night.

"Now, I do bequeath to thee, my son Mallory, known before the world as the Pendragon, all that remains of my powers! Thou art the last High Lord of the Fairie! In thee is all that remains of the substance of my people! And, to thee, I bequeath a life in the world of men. Go thou to thy duty with honour and my blessing, for thou shalt not know my presence again. As with my brother Merlin before me, I depart to my final sleep!" Mallory raised his face at that.

"Nay! My father!" He cried out.

"I must, my son." The warlock's voice was whisper soft. "Thy love brings me peace. Of all my children, thou alone . . ." His form began to shrink, his voice fading with him. Mallory stood, his face distraught, unseeing, and Lord Reginald shivered violently as he found himself staring at a withered old man leaning on a staff. His face, turned toward them, was ancient beyond belief, unaccountably weary, drained of life, yet peculiarly wise.

Then the old man, little more than a shade, turned and hobbled into the night, fading to vanish entirely just before he reached the trees.

Even the wolves had gone. Nothing stirred. There were no noises from the forest, nor night creatures about. Only the crackling of the campfire and the sounds of breathing from among the company. And, the single, hoarse outcry of Lord Mallory's grief as he stood before them all, tears of blood slipping down the taut planes of his alabaster face, the sword still held in his hands, the name inscribed in the sparkling blade clear enough for all to see—

EXCALIBUR.

As with the rest, Rosamund, too, stood very still as she understood the full import of what had happened. Her father had made of her a mortal. She was disinherited. Her fists clenched slowly.

Mallory De Cheiney had stolen it all.

# FOURTEEN

Gone. He felt it. The warlock was gone. All sense and understanding of his presence, however remote, were entirely void. And, save for that single outcry, Mallory stood very still, his breath rasping awkwardly, liquid drops tracing down his face as he knew his own profound sense of loss.

He felt, as well, the subtle movements of new energy that flowed through his body, power that gathered, sifted, furled, and lived to make of him something he had not been before, somehow given into him by the lord he loved above all others.

Yet, it could not change his grief. He drew up the sword Excalibur until it lay cradled like a child in his arms, and found control. His brother's sword. It was a trust that had been given to him, an honour beyond his worth, despite the strange sensations of strength that coursed through him. His brother—Arthur, as the warlock had made it to be.

"My lord Reginald?" he spoke with slow quiet. "Sirs, my lady. Do thou rest. We have a great distance to journey tomorrow, for we must come to the King's court at Winchester tomorrow eve." He turned away from the sounds they made, seeking only to be alone. He heard the owl that had served his father call out differently in the distance, and felt his stallion cropping grass peacefully nearby. He strode toward a tree, reaching out to find it with one hand, then drew his cloak about himself and the sword, and crouched down to sit in the grass.

He bowed his head, his face stern.

From across the clearing, he could feel Rosamund's fury, her jealousy.

"There is Winchester, my lord!" The Earl of Arundel was the first to proffer more than murmurings since the mysterious events of the night before. "It lies ahead, and somewhat to thy right side, down in yon valley beside the river Itchen."

Mallory nodded. "I thank thee for thy direction," he said courteously, forbearing to explain that he could scent the township, and the eagle circling overhead had informed him of his approaching destination. He reached for the pouch at his belt and drew out the crystal sphere. Cupping it in the palm of one hand, he stroked its surface with the fingertips of the other—so much easier to perceive now that he had his father's final bequest inside him.

He felt the form of the land that lay before him, the curve of the river, the cathedral that rose gloriously beside a castle to the right. He felt the cottages and other constructions contained behind the stone walls of the town, and probed more fastidiously, finding the ways that wound between the buildings, and the entrance to the great, six-sided keep. Aye, that of a sudden he recognized. It was all that remained of the castle that had once been his brother's.

"Camelot . . . !" he breathed aloud. Lord Reginald, who had been uneasily watching the play of white fingers across the translucent crystal sphere with its sorcerously swirling, smokey depths, glanced abruptly at Lord Mallory's face.

"My lord . . . ?" But the blind man did not answer, and De Beauvais determined to ask about the disturbing crystal. "What is it that is in thy hand, my lord?" Lord Mallory smiled slightly.

"An instrument, my lord, it is not to be feared. It is a gift of my father, and, mayhap it can be said that it is the means by which I—see."

"Jesu!" De Beauvais muttered, instantly aware of macabre associations with a man holding his eye in his hand. But Lord Mallory was unperturbed.

"It is an instrument," he reiterated. "For perception, such as are the senses that are a part of the flesh. That is all!" Lord Reginald did not comment further, but let his mount fall back until he flanked the others. Lord Mallory chose that moment to set his blue stallion into a faster pace, and the beast sprang forward to canter down the long slopes of the downs. Lord Reginald put spurs to his own horse and pursued, aware of his considerable relief in knowing that it would all be in the King's hands soon.

The blue stallion slowed of its own accord as it neared the river. Mallory groped for the helm that was afixed to the front of his saddle, unfastened it, and set it upon his head. Then he drew his cloak about him, concealing the shield on his saddle

bow, and drew the hood over his helm. Settling his grip upon
his lance, he held out his other arm, and, with a single cry,
summoned the eagle.

He is like my father already, Rosamund thought bitterly as
she watched the great bird settle upon Mallory's gauntlet, then
hop to his shoulder.

Using what he had felt through the crystal, Mallory allowed his will to converse with the stallion. The horse snorted
once, then began trotting boldly toward the main gates of the
town and through them past guards that looked their surprise
at the shrouded knight, then at the sober, open countenances
of those that followed him, recognizing at once the arms of
the Earl of Arundel.

The blue horse halted nervously in front of the castle bailey
where guards strode forward to hold pike points toward its
breast.

"Who goes there?" a harsh voice rang out challenge.

"One who brings petition to the King." Mallory's voice,
slightly hollowed, echoed calmly from the interior of the
helm.

"Thou art unknown, my lord!" The sergeant persisted,
eyeing rich attire and the magnificent warhorse. Lord Reginald rode forward, his mouth set.

"I am Arundel!" he barked. "Do thou let us pass!" The
guards bowed and retreated at once, murmuring apologies, as
Lord Reginald thrust his destrier through their ranks. Listening, Mallory let his horse follow until Lord Reginald brought
his animal to a halt a few moments later. The blue horse
stopped, and Mallory slowly let his lance slip to the ground as
he heard the Earl bark more orders. He dismounted and
reached to touch the wolf that had set itself by his left leg once
more. Someone who sounded young stepped close to him.

"I will tend thy horse, my lord?"

"My thanks," Mallory said slowly, feeling sound character
in the youth. The lance was taken from him, and he reached
for the shield on his saddle bow, important for the emblem
upon it, likewise, the pack he had set with it. He did not see
the puzzled look that was given him as the blue stallion allowed itself to be led away.

Instead, he stood very still, trying to find perspectives in
the spaces and sounds around him, to sort through the array of

noises that revealed the bailey to be a busy and populous place.

Somewhere ahead of him, he heard Lord Reginald's voice, clear and confident in attending to the details of their arrival.

"Do thou come with me, Lord Pendragon. Quarters have been arranged for us, and for the lady Rosamund." Mallory heard the Earl approach him. He stepped forward, keenly aware of how much more difficult it was to feel through the helm and the chain-mail armour that covered him

He followed, attentive to the sound of the Earl's footsteps and the lithe movements of the wolf. Up steps, along corridors, changing direction to spiral upward into a moderate chamber.

"We must share, my lord Mallory," the Earl said a little tautly. "Space is often inadequate at court, and I do not favour the public houses with their rats! The lady Rosamund will be quartered with the Queen's women." Mallory slipped back the hood of his cloak and held out an arm. The eagle jumped from his shoulder to clasp its talons about his gauntlet. He loosed his helm with his own hand, removing it with a sigh.

"This casque makes hearing difficult," he commented, then. "I am content with thy will for I know nothing of court beyond perceiving the presence of many people." Lord Reginald continued to watch from his position in the middle of the chamber, as Lord Mallory began to grope his way about the room with—almost reassuring hesitancy. Mallory felt the walls, the door, the narrow window where he gently set the eagle, the sparse furnishings of a pair of truckle beds, and a chest. Then, hc set pack and helm and shield beside one of the beds and sat down to thrust back his coif and put his white face into his hands with a deep sigh. Lord Reginald swallowed uneasily, aware that, save for such moments as this, how easy it was to forget the Pendragon's blindness.

"My lord . . . ?" he ventured.

"I am called Mallory, wouldst thou be my friend, my lord?" Lord Pendragon said at once through his fingers, then straightened, removing his hands from his face. Lord Reginald glanced at the great sword that hung from the Pendragon's hip, then at the scarlet, unfocused eyes.

"And I am Reginald!" he said gruffly, commiting himself. Mallory stood.

"I grieve for my father," Mallory softly answered his first

query. "And I think on what I must do to accomplish the fulfillment of his will."

"It should be simple for thee," Lord Reginald ventured carefully, after a moment. "Thou art a warlock, surely. . .?"

"Which frets thee!" Mallory said ruefully. "Mayhap I am a man as well, as my brother."

"Brother?"

"Arthur. Or I am something between the two. I feel the—strength my father bestowed upon me. It feels, inside, a most curious balance."

"I do not understand."

"Nay. I think thou cannot know this!" Mallory said ruefully. Lord Reginald shifted, still shocked by Mallory's reference to the legendary King Arthur as his brother—as well as by all the impossible things that had happened. Sufficient to terrorize any good Christian soul. Yet, he was compelled to remain, to see this peculiar business through to conclusion by those very qualities in Lord Mallory that commanded his respect as a man. Strangely, he felt a thread of confidence in this equally peculiar association between Lord Pendragon and such an ancient and revered King. Impossible? The events of the night before had torn apart the restraints on his credulity.

Mallory drew his hood over his head once more, all but concealing his face, and drew his cloak about him to shroud his armour and the dragon emblem on his surcoat.

"And, now we are at Camelot, Reginald!" he said softly.

"So legend hath said." Mallory smiled.

"From truth, legends are sprung! That was another aspect of my father's last bequeathing to me," he said. "His memory. His—vast memory."

Lord Reginald did not, could not answer, but strode forward to open the chamber door and lead the way down to the great hall and the King's presence.

From her position beside Sir Geoffrey, who hovered with belligerent protectiveness, Lady Rosamund glanced about to see the bold looks of young men throughout the heavily populated and enormous great hall. She looked well, she knew, gowned as before in scarlet and green, finding interest in the looks that came her way. Her shield, the grizzled knight, exhaled relief as Lord Reginald strode up to them, Mallory behind him, still oddly shrouded by his cloak—the wolf, as ever, at his side.

The Earl's blue eyes flared as she smiled at him, then dipped a slight and elegant curtsey.

"My lord . . .?"

He took her hand and bowed over it. "My lady. . ."

To Mallory she said nothing. Even the sight of him was fuel to her rage.

"My lord Reginald, I would be thankful for thine escort. Lord Mallory is not so well able to find his way through the crowds here gathered, nor to see the dangers lurking for such a maid as I!"

Lord Reginald flushed, and shot a look of discomfiture toward the slighted blind man. But Mallory smiled, seemingly unaffected.

"My lady chooses well. The Earl's honour is a puissant shield!" he offered pleasantly, and Lord Reginald felt his flush deepen at his predicament of being impaled upon the lightning that sparked between the pair.

Without a word, he took the lady's fingers and escorted her toward the table where lords of his station were seating themselves for the evening feasting. He glanced at her, and succumbed again to the tug of her beauty as he recalled the warlock's last words to her, and thought that her anger was not unreasonable.

Looking up, he caught sight of Lord Fulk, the Earl of Wallenford, and his son, Sir Ranulf, both engaged in some intent conversation with the Earl of Sussex. He frowned, and wondered at Wallenford's presence at court. Then, as he seated himself on one side of the lady Rosamund, he saw Sir Ranulf's gaze move, then stop abruptly—to stare with widening eyes and the interest of a rutting stallion upon Rosamund.

He frowned.

Mallory listened to tapestry of voices around him, the interweaving scraps of conversation that threaded through all manner of subject matter and interest. Then he heard the herald who bellowed:

"All rise for the King!"

Mallory stood up carefully as voices died away to silence, and listened to the feet that passed a brisk description of the length of the hall before stopping on the hollowed dais. Other footsteps, muffled by the ruffling of skirts, were the only accompaniment. He sensed vigour, ferocious and disciplined energy and will. Mallory smiled and seated himself with the rest. With one hand he reached into the pouch at his waist and explored the surface of the crystal sphere, feeling the figure of a moderately tall man of remarkable fitness. Still young, with close-cropped hair upon which a crown had been carelessly set. He was richly attired, but without armour.

He felt, also, the form of the woman beside the King, and knew she was Queen Elinor. Older, but as slim and hard as her lord. Elegant and with a shrewd proud wit.

Conversation began again. Servants pattered back and forth, setting dishes on the tables with decisive thuds that spoke of the weight of their contents, pouring wine as liberally as water. Mallory ate little. He fed the wolf most of his meat, and listened to Rosamund's flirtation with Lord Reginald, his answers and comments. He felt a fleeting pity for the Earl whose personality was softened by humanity. He was no match for Rosamund, he thought, for she had become as a young bird of prey discovering the power of her talons, dangerous.

Then, Mallory knew it was time to begin that which he had to do. He pushed himself carefully away from the table and stood.

"Lord Mallory. . .?" he heard Arundel's voice.

"Be thou still, my lord," he told the other quietly. "I must make my beginning. Alone!" With the wolf guiding him, Mallory found his way down the side of the hall and around the end of the long table. He sought and discovered the balancing point near the center of the hall midway between the waves of myriad voices that were already becoming stilled as people directed their attention toward him. Curious, he thought—how he could perceive the direction of the sight of others, yet could not find even the slightest understanding of the sense itself. He began walking forward, straight toward the dais where the King sat with the restless discomfiture of one who knew not how to be still.

"Who goes there . . .?" a voice challenged loudly from some place to his right, but Mallory did not answer, and held out a hand before him as he continued toward the dais, toward the King, who was now, he felt, aware of him.

"God's Blood! What is this?" he heard sound clearly before him and felt the air, the boldness, and curiosity of the one before him. He stopped and bowed gracefully.

"I am the King's good servant!" he said in clear tones that somehow were changed to carry the depth that had been a part of the warlock's voice. "I am come to petition my liege lord for the bestowing of knighthood by the King's own hand! And for the justice that makes of my king a legend!"

In the absolute silence that followed, Henry Plantagenet stared at the tall, shrouded figure before him, the wolf that was of menacing proportions and colour, and the uncommonly white hand that seemed to reach toward him. He stood up himself, never able to find repose for long.

"Prettily, if boldly said!" he commented. "Who art thou to make such request for us?"

Mallory raised his hands and pushed back the folds of his cloak, thrust back the hood. He heard a ripple of wonder.

"I am the Pendragon!" he called out with bold pride. "I am Mallory Pendragon, once called De Cheiney, begotten of the loins of Lord Robert De Cheiney upon the lady Edwina, within the sanctity of Christian wedlock. I am now the son of one known by the name of Uther Pendragon!"

Shocked raspings, gasps of astonishment all melted away as the crowd of nobles stared at the young man who stood in the midst of them. Startlingly white—his red eyes gleamed like pools of blood.

The Earl of Wallenford paled, clenched his fists and half-glanced at his son as he began to rise from his seat, then thought better of it.

De Cheiney? He had thought the boy long dead. But there was no mistaking that uncanny—unnatural look.

"Witchcraft!" he hissed loudly enough for those around him to catch it. "'Tis witchcraft!"

The King, very rarely caught unawares, stood alertly, surprised to realize that this was one of those occasions. He absorbed the tall, muscular body that was richly armoured and attired to the envy of any prince, the dragons broidered on a field of green, the silver hair, and death-pale face . . .

The strange red eyes that did not seem to focus.

De Cheiney. He frowned, remembering the name with a mind gifted with an acute sense of detail. Aye. He had heard strange things about the son. He shot a glance toward the Earl of Wallenford's face, his look hardening as he saw the tight, flushed expression there.

"If thou claim to be one Mallory De Cheiney," he said slowly, "we desire to know how it is that thou use the name of Pendragon and claim kinship to a prince of legend, dead these many ages, and known only to have sired none other than that favorite hero of minstrels, King Arthur?"

To the King's further surprise, the Pendragon smiled confidently.

"Arthur was my brother, Majesty! Got of the same father as I, for the Pendragon was the wizard Merlin's brother, and longer lived than mortal men!" The King leaned forward, well aware of the restless murmuring that had begun. Madness . . .?

"How may thou claim to be Mallory De Cheiney then?" he demanded.

The response was offered in a like, calm voice.

"As a man is given two beings, my liege, one material, and one of the spirit, so, too, I am endowed of two fathers. Robert De Cheiney sired my flesh! The Pendragon hath fathered my spirit and my mind!"

From the edge of his field of vision, Henry Plantagenet saw his friend Thomas lean forward abruptly and cross himself.

"This is heresy, Majesty!" Lord Fulk shouted protest as he strode from his place. "This is blackest heresy! The spirit comes from God, as is known to every man!" His voice rose in outrage. "This creature is mad! Or worse!"

"So we would suppose, my lord, being devout in our faith," the King responded with curious mildness, watching Lord Pendragon hold out a hand and cock an ear as Lord Fulk strode toward him. He felt a start as he realized that the pale young man was unable to see. "Nonetheless—my lord," the King said sharply, "we are interested in this diversion!"

Lord Fulk stopped at once, his hand abandoning his sword hilt at the implicit command.

"Thou suggest new exercise for our wits, Lord Mallory," the King continued to stare at the scarlet eyes. "By giving us to understand that fathering may be done by other than God, or through His Will. Likewise, it is in us to know that only Satan begets children as well!" The reply that was given immediately was offered in a voice that softened remarkably to reflect the serene confidence of certain knowledge.

"From the power that is God, *all* life is given, even unto those composed entirely of spirit!" With those words, the King sat down and grinned with delight as he glanced at his friend, Thomas A'Becket, whose intense stare was fixed upon the unusual man before them. Becket who had become a favourite to cross the swords of reason with. Henry leaned back in his seat and returned his gaze to the Earl of Wallenford, whose rigid stance and vehement demeanor alone were sufficient to cause him to hesitate in disposing of this mad, peculiar boy. That, and some equally insane wish brought to him in private audience with the same earl, that had to do with the deforestation of his fiefs.

"Do thou tell us, Lord . . . Pendragon," the King said slowly. "What proofs thou may offer to thy claim?" He stood again and committed a breach of etiquette only he could indulge by seating himself on the edge of the table before him.

"There are witnesses sufficient to testify to the truth that I am Robert De Cheiney's heir. And to the rest, I have proofs of another nature! Majesty, as thou reside now in was was once a part of Camelot, know that I, who am now the Lord Pendragon, may show thee Avalon where my brother's tomb may be found!" Mallory reached with his right hand and grasped the dragon hilt of the sword that hung from his left hip, slid it from its scabbard, and held it aloft.

"Here is my brother's sword," he called out. "Excalibur!"

Unsettled murmurings died away. All eyes fixed upon the shimmering brilliance of the wide-bladed sword, and the interweaving of the golden dragons that comprised its hilt.

"This is madness or contrivance, Majesty!" Lord Fulk bellowed furiously. "Or sorcery, and most clearly heresy of absurd proportion! Thou have but to look upon the face of this unnatural creature to perceive its unnatural source!"

Again, the King glanced at Becket. Thomas shook his head faintly, his expression grim as the Pendragon lowered the sword and resheathed it.

"And this were a jest, Sire," Becket murmured very softly. "It has gone far enough." Henry frowned, finding himself inclined to agree. He sternly voiced his most reasonable pronouncement.

"Lord Mallory. We are well familiar with the madness of the House of De Cheiney, and do now perceive the Devil's curse as well!" Mallory stepped forward to meet the challenge he heard in the King's voice, but Lord Fulk spoke from a close distance behind him.

"Here is final proof, my liege, on those matters to which I have already addressed. The forests of Wallenford must be cleared. Sorceries and evil abound there to haunt the lands and steal the faith and wits of all who dwell upon them, even as they have stolen the mind of this pitiful youth who conjures such magnificent fantasies! Aye, Majesty, he was found those years past, locked by his sire into a tower where his madness was given to howling in the manner of wolves. He was as one possessed. And, for charity, he was given care and well tended. Yet he fled and vanished, and, it was thought, was consumed by the wolves that are a very pestilence to my lands.

"It would appear that he was found by the old man, a sorcerer, who dwells there, and now he comes before thee filled with confusion and dreams of glory from tales of times long past us all!" Lord Fulk snorted. "Knighthood! My liege, he is blind! He is no more fit to bear arms than a leper!"

"I am come to petition the King's justice in the return of the fiefs of Wallenford!" Mallory's voice rang out with thunderous clarity. "It is mine inheritance! It is the fief of the Pendragon, favoured and beloved of my father, and bequeathed in trust to me. Likewise mine by right of inheritance through gift to Robert De Cheiney!" Lord Fulk strode forward.

"Majesty. He speaks again in bewildered riddles. This is utter blasphemy! And it is the same heathen madness that torments Wallenford, that I struggle to free my lands from!"

"Thou may not persevere against the wolves, my lord. For they are the guardians, and they hold mine inheritance for me until I am come to claim it!" Mallory inserted calmly.

"The wolves are Satan's own pestilence, Majesty, and must be destroyed to the safety of Christian souls! Even as that one!" Lord Fulk roared, pointing toward the great black wolf at the Pendragon's side. It snarled and bared its fangs, its hackles rising. Mallory touched his friend and spoke to it without sound.

'Go thou to my lady. Guard her as thou would myself.' The animal closed its jaws, shook its great head, and padded tamely away down the length of the hall.

"See?" Lord Fulk spun about to address the entire company. "Even now, he conjures in the manner of witches as he hath been taught by that ancient wizard that plagues my fiefs with evil! I declare him heretic and witch!" He swung again to the King. "Majesty?" His tone changed to another kind of earnestness. "I am thy true and loyal vassal, and I do plead for thy intercession to rid myself and my fiefs of this curse. I would bring Godliness to my lands as thou hast brought peace and justice to all England!"

Cleverly done, Henry thought, slipping from the edge of the table to settle into his chair. And reasonable. He reached for his wine goblet and sipped sparingly. Listened to the mutterings of assent that were growing among the crowd of assembled nobles in his court. Just then, the one called the Pendragon stepped toward him.

Mallory felt the moment, and the tempest of suspicion and fear that was brewing within it. He stepped forward, concentrating on the feel of the space before him, and drew Excalibur. He almost tripped as his feet found the dais, then he stepped up and held out the sword, hilt first.

"Majesty, I am thy true liegeman. And into thy hand I give my brother's sword which hath been given unto me," he said quietly. "Whether thou condemn me, or knight me, I pray, it will only be by the blade of this untainted weapon! For the rest. I am thine." He found the surface of the table and set the sword upon it, then stepped back.

"Seize him!" Lord Fulk roared. "He threatens the King!"

Mallory stood. He felt them rush toward him in a wave. Hands that clawed roughly, jerked and pulled, then dragged him through space gone askew, tumbling into chaos.

He felt himself assailed by old terrors that were not forgot, nor, of a sudden, at all remote . . . And he felt, likewise, the power inside rise and gather itself in the manner of a lion preparing to spring.

But. This was the world of men. He could not, he knew, he could not use the power in that way.

# FIFTEEN

Lord Reginald watched with rigid posture and intense concentration as the Pendragon was dragged, unresisting, from the hall. If Lord Fulk won in this, he thought, then there would be little to limit his power in the southeastern part of the kingdom. He looked at Rosamund, and saw her grim, ashen hue, a cauldron set to overboil. He caught her arm.

"For thy safety, be still and silent, my lady!" he hissed. Her eyes widened half defiantly as she met his look. "Should they know of thee, thou wilt be burned for a witch in an instant! 'Tis best left in Lord Pendragon's hands!" She continued to stare at him, impossible to decipher, yet, he thought, young and defenseless.

"What will happen now?" she whispered.

"I know not, my lady," he told her honestly. "I will go now to do what I may!" She looked away, down at the white protruding knuckles of her clenched hands. Fear, he thought, and looked to Sir Geoffrey. "Guard this lady, sir knight!" he breathed and moved away.

Rosamund did not look up as the older knight took his place beside her. When he was settled, she glanced up to see Lord Reginald disappear in the same direction they had taken Mallory, then caught the gaze of a tall, strong, handsome man with dark, curly brown hair and eyes of warm hazel. He raised an eyebrow, and smiled very slightly.

Lord Reginald marched briskly, having no difficulty in pursuing Lord Fulk and the personal guard who had seized Lord Mallory. He took the steps two at a time as he hurried down toward the dungeons of the castle, following the echoes of the voices ahead of him. Then, he rounded a corner, his nostrils flaring at the foul stench that announced his destination, and stopped abruptly.

"Strip him!" he heard Lord Fulk's vengeful bark. "The King will be eager to know what other marks of Satan may be found upon this creature! Then, bind him with chains, lest he attempt to take flight!" Very carefully, listening to the scuffling sounds ahead of him, Lord Reginald found mastery over his expression and walked around yet another corner.

Lord Fulk turned at once, his eyes widening in surprise. "My lord of Arundel?" he exclaimed. "How are thou so interested in this mad witch?"

Lord Reginald stared at the open astonishment that flickered across Mallory's face as he was spun about and the last of his clothing jerked away to reveal a body so different—than before. Perfect . . . Contemptible to dissemble so, Lord Reginald thought of, frowning as he looked at Wallenford.

"The wolves of which thou hast spoken, my lord," he said with an edge to his voice. "They begin to plague my lands as well."

"Aaah!" Lord Fulk nodded in the manner of one who has found an unexpected ally.

"I fear God as well as thee," Lord Reginald pursued deliberately, "and I would see an end to such evil!"

The look on Mallory's face was a hideous reflection of betrayal as he was dragged backwards, manacles bound about his wrists and ankles. Chains were passed through these and attached to the wall.

Lord Reginald looked away. "Are these his garments?" he asked. "I will remove them to the Bishop for exorcism and the fire, my lord!" Quickly, he bent and scooped up the scattered pile of armour and clothing. "Unnatural material!" he stared grimly at Lord Fulk. "I must trust to the relic of the Baptist's Hair to preserve my soul from harm!" He crossed himself as Wallenford studied him for a moment with less pleasure. Aye, think me superstitious as thou wilt, Lord Reginald thought as he shook his head and strode away. Mere wolves! He thought, startling himself. What did the rest of them begin to know of witchcraft that could compare . . . with his own recent experience?

He hurried back along corridors and stairs to the chamber that he shared with the Pendragon. There, he concealed Lord Mallory's belongings among his own. Then, he strode briskly back to the great hall to seek out the lady Rosamund. To consider their next move. Lord Fulk, he thought, surely would not dare to kill the Pendragon at once, but was wise enough to wait on the King's disposition.

Henry Plantagenet ignored the conglomerate uproar of voices that filled the hall and frowned as he stared at the sword still lying on the table before him. A composite design that combined ancient Roman breadth and the current length for a two-handed sword, it was jewel bright, sparkling with an unnatural-seeming, almost fluid brilliance such as he had never seen in steel before. And the letters inscribed in the upper length of the blade were ornately imbedded. Unmistakable. They spelled out the name "Excalibur."

He leaned forward abruptly and brought his strong fingers around the wondrously contrived hilt that was composed of two, intricately detailed golden dragons, each, he noted, with glinting ruby eyes. He stiffened a little, feeling warmth, then a faint stirring beneath his hand, as though the golden creatures were alive. Aye—and another such movement. And he knew, beyond question, that the sword was magical.

Frowning, he sat back and set the weapon across his knees.

"Mayhap, this—Lord Pendragon spoke the truth?" he murmured very softly.

"Mayhap, my liege, this is Satan's cunning made manifest?" Becket spoke suddenly beside him. The King looked at his liegeman.

"Do thou consider it so, Thomas?" Henry enquired in another tone. " 'Tis certain that Wallenford would have us believe so!"

"God hath not the need for witchcraft, Sire," Becket began. The King smiled.

"Nay, Thomas! On that we must agree. God hath the use of miracles instead! But, where to draw the distinction? That is the puzzle!" His smile widened to a grin. "As thou hast said to us on more than one occasion, Thomas: Under God, all things are possible! Consider. Should this strange, white youth indeed be such as he claims, mayhap his right to the throne of England hath more sanctity than our own!"

"Never, my liege!" Becket rasped in horror, and the King's eyes narrowed a little as he studied his friend's face.

"I begin to detect an inclination toward sanctimony in thee, good Thomas! I caution thee. It does not sit well upon the shoulders of statesmen!" He stood up abruptly, still holding the bright sword, and offered his arm to the Queen. "I hold what is mine, my friend. Know that!" he said with potent quiet. Feeling Elinor's grip upon his forearm, he strode away from both table and hall, briefly exchanging glances with her as they reached the corridors that led to the Royal Chambers.

Rosamund saw the brown-haired young man who had met her look with a smile begin to stride purposefully toward her. She glanced at Sir Geoffrey. The knight's mouth was set in a thin line, and she stiffened her back. Reaching her, the young man bowed courteously. He was somewhat shorter than Mallory, she noted at once, but much thicker—more powerful.

"Thou art newly come to Court, my lady?" he enquired politely, his eyes intent. "Such beauty as thine could not be forgotten by any who are so privileged as to behold it!" Charming, Rosamund thought and smiled a little.

"This is the Lady Rosamund, ward to my lord, the Earl of Arundel!" Sir Geoffrey inserted crisply. The young man glanced at him.

"And I am Lord Ranulf of Wallenford, my lady!" he introduced himself with equal clarity. Lord Fulk's heir. Rosamund looked at him with new interest. Her mind began to thread and weave in the manner of cat dissecting a vole.

"Well met, my lord!" she said more gently and held out a long-fingered hand to the accompaniment of a slightly warmer smile. He bowed again, and kissed the back of it with soft, full lips.

"Lord Ranulf?" He straightened abruptly, as the Earl of Arundel strode forward to stand at Rosamund's other side.

"My lord," Sir Ranulf responded politely, smiling a little as he saw himself caught between the knight's disapproval and the Earl's cool formality. Truly, he thought, this lady was uncommonly well guarded!

"Sir Ranulf is betrothed to the Earl of Sussex's daughter, my lady," Lord Reginald told Rosamund. She glanced up at him.

"Should my father and Lord Sussex ever agree to the dower!" Sir Ranulf said cheerfully, opening channels once more. Lord Reginald's expression grew sterner still, for he had not known of that, nor was he convinced it to be truth. Instead, he turned to Rosamund.

"My lady," he told her. "After so long and arduous a day's

travelling, it is past time for a maid as thyself to retire. I will escort thee!"

Sir Ranulf recognized the dismissal and bowed. "I bid thee good night, my lady. My lord!" he said and turned away.

Rosamund, stung by the commanding tone that Lord Reginald had used, shot him a dark look as he reached for her hand, and began striding away across the hall, furious at his management. Lord Reginald set out in pursuit, Sir Geoffrey behind him.

"That wench needs a thrashing!" he heard the other mutter and glanced back to give the knight a startled look.

The black wolf glided to a corner and crouched unnoticed, and Rosamund turned as Lord Reginald closed her door behind him.

"Though thou art safe in my care, my lady, it does thy honour little good for me to be seen here with thee."

"I am well able to tend to mine own honour, my lord!" she retorted sharply. "Indeed, I will do better than Mallory!" She held out her hands, fingers spread, and uttered an ancient word with clear command. But the spell did not work. The flames she summoned did not come. Her eyes widened and she looked at Lord Reginald, seeing for the first time, a glimpse of wariness directed toward herself in his expression.

Again, with vehement determination, she conjured. And again, she was answered with absolute silence. And then, she understood.

"Mallory has it all!" she hissed, her fists clenching. "Even the power that was mine from birth is gone!" Her tone strengthened with anger, and she began pacing with furious vigour. "The fool! The crass stupidity he hath exercised. To so stand before the King with all the manner of an innocent child. And, then—to allow himself to be so taken when he hath the power to prevent it!"

"Had he so?" Lord Reginald gasped his astonishment, still troubled by the sight of Lord Mallory's naked body being bound in chains against the dark stone wall of the castle dungeon—that look upon his face. Rosamund glared at him.

"He is the last Prince of the Fairie, as my father hath decreed!" Her tone was bitter. "And now, as I suspected, I am become a mere mortal!" Lord Reginald watched her with mixed feelings of confusion and sympathy. To be disinherited was something he could well understand, but from such as this?

"Is it so bad a thing to find thyself human, my lady?" he tried. Rosamund stopped pacing and faced him, her eyes, for the first time, enormous with pain. She did not answer at once, and when she spoke, it was in a whisper.

"I loved my father as well, my lord. I was ever obedient to his will. As he directed, I have learned to hunt, to bear sword and armour, to fight, to be—a man. At his command, likewise, it was I who taught Mallory all he knows of horsemanship and weaponry." She challenged him with her head held high, her pride ferociously apparent and powerful. "And now, I am to be a woman? To yield to my father's last caprice and surrender all in taking Mallory to be my lord? To become in all things second to him, his servant and chattel? Nay, my lord! It will not serve!" She spun away in a swirl of green and scarlet, her fists still clenched, her back straight.

Lord Reginald stood helplessly, his heart thudding uncomfortably in his chest. He understood that her sullenness had a goodly measure of reason, even of justice. Aye, she was strong. Not like other maids he had encountered. Hunger flared in him and he took a step toward her.

"My lady?" It were the soft expression of his concern, and more. He watched her head bow down, touched her shoulder, and spun her supple warmth into his arms, burying his face against her hair as he felt her shudder.

Aaah, she was a woman such as to make a man dream of impossible things! He felt his loins flare with heat, and sought refuge in his own pride.

"I would be content to be thy true knight, Lady Rosamund," he whispered fervently against the fresh, silken fragrance of her hair. "I would love thee, and honour thee." Her face turned up to him, eyes wide, and, unable to resist, he bent and kissed her with all the passion he had been confining since he first really saw her. He closed his eyes and moved his lips to her eyes, now veiled by those miraculous lashes, and murmured. "I will find a way to secure Wallenford for thee." He felt her arms close about his waist and shivered for the fire that shot through him and groaned a little at the violent urgency caused by the feel of her body against his own. "This man is most glad of thy humanity," he whispered hoarsely, "for there is no greater miracle than woman!" He bent his head and found the pulse at the base of her throat, drew up a hand to cup the softness of her breast, and bore her backwards to the bed.

He found the laces of her gown, the silken samite of her chemise, and the velvet softness of her skin. Rosamund closed her eyes as well, savouring the reverence of his touch, and the pleasure that swirled through her belly to weaken her knees, a sweetness such as she had only known once before.

She surrendered to it, relishing the smooth, tawny-skinned, hard-muscled frame he revealed to her, and opened herself to his entry. She felt him thrust, then shudder in violent explosion as her pleasure began to build, then shrink inside, fading away to leave her to pulse alone. Seeking. Abandoned. Disappointed.

"Forgive me, sweeting," he murmured, drawing her into his arms. But Rosamund turned her back to him and curled herself up to stare at the cold stone wall. She ignored the hand that reached to stroke her hair. "It will be better next time," she heard him say. "The fire in me was beyond my mastery of it."

She did not answer. Or move.

Uncertain, Lord Reginald drew away to find his clothing. He dressed quickly, still watching her.

"My lady?" he asked unhappily, acutely aware that somehow she had withdrawn from him, thrust him out. He covered her with the bed furs, looking at her once more, but she did not utter a sound, or move, save to bury her face against her arms. Not knowing what else to do, Lord Reginald stepped back, realizing as he did so, that she was not the virgin maid he had expected. He slipped quietly through the door, shocked by the importance he had attached to that.

For he had thought to wed her . . .

"I will know from thee, Mallory De Cheiney, where it is that the old man may be found!" Lord Fulk's voice stabbed the air with temper. "Aye, that old man who haunts the forests of Wallenford, and who hath, likewise, filled thy mad brain and Devil's soul with mischief!"

Mallory shivered at the feel of the dank, almost slimy cold stone against his naked skin. He pulled at the manacles that held him spread-eagled against the wall. He did not answer, but closed his eyes, and thought again of Lord Reginald's words.

Was it always so in the world of men? Had these been his

brother's difficulties? Was it worse for the nightmare memories that comprised the entirety of his childhood, or for the understanding in him that so clearly perceived other alternatives?

"Answer me!" Lord Fulk roared.

"To what purpose, my lord?" Mallory released the words with soft-toned courtesy. "He is not for thee."

"Witch! Heretic!" Lord Fulk's voice dropped to an enraged snarl. "I can make thee suffer."

Mallory breathed deeply, feeling the power shift restlessly inside him again. He confined it and collected himself.

"I doubt it not, my lord!" he said in the same tone, then let his voice reflect the power within, becoming deep and somber. "But I do give thee honest caution. As thou sow the seeds of my blood, so, too, thou shalt reap the harvest of the same!" He heard Lord Fulk's sharply indrawn breath. Then, the snarled order:

"Flog this monster!"

Mallory felt hands at the manacles that held him pinioned. He was loosed, seized, twisted about, then flung, belly first, down, against the damp, foul-smelling litter that covered the floor. Before he could shift, he was bound to immobility again.

There was a hissing sound in the air, and splintering pain sliced in a line across his back. He gasped from the shock of it. But then there was another blow, lower down. Mallory's body jerked involuntarily, and he felt the shattering of the third blow that sliced across his shoulders, causing an agony that slipped inside to make a swirling chaos of his strength. And, with the fourth blow, he cried out a little, as he understood other levels of vulnerability beyond the kicks and crude blows that had been his lot from Robert De Cheiney.

He lost count after that. Nor did he notice the hissing sound of the whip preceding each blow. There were only succeeding waves of pain that moved and swelled into a crescendo, that held him suspended before he began to drown in the surcease of unconsciousness.

The Earl of Wallenford stared at the limp white body that had proved as responsive as that of any other man. Scarlet blood trickled across white skin of incredible and pristine purity, oozing from open slices that formed an irregular tracery of damage across the well-muscled back, in drops that did not darken or dull. Lord Fulk shifted, half-reaching to touch, his mind caught by the unsettling contrast and the image of blood on snow. But he jerked back, and shivered a little, remembering De Cheiney's ominous promise. He turned, and strode from the dungeons, his skin crawling abruptly in response to his fear that so it would come to be true.

# SIXTEEN

With the closing of the door that heralded her solitude, Rosamund loosed herself from the tense bonds of her rigid self-containment, and began to weep the pain of her confusion, of her disappointment. . . .

Lord Reginald had spoken of devoted and serving love. Yet, he had spilled his appetite into her with intemperate haste, and fled from her unfulfilled pleasure. And, he had not wooed her further, but had gone entirely.

"Why?" she whispered hoarsely to the silence about her. "Why am I born a woman when I should be my father's son? Why must I be dependent where I should be free, I, who was taught the nature and feel of that same freedom. Aaah, my father, what hast thou brought me to?

"And, why hast thou so favoured Mallory? For all that he is a man, he weeps if he injures a foe, and hath not stomach sufficient even to undertake his own defense!" Her voice gained power as anger stirred, began to brew. She clenched her fists. "It was supremely unjust of thee, my father!" She sat up and turned about to see the gleaming brilliance of Mallory's wolf from where the beast lay in a corner across the chamber. She remembered then, another afternoon of loving, filled with Mallory's lean white body, the gentleness of his hands, the softness and delicacy of his mouth.

And how she had ridden him in triumph like the warrior she was! How he had rejoiced in that. Her mouth tightened with contempt for Lord Reginald, and she wiped the moisture from her eyes and stared at the tears smeared across the back of her hand. Tears of blood—such as only came from those of the Fairie.

She frowned more deeply. Aye. Mallory had brought her to softness and compliance that time. It was that, she knew, which had betrayed her, for the old warlock had given all of it to him, even herself. And now, in a female form she were powerless to change, she was now condemned further, to dwell in a world where men ruled, where she was viewed as little more than a vessel for their passion. Or a mare for the begetting of sons—who grew to become other men.

It was a vile destiny.

Mallory's eagle had disappeared when Lord Reginald reached his own chamber and closed the door behind him. He looked about him, but the rest of his own and the Pendragon's belongings were undisturbed. He sighed and undressed again, eager to seek his rest for his body was replete with satisfaction. He settled himself on one of the truckle beds and drew his cloak lightly over his lower body.

He closed his eyes, and, at once, thought unhappily of Rosamund. His self-conscious chagrin at his own failure was contradicted by his deep anger in the knowledge of the impurity of her body. She had known others! He felt betrayed, and it was worse for the way she had withdrawn from him, turned away so completely as to deny him opportunity to undo the consequences of his haste. Worse, for being left to stand like a callow boy compared—to whom?

He sighed uncomfortably, and thought, as well, of Mallory. That kindred expression he had seen that was chastisement for his ploy with Lord Fulk, rendered worse for seeing the other stripped, bound in chains.

Yet, Rosamund had said . . . Bewildered, Lord Reginald tossed restlessly.

"What is there without honour?" he asked the unresponsive air. Nothing, he knew. This was a chaos he had brought on himself.

Rosamund was again attired in her boy's garments when Lord Reginald came upon her the next morning.

"Good morrow, my lady," he said with some slight hesitation, his eyes travelling to the sword that hung from her left hip, then back to her face.

"My lord," she responded, meeting his look with lethally cool composure. Beyond his ability to prevent it, he felt a flush creep up his neck in response to the penetrating clarity of her incredible eyes. Again, he was brought to feel like a callow boy, and he stiffened, disliking the sensation.

"While we are at court, my lady," he said frigidly, "it is best to let it be known that thou art my ward! By the same, I may defend thy name—and honour!" Her eyes narrowed at the barely perceptible hesitation.

"Should I be grateful, my lord of Arundel? For I am well acquainted with the use of arms, and capable to mine own defense!" She set her hands on her hips, aggressively facing him. "Though, it would appear, from thy expression, that honour is one thing for thee—a man, and another for myself—a woman!"

Lord Reginald went scarlet under this direct attack, and the contempt that followed.

"Feeble creatures, men! Thou. And Mallory!"

Lord Reginald glanced furtively about him to be sure that no one else was close enough to witness this diatribe, and felt the rise of his own jealousy.

"It is honour in a highborn maid to husband her virtue!" he retorted.

"Thou were willing enough to dispose of it last night, my lord!" she shot back in scathing tones. "All clothed in protestations of love! No longer am I innocent of the manners and hypocrisy of men who rut with the grace of the wild boar!"

Lord Reginald scowled angrily. "I have thought to wed thee, my lady, though thou art not dowered . . . ," he began.

"Am I not?" she cut through with silken tones. "There is more to me than the claim to Wallenford!"

He ignored that and leaned forward. "But, my lady, I expect virtue in my bride. How many others hast thou bedded, woman? Aye, how many, roaming about without chaperone, or maid, and with but a blind man to guard thee?"

Rosamund smiled. He was jealous.

"But one, my lord!" she said quietly, triumph glinting in her dark eyes.

His mouth went white. "Can it matter so much to thee?" she challenged. "Thou were virgin once, I warrant! Virginity is but a condition for children!"

His flush returned at this last sally. "Who . . . ?" he demanded, goaded by both his feelings and her barbs. She eyed him from head to toe and he stiffened.

"Mallory Pendragon, my lord," she said very softly. "Who, other?"

He exhaled violently, for it was as he had thought, but to hear her say it was different from the speculations that tormented his mind. "Mallory was virgin likewise . . . ," she added.

Silence hovered for a moment. Then Lord Reginald found his voice.

"I thought—thou hast a deep misliking for Lord Pendragon?" he asked slowly, feeling bewildered by the awareness that, somehow, Rosamund was shredding all his values and many of his beliefs, turning them into a quagmire.

She sighed wearily, spoke quietly this time.

"Lord Reginald. Mayhap thou can understand this. I am not Eve made from Adam's rib. I am the daughter of the High Warlock Pendragon! My soul is mine own. In bondage to no one! My body is mine own to bestow as I will! I am neither property, nor chattel to be disposed to the will of others. And, my love is a gift to be earned. It is not obligation, nor yet, to be taken by force." He swallowed and she looked at him steadily. "For all, I wear the form of a woman, I am spirit, as thou! Think on that!" She turned and strode away with masculine vigour, her stride buoyant in the manner of a deer, yet, he saw, with a woman's unconscious sway. The black wolf padded disconsolately behind her.

"Yield thyself, my lord! For the Lady Rosamund hath conquered thee!"

At the sound of the voice, the Earl of Arundel spun violently about to see Sir Geoffrey leaning against a nearby stone wall, his eyes twinkling merrily, his lined face alight with amusement. Lord Reginald glowered as his flush rose to beyond the roots of his hair. Sir Geoffrey laughed.

"She will make a boy of any man, that one!" Sir Geoffrey chuckled. "Me . . . ? I learned long ago it was safer to pay monies for a woman's favours toward the easement of my flesh! Thus I safeguard myself from such complexities. Women are not made to be understood by men!" Thoroughly annoyed, Lord Reginald clenched both his teeth and his fists.

"If thou wish to stay in my service, sir knight," he growled menacingly, "thou will keep a still tongue in thy head!" He turned and strode away in the manner of a man engaged in war.

Sir Geoffrey watched him, chuckled again, and shook his head. Nay, he thought, his young lord was no match for the lady Rosamund. Nor, it seemed, was the lord Mallory to whom she were, rather dubiously, he thought, betrothed.

Nay, she was not unlike a she-wolf loosed among a pen of

tame fowl! He grinned at his own analogy, and sobered at once as he thought of the blind young man in chains below. Lord Mallory seemed a truly noble soul, for all the mystery that surrounded him.

The King paced restlessly back and forth across the antechamber, pausing to kick at one of the fur rugs that littered the floor, shoving it out of his way. He frowned.

"It is a most curious case, is it not, Thomas?" he muttered. "We confess ourself to be fascinated by it!" He stopped abruptly to stare again at the magical sword that lay on one of the oak tables in the chamber, amid a littering of scrolls and documents.

Becket, seated by the privilege of his friendship with the King, did not respond. Henry Plantagenet eyed his friend, somberly dressed in the daily garb of his new posting.

"We did not make thee Archbishop of Canterbury in order for thee to sit about and fatten like some pedantic lamb, Thomas!" he commented. "Or, are we growing old so rapidly, then, that thou recline thus to remind us of the years that have slipped away?"

"Thou art still a young man, my liege. In the prime of thy years!" Becket answered.

At thirty-three, Henry knew it so. He looked again at the sword. Yet—he thought, life was an uncertain commodity. And he had so much still to do . . . Thomas, who had been his gay, wily and vigourous friend, now, since his appointing, was becoming another kind of man. Hardened, old-seeming, unknowable in other ways, concealed behind the sanctity of the Cloth.

The King's pacing reflected his growing unease, for he had thought Becket's loyalty sufficient to counter any ambitions he may have harboured. But it was beginning to appear that the piety of a new-found, even sanctimonious disposition could well alter that. He stopped pacing at the far side of the chamber, and turned to face his friend.

For an instant, Church and State stared at each other. Becket got to his feet, his gaze falling with the appearance of meekness.

"This is a matter for the Church to try, Majesty," the Archbishop pursued, "for it must be determined how the Devil hath undertaken to contort and steal the soul of this—Lord Pendragon. Likewise, the extent to which his powers are given to unnatural creatures and witches."

Henry continued to stare cautiously, thinking of the sword, Excalibur, its meaning, and the trust that had been placed, thereby, in his own hands.

"This is a matter for the State, I think, Becket," he answered in a harder voice. "For it involves the disposition of one of our greatest southern fiefs. If this youth is the same Mallory De Cheiney, and witnesses can be found to attest to it, then his claim is just. Which impels us to examine the eagerness with which Lord Wallenford disclaims him. We do not forget that Lord Wallenford proclaimed the youth's death to us these six years past."

"The Pendragon is accursed!" Becket protested. "He is a creature of madness and sorcery. All could see plain enough the fire of Satan in his eyes."

"He is blind, Thomas!" Henry broke in with hard asperity. "And he is white beyond the norm for men. Nay!" He raised both a hand and his voice as Becket stiffened, opened his mouth. "Listen. Once, when we were courting our Lady Elinor many years ago, while we were hunting in the forests of Acquitaine we did spy a white hart.

"We put chase to the beast and followed it for some few miles. Finally, we trapped it in a gorge. And, when we were about to loose the hounds upon it, for it is well known that the meat of the white hart is a blessing, it was the Queen who pointed to the rare beauty of the beast that was clothed, she did remind us, in God's own colour." The King's eyes locked with those of his Archbishop. His tone softened for emphasis. "Its eyes were red as well, Thomas. Red and white. Are these not the colours of those who undertake God's Holy Cause?"

Becket opened his mouth, but could find no response. The King took a step toward him, his gaze unwavering.

"Thou art bred a Saxon, Thomas, and surely thou must recall that Pendragon is an ancient title for princes of this realm. Or is that fact forgot in this fervent preoccupation with the duties of the Church? Even King Arthur was known to be a most puissant Christian prince in those barbarous days."

Again, Becket did not answer, but his lean face tightened.

"Nay," Henry told him, "we choose to pursue this matter ourself, and—should it come to the *thee*, Thomas, know that the Church will intervene only at our discretion!"

Silence hovered between them. Then, Becket bowed.
"Majesty!" he said softly.
The King watched him turn and walk away.

When the door had closed behind him, Henry Plantagenet exhaled sharply and turned to the Queen, who had been broidering in silence in another part of the chamber. She looked up and met his grey eyes.

"Becket will serve thee ill, Henry. When he finds the courage for it!" she said baldly.

He sighed. "I had hoped he would be my ally in what I would accomplish, Elinor," he said slowly. "I will have this kingdom to prosper in economy and peace and justice! And, for that, power must come from a singular, divinely endowed source, which is the King! Look at the wars that preceded us, and consider the strife that will result should we be swayed in this purpose. . . ." He stepped to the table and touched the hilt of the sword, feeling again the fascination of the almost living golden dragons. He heard the Queen stand, the rustling of her robes as she approached him.

"Wouldst thou be another Arthur, Henry?" she asked fondly. "It is that manner of greatness that I see that brought me to love thee." He looked up and held out an arm. Smiled. She moved into the embrace. "Thou art still the youth I saw, endowed with great beauty, and filled with dreams of great breadth and depth. God pray thy sons be worthy of thee!"

He bent and kissed this lioness of womankind. "And, mayhap—this is Camelot!" he murmured against the gold of her hair.

Mallory hung from arms that ached unbearably, and struggled against his growing exhaustion for new air to fill lungs that could not properly function. Once or twice, he gulped awkwardly at water that was carelessly poured against his mouth to trickle for the most part down his body. . . .

And, when he was beaten again, he cried out, and struggled for mastery of the swirling power inside him that gathered itself like an enraged dragon. That was the hardest thing of all—to leash that defiant beast. Pain gnawed at his flesh and chewed through his will with relentless determination, making him tremble with the raw acuity and depth of all his knowledge of fear, demanding his surrender.

* * *

He was only vaguely aware of crumpling to lie shuddering and gasping on another plane of cold stone when they loosed him eventually, and he tried to twist away when someone covered his raw, chilled body with a garment like a surcoat, binding it at his waist with some manner of cord. He could not react to the hands that bound his wrists together, nor to the men who dragged him through spaces that swooped with sickening lack of direction until he heard the murmurings of voices all about him. He gasped awkwardly and realized he was being held upright, and listened to the mutterings that died away to tense silence. Then he heard a single voice, a lion's roaring.

"What hast thou done, my lord? We did not order this?"

Mallory felt the hands leave him, and he dropped to his knees, falling forward to lie panting with effort on the rushes of what was, surely, the great hall.

"I feared the harm this mad De Cheiney might bring upon thee, Majesty!" Lord Fulk's voice above him was tinged with defensiveness. Deep inside, the dragon sighed fire, and settled a little to coil itself.

"Thou hast overstepped the charge of thy office, my lord!" The King's reprimand shattered the air like a lash. "Loose his bonds. This man is of noble blood, and is deserving of our justice, not such as this."

Mallory felt the manacles being taken away. He groped and tried to sit up, but fell back with a gasp. His flesh—his flesh, that was so much weaker than the forces he held inside him.

Lord Reginald stared in sober horror at the changes two days had wrought. Lord Mallory looked worse, if it were possible, than the scarecrow grey boy he had found imprisoned in Wallenford Castle six years before. Streaked with grime and blood, the tattered surcoat could not conceal the terrible beatings he had endured.

"I had not thought," Lord Reginald half-whispered, "that Wallenford would dare so far." His mouth tightened. Nothing, so far as he knew, that Lord Pendragon had done, warranted this.

Out of the corner of his eye, he saw Lady Rosamund slip into the far end of the hall, saw the way she stopped abruptly and stared, the colour draining from her face as she caught sight of Mallory. She looked wildly about. Lord Reginald beckoned discreetly, and she strode around the periphery of the hall toward him, slipping silently, like a shade into the space between himself and Sir Geoffrey. He glanced down and saw the haunted, terrible darkness of her eyes, and flinched.

The black wolf that had been following growled and raised its hackles, then left her side to slink across the hall with bared teeth, flattened ears, and eyes of golden menace. It dropped to glide arrow-true toward Lord Fulk, whose face whitened as he spun to face the beast and grope for his sword.

The wolf snarled, tensed. Another low call penetrated the hall, and the wolf stopped in its tracks as Lord Mallory struggled to raise himself a little and held out a hand toward the beast.

In an instant, the wolf abandoned its attack, and padded toward the white hand, dropping down to lie beside the long, abused body. The white hand settled on black fur, and with clearly heard gasps of pain, Lord Pendragon sank back on the rushes that covered the floor.

All was silence. Some crossed themselves. Lord Fulk shivered for the chill that crawled across his skin and stared at the King.

Henry Plantagenet rose abruptly from his throne and stepped lightly down from the dais to stop, legs apart, in front of Lord Mallory. The Earl of Wallenford bowed his head uneasily, and the wolf simply looked up with tame-seeming interest.

"Lord—Pendragon?" the King spoke clearly. Mallory struggled again, managing to push himself up onto his arms and draw his knees under him as he turned toward the King's voice with a haggard grimace.

"Majesty . . . ?" he whispered through dry lips.

"We wonder how is it that thou didst not loose this beast upon this man who hath so damaged thee?" Henry Plantagenet asked very softly, staring hard into those peculiar, scarlet eyes, his own widening slightly at the slight smile that flickered across firm white lips.

"The wolf is my friend, my liege. Not my instrument," Mallory answered hoarsely. He gathered himself with hard effort. "I am thy true liegeman, and must, accordingly, give the entirety of my trust to the King's justice!" His strength failed, and he sank down breathing heavily, into the haze of pain that beckoned him.

As the scarlet eyes closed, the King thought again of the

white hart, and wondered with something of conviction, if there were some connection. Trust, so absolutely expressed.

He turned to Lord Fulk. Wallenford's face was a flushed blend of anger and nervous chagrin. Then he raised his head to pass his gaze about the rest of the company of his court.

"Would that all our liegemen show such faith!" he said with slow, toneless deliberation, letting his gaze linger on Becket a moment longer than any of the rest. "For, by such, we may hold the peace of our realm!" He glanced down again at the pale bloody form at his feet, and the wolf that crouched protectively beside it. Another kind of dog, he thought. And just as loyal. Something more was called for here. He again scanned the gathering.

"Are there none to tend the lord—Pendragon until he may be brought to plead his case before us in a manner befitting his rank?" he asked, then turned, and again thinking of the white hart, strode back to his throne. Reseating himself, Henry's gaze sharpened with interest as he saw the Earl of Arundel step purposely from the ranks of the company and walk toward him, flanked by four knights who wore his emblem.

The King sat back as Arundel bowed, remembering that it had been this same young lord he had dispatched with Wallenford to attend to that business six years past. He noted the grim composure of that pleasant face as the Earl straightened.

"Majesty," Lord Reginald pronounced firmly. "I will gladly give attention to the lord Pendragon."

Henry nodded.

"So be it," he said quietly, and watched as the Earl's knights raised the injured Pendragon, then carried him from the hall. He frowned a little, connecting another piece of information as he thought on how he had noted the Earl's reluctance to ally himself through marriage to Petworth. Then, he caught sight of a female form in boy's garb, striding from a corner of the hall to follow the small party. Nay. He had been right. This was not a simple matter.

# SEVENTEEN

Lord Mallory was entirely unconscious when they laid him on the truckle bed, and remained so as the other three knights departed the chamber. Sir Geoffrey began to strip away the soiled and shabby garment that covered him, exposing the long, intercrossing gashes that laced his back.

Rosamund stood by the door unmoving, simply watching, hardly aware of the way Lord Reginald's eyes flitted from her to Lord Mallory and Sir Geoffrey, who had taken silent command of his care and cleansing. She watched as the knight washed away bloody debris and filth, then rubbed salve into the hideous weals, and, as Mallory began to rouse, raised him gently to drink from a cup of watered wine.

"Sir Geoffrey . . . ," Mallory murmured recognition as his fingers groped unsteadily and touched.

"All will be well, my lord." Gruffly soothing, the aging knight tucked soft blankets and furs around Mallory's lower body. "Do thou sleep, for thou hast the King's protection now!" Mallory smiled a little as he sank back.

"Aye!" he whispered in a tone of great content.

Lord Reginald shifted, thinking of a time in his boyhood when he had known a like degree of care from this same vassal, and realizing with surprise that his knight had come to love the lord Pendragon.

Rosamund's frayed nerves snapped in an explosion of rage.

"Thou art a fool, Mallory, to let thyself be so used when but a simple exercise of power would suffice prevent it!" She spat her contempt.

Mallory's smile faded in a face that had become weary. His eyes opened again.

"Rosamund . . . ?"

"Pah!" she hissed. "I have naught but contempt for thee! I despise this weak-mindedness in thee. Thou—thou, who art the Prince of Fairie, to so let thyself be bound in irons and flogged like that weak creature my father found! Thou art unfit for that which he hath bestowed upon thee! Then, to lie there like a babe and let others tend thee when thou may heal thyself! I cannot comprehend this disgusting weakness, nor thy lack of pride in thy high office!"

"This is the world of men . . . ," Mallory began mildly.

"Is it so?" Rosamund snarled furiously. "Then, do thou be a man and deliver unto me, who art my father's daughter, that which rightfully belongs to me so that it may not be so shamefully misused! I am not such a prince to allow myself to be butchered like a mortal criminal! Aaaah—how much I despise thee!" She spun on her heel, and the door closed behind her with a resounding crack.

Lord Reginald swallowed discomfiture, and, strangely, Mallory grinned with seeming delight, certainly untroubled by her temper. He sighed then, and murmured. "Pain is exhausting!"

Goaded, Lord Reginald found some expression for his feelings.

"The lady Rosamund is a termagant!" he grated harshly, thinking that she was most unpleasantly devoid of any trace of womanly tenderness.

Mallory turned his head a little, continuing to smile. "Aah, Reginald!" he said softly. "But she cares! That is the chief thing. She cares . . ."

Lord Reginald stared at him, completely bewildered. He ducked away to another question that troubled him. "Did she speak truth, my lord? Have thou such powers as to prevent what hath occurred?"

Mallory's face sobered as he let his head sink carefully down onto soft pillows. "Aye." He whispered.

Lord Reginald frowned. "Then, I do not understand whyfore thou hast not undertaken to use the same," he pursued.

Mallory sighed. "Then know this," he said. "The powers my father bequeathed to me are vast beyond thy comprehension, and I must be master of them. I must use them with discretion, if at all, for the might of power is not in its use, but rather is found in the manner and direction of its constraint. Passion, of any kind, is the least of reasons to engage the same!" His voice faded, exhaustion clear in the drawn look of his face. "Now, I would sleep and let my flesh heal itself," he murmured and went lax. The wolf, lying at the foot of the bed, set its head on its forepaws and did likewise. Sir Geof-

frey settled himself in a nearby chair with a protectively pater-
nal air. Lord Reginald gave him a considering look.

"Dost thou guard Lord Pendragon then?"

"Aye, my lord." De Beauvais hesitated.

"Hast thou no fear of him? This magic . . . ?"

The knight shook his head. "Nay, my lord," he said in the
same tone, then smiled ruefully. "Now, were the lady Rosamund so endowed, then I would tremble, for she is witch
enough to terrify any man as it is!"

Lord Reginald did not answer that, but thought grimly of
her temper, and resolved to find out what the wench was about
now. Turning suddenly, he left the chamber.

Rosamund ducked easily as the quintain swung its lethal
mace toward her back in answer to her blow upon the shield.
She spurred the silver horse on to the end of the field and
brought him to a plunging halt, glowering at the teaching device. It was too tame by far to suit her mood.

"Well ridden, lad!" a cheerful voice exclaimed behind her.
Rosamund spun the silver horse about. "From the temper of
thy charge, I'll warrant thou prefer a real foe!" A large knight
on a bay warhorse that was obviously fresh smiled at her from
behind the nasal of his helm. She recognized Ranulf of Wallenford at once, and knew he could not identify her beneath
the casque helm that covered her own face.

"I see thy skill, squire," he continued. "Would thou couch
a lance against me?"

It was intended as a kindness, she recognized. She nodded.
He was a man, and she was eager to best a man. And, for the
moment, any man would serve.

His eyes passed over the horse beneath her. "I fear thy
mount has a palfrey's lightness," he pointed out, generously
thinking to even her odds.

"What he lacks in substance, my lord, he recovers in speed
and agility!" she growled.

Sir Ranulf looked at her. "So be it then," he said mildly,
and, putting spurs to his own animal, galloped to the other end
of the field. She waited as he set his shield upon his arm,
couched his lance. Then she lowered her own, and charged.

She shifted a little to one side in the saddle, and Sir Ranulf's lance slipped off the side of her shield. Her own lance
caught him squarely on the middle of his shield, the force of
her blow against the much heavier man, almost unseating her.

She swept past, furious that she had not tumbled him.

Sir Ranulf's eyes widened with surprise as he spun his stallion about at the end of the field and reset his lance. For all his lack of size, the boy was uncommonly skillful, he acknowledged. And eager, too, to judge from the way he brought his lighter horse about and lowered his lance again.

They met at midfield, and Rosamund heard the loud crack of her lance splitting as it was torn from her grasp. She felt the blow that thrust her upward, above the high cantle of her saddle, and sent her through the air to land in an ungainly heap in the dust. She shook her head to clear it, as the knight discarded his lance and leaped from his horse, striding toward her as she began to pick herself up.

He held out a hand, confident in his superior strength.

"I did not mean to give thee so great a buffet!" he began. Infuriated, Rosamund snarled, drew her sword and went for him. Leaping back, Sir Ranulf barely had time to loose his own weapon as she attacked. Skill alone saved him from injury.

"Brat!" he shouted angrily. "Where is thy courtesy to thy betters?" He countered her lightning moves with confident dexterity, now determined to teach this brash, ill-tempered squire a lesson he would not readily forget.

Now she had found vent for her fury, Rosamund attacked viciously defended, with lethal intent. She hardly felt the shocks of his definitively greater strength.

"Little cockerel!" he muttered once as she sliced through his surcoat. Stronger, and well aware of it, he pressed her back until he forced her to stumble, loosing the use of a leg. He struck the sword from her hand and leaped for her, knocking her to the ground where she lay under him, heaving for air.

"Well fought, lad!" he panted over her. "But this was too vicious for sport. Learn to confine thy rage to the battlefield where it is needful!"

"Get off me!" Rosamund screeched, remembering another time.

Sir Ranulf laughed. "Nay, lad! I'd not like to find a dagger between my ribs!"

Rosamund squirmed violently as he pinned her arms. "Pig!" she hissed.

Sir Ranulf's patience snapped. "Enough!" he roared. "Who is thy lord to allow thee to be so ill-mannered to thy betters, boy?" Rosamund did not respond. "Then I must discover for myself! I think thou hast never been given the thrashings that are so clearly thy due!"

Rosamund felt the pressure of his weight ease, then she was hauled roughly to her feet, and, an instant later, was being hauled along the courtyard by the neck of her short hauberk.

"Whoreson!" she shrieked. He did not answer, but pushed her forcibly through a wide doorway into an empty part of the stables. She spun around and lashed out with a fist that was easily caught. Then she was slammed back and pinned against a stall. Her helm was torn away.

Sir Ranulf's eyes widened and the anger in his face vanished entirely.

"God's Blood. Lady Rosamund!" he exclaimed.

"Let me go!" she snarled. But Sir Ranulf did not release her. Instead, he looked at her, his expression changing to intent consideration.

"How is it that my lord of Arundel forgets his duty to allow his ward such freedom as to indulge in these unwomanly pastimes?" Rosamund glared at him.

"That is not thy concern!" she snapped. Sir Ranulf tightened his hold, moved closer.

"What is thy house, my lady?" he asked.

"Neither is that thy concern!" she spat. His eyes narrowed a little as he continued to stare at her, moved his body to press against her, and reached a hand to cup her chin.

"I think mayhap thou art Arundel's mistress?" he murmured. "For, in truth, I have not seen thee with another woman as it should rightly be for a highborn maid." She was close to his own age, he noted. And a beauty. And, lithe and supple beneath the steel that separated them. Desire flared.

"I am no man's chattel!" she growled, and Sir Ranulf flung back his head to laugh delight.

"Nay, lady. That is abundantly clear!" he chuckled. "But," with abruptly increased intensity, "I'll warrant thy loving is made of fire enough to tame most men! Come. We shall have a good frolic, for I vow I will find the softness in thee!" He thrust her back along the boards, toward a corner.

"Nay!" Rosamund shouted, alarmed now, and struggling to loose the arms he held pinned to her sides. "Nay!" But he flung her down.

"Arundel is too tame for thee!" he said. Rosamund did not

waste breath, but picked herself up and lunged for the opening to his left. He caught her easily, and flung her down in the straw, landing full length on top of her. "I will show thee a man, wench! I like fire in my women, and thou hast sufficient to delight us both!" Afraid now, she jerked, and found his hand, bit down hard. Sir Ranulf pulled back, roaring in anger.

"Thou art an unbroken mare!" he growled. "And I will teach thee the meaning of bridle and spur. Thou shalt be well ridden, mistress!" he promised furiously. But Rosamund jerked and thrashed, kicked and hit out as he tried to hold her, then rolled her onto her belly. He jerked an arm up behind her until she gasped from the pain of it and lay still.

She felt his other hand undo her hauberk, find her waist, and loose other garments to tug and pull. She bucked violently.

"Aye! That is the way of it!" he told her more cheerfully. He bound her wrists together and rolled her over to lie painfully on top of them, trapping her between his thighs. She spat.

"Thou art no knight to use a lady so!" she snarled. He grinned unpleasantly.

"I recall the interest of thy look." He told her, thrusting a finger toward that place between her legs that he had exposed, drove it upward, learning what he wished to know. "But, then, mistress, thou art no lady!" he finished his retort, glancing down toward the rest of her body that his hands were rapidly exposing. "Aah! It will be delight to play stallion to such a well-made mare!" He mocked her now.

Rosamund bucked as his fingers found a breast, pinched and tugged crudely at the flesh. Then she closed her eyes, hating him—hating herself. And, truly afraid, she clenched her jaws as he jerked her legs apart, wrenching the joints of her hips. Pride of silence was all that she had left as she felt heat and steel scrape at her. He grunted, thrusting into her woman place without courtesy, his upper body falling forward to smother her.

Raw intrusion... stabbing pain... It was impossible to breathe as he prodded her depths with increasing urgency and force. Then he groaned, and stiffened, shuddering—eased, and fell away. Rosamund opened her eyes as he drew back, then shifted her gaze to stare at the wooden beams far above her head.

"Even a dog covers a bitch in heat with better skill than thou!" she said in clear, frigid contempt.

Sir Ranulf froze, then scowled in self-defensive anger as his eyes travelled down from breast to hip, and back to the beauty of her face and the deep cold wells of her dark eyes that could drown a man. Who was she to complain . . . ?

"Were thou a virgin, mistress, or, even as highborn as thou pretend, I would not have taken my way with thee!" he growled. "But thou art Arundel's whore, and something unnatural as a woman in the wearing of men's garb and the practise of arms! Such is the price."

Her eyes turned to lock with his.

"I am Rosamund of Wodensweir," she said in a terrible voice. "And thou art a falsely titled lord!"

Sir Ranulf froze entirely. The old man in the forest? The one who dwelt unharmed amid the pestilence of wolves harboured there? He bore the same name. Sir Ranulf's face paled a little as he remembered something else. How it had been told that Lord Robert De Cheiney had raped and killed that same old wizard's young wife. This, he knew suddenly, must be the child that remained.

"Thou art a witch!" he rasped. She continued to stare at him, compelling him to return her gaze.

"Aye, I am that, Sir Ranulf of Petworth," she said with quiet ferocity. "And my lineage is of greater antiquity, of purer blood than thine. Thou, who hast despoiled my body, likewise, falsely hold my fiefs!"

Grim now, and disconcerted, Sir Ranulf attempted to tug her garments back into some semblance of order. Then, he dragged her to her feet, and bore her across the court toward his quarters in the great keep. He thrust her along shadowed corridors and up winding steps to the chamber accorded him, then pushed her through the door so hard she tripped and went sprawling across the stone floor, her arms still bound behind her. He slammed the door behind him.

Rosamund twisted and rolled onto her side, aware of bruises and sore places as he strode forward to stand over her.

"What is this claim thou makest upon the fiefs of Wallenford?" he demanded, acutely aware of the furor in the court over the blind knight's claim. Now he had discovered there was another. She glanced up at him. "I am the daughter of Lord Wilfred of Wodensweir, which is the ancient Saxon name for Wallenford. I have proofs of my entitlement to that fief which was taken from my father by King Stephen and given by grant to Robert De Cheiney, then was stolen from his heir by thine own sire, the Lord of Petworth!" she told him in frigid tones.

"What are these proofs?" He grated.

She smiled grimly. "Thou art unsubtle, Sir Ranulf!" she sneered. "They are well hid! And beating me will not serve as it did with Lord Mallory, for I am made of sterner stuff!"

That last claim, from his experience of her ferocity, he was beginning not to doubt at all. He frowned thoughtfully, hesitated for a few moments, then, abruptly picked her up and dragged her over to the bed. There, he bound her down to complete immobility and gagged her.

He left her there, departing the chamber to seek out his father and relate what he had learned.

Some time later, Lord Reginald found the silver horse, still saddled, standing in patient resignation in a corner of the bailey. There was a broken lance left uncollected in the dust of the training area, and he led the strangely docile animal back to the stabling, puzzled, for it was unlike Rosamund to neglect her beast.

There, after unsaddling and attending to it, he found the helm he had seen before attached to her saddle, and a short, training hauberk, such as he had seen her wear. But, of the lady, he found no other trace. Neither in her chamber, nor by answer to his enquiries after the squire she was pretending to be.

Troubled, he did not neglect to wonder on the coincidental disappearance of the greater part of the Court, for most had gone hawking with the King in the hills above Winchester.

# EIGHTEEN

Mallory pushed himself off the bed, wincing as the movement tore at the weals on his back, and stood up. He felt much stronger after the long sleep, yet was acutely aware of the sheer draining effect of the damage on his physical resources. He groped his way to where the window focused a gentle influx of warm summer breezes and external sounds, then cried out through the aperture, summoning the eagle.

He left the window, and carefully found his way back to the bed, sitting down once more with a short grunt. Hearing Sir Geoffrey suddenly rouse from a light doze nearby, he softly requested his pack from the other. The knight found the required item of baggage amongst others of Lord Pendragon's belongings, under the clothing and armour that Lord Reginald had rescued. He hefted the pack, and was startled by the lightness of it, totally disproportionate to its size. He opened the flap and peered inside. It was empty.

"There is nothing in here, my lord?" he said in confusion, looking at Lord Mallory as he held the item out. The Pendragon showed his surprise.

"Is there not . . . ? I had thought it contained all I need," he said and held out his hand. The knight put the pack into his grasp and watched as Lord Mallory set it upon his bare knees, opened it, and, after rummaging about for a moment, began to extract clothing. "Aye," he said softly. "It holds all I require."

Sir Geoffrey stared in mesmerized fascination as chausses, undertunic, calf-length robe, surcoat, and cloak were set one by one on the bed beside Mallory. Then, he drew out all the attendant accoutrements: boots of soft leather, belt, cloak brooches.

"Aye, no armour this time, I consider," Lord Mallory murmured.

"My lord. That was an empty pack!" Sir Geoffrey exclaimed. "I could see . . . ,"

Mallory smiled. "I do not suffer the constraints of thy vision, Sir Geoffrey," he suggested gently, and immediately preoccupied himself with the business of dressing.

Sir Geoffrey subsided into the chair he had occupied for so many hours, glancing once to see the great eagle thrust its way through the window, then hop down to perch on one of the chests in the chamber. He wondered briefly at his own acceptance of all this, and thought that, mayhap, it was the consequence of those qualities of easy naturalness attendant upon the mysteriousness of Lord Mallory's person. . . .

Feeling vastly improved by his fresh attire and the large meal Sir Geoffrey had provided, Mallory set the eagle upon his wrist and stroked the wolf that lay across his feet. He thought of Rosamund and wished—wished that she would come to that understanding that her father had intended for her.

Wished . . . Aye. For he felt lonely.

"Thou art recovered, Lord Pendragon?" The King's voice was courteous as he studied the strangely pristine young man who stood before him as richly attired as he was himself, distinctive, also, for the eagle that rode upon one broad shoulder and the black wolf that flanked him, and the empty scabbard at his hip.

"Sufficiently recovered, Majesty." Lord Mallory's reply was accompanied by a fleetingly rueful, rather elfin smile. He could feel the presence of other people in the chamber to which he had been escorted, and the King before him, moving as ever, restless with vigour.

It was disconcerting indeed, Henry Plantagenet acknowledged, to be unable to meet the aimless stare of those sightless red eyes.

"We wish to fully understand, Lord Pendragon, these claims thou have made upon us. For that, we must know how it is that, on the one side, thou may declare thyself to be the son of the late Robert De Cheiney, liegeman of Stephen, and, on the other, likewise proclaim thyself son to this other—this, Uther Pendragon, who, by legendary repute, fathered King Arthur?" Lord Pendragon's face retained the smooth, relaxed composure of confidence, the King noted.

"Lord Robert De Cheiney, Majesty, sired my body on his lady wife, and I am, by that means, got as any other man. For the other—the Pendragon fathered the being that I am within this garment of flesh, and likewise, affected such changes in my flesh as to make me this mysterious thing called white, and took from me that sense known to others as sight."

"Sorcery!" someone muttered. Mallory cocked his head toward the voice. The King glanced at Becket, sitting with frigid sternness nearby.

"Was it sorcery?" Lord Pendragon responded at once. "If it were so, then I am glad of it, for I was otherwise condemned to be Lord Robert's son in all other ways, even to becoming the bestial, injust, and dishonourable creature his loins and his disposition were impelled to make! Lord Robert brought little good to the fiefs of Wallenford!"

The King frowned, and recalled the things that had prompted him to dispatch Petworth and Arundel to Wallenford in the first place. The subsequent reports . . . he had received.

"It is not possible for the Prince who sired King Arthur to have sired thee," Henry pursued. "He, with the rest of those legendary times, is dead five hundred years and more!"

Again, Lord Mallory's response was direct, sure.

"This Lord, the Pendragon, whose name I am given to bear, undertook the form of that same Lord Uther for a time. More recently, he was known as Lord Wilfred of Wodensweir." Mallory heard a hiss of indrawn breath to his right. "Wodensweir is the ancient name for those lands now called Wallenford, my liege, as it was until the time of the coming of the Conquerer. And, I am given to understand, it is so recorded in the Domesday Book."

Henry's eyebrows rose a little as he noted the reference to that document, and in the same instant, he caught Lord Fulk's stiffening, the exchange of glances that passed between father and son.

"Lord Pendragon. Thou suggest that this one—this father—was no mortal human soul," Henry said as he leaned forward.

"Satan, rather!" The same voice as before muttered. The King shot Becket a quelling look of annoyance. Lord Mallory's open expression did not change.

"The Pendragon was not mortal in the way of men!" Lord Mallory answered with composed clarity. "He was of the same blood as great Merlin, being Merlin's full brother. Likewise, he was the last High Warlock of this realm. And, I am the son of his contrivance, which is something different from the manner of human begetting!"

"Majesty!" Mallory heard the outraged tone, heard footsteps and the flurry of robes as someone moved closer. "This goes too far! This is heresy of the most heinous and terrible sort in defiance of God's laws! This creature is bewitched and got of Satan, and, even now, through him it is plain enough that the Devil casts his evil eye upon this gathering, even unto the seduction of thine own sacred Majesty by these cunning words!"

Mallory stiffened. "I speak truth!" he declared in clarion tones. "I have no need for falsehood or dissembling, for I am the Pendragon now!"

"Satan, Prince of deceit!" Becket shouted, raising an arm to point accusingly.

"Silence!" the King roared. In an instant, every soul stilled in obedient attention. "We will know. Art thou human, Lord Pendragon?" Henry demanded with frigid calm.

"I am a man, Majesty," Mallory answered softly. "I bleed of my wounds! I am mortal, after a fashion!"

The King sighed and shifted, fidgeted with his fingers as he scanned the gathering, then scowled.

"Are there none among this company who may bear witness to the identity of Mallory De Cheiney?" he demanded, then arched an eyebrow as the Earl of Arundel strode forward, one of his household knights flanking him. The Earl bowed. Henry waved an impatient hand.

"Majesty," Lord Reginald spoke clearly, straightening. "Six years past, while attendant to my duty in accordance with thy command to investigate the fief of Wallenford, I found Lord Mallory in the north tower of Wallenford Castle, where Lord Robert had kept him locked away from all traffic with people since the time of his birth. Worse. Then but a boy, he was found to have been beaten and starved, denied even garments to cover him, and kept in a most hideous condition for the heir to such a great fief. Having discovered him, I did leave his care to Lord Petworth, who had undertaken to set aright the terrible conditions at Wallenford. The next word I received was that this same boy was dead."

"Majesty!" Lord Fulk strode forward. "It was a mad, blind boy that was found, and now it is a madman, or worse, that stands before thee now with these preposterous claims!" He glared at Lord Reginald. "Only by strenuous effort have I brought some measure of order and prosperity to Wallenford, being in that, thy good servant."

"Aye, so thou hast done," the King muttered. "Save for this matter of wolves." His voice sharpened. "But, it was thy obligation to bring the boy to us to be our ward as is customary, and this thou did not fulfill."

"He was lost, Majesty, before..." Lord Fulk began.

"Strange, how that should occur, my lord!" the Earl of Arundel broke in acidly. "For I clearly recall he could not find his way about without a hand to guide him!"

Lord Fulk did not look at the younger man. "Majesty. He was a mad thing, howling like the wolves that plague those lands, and seeking the company of dogs. I thought to exercise charity—to avoid locking him away after the manner of his father...!"

"Aaah!" Henry sat back. "So he is De Cheiney's heir!" Lord Fulk whitened as he realized he had been caught out.

"I heard testimony from some who were witness to his birth, my Liege," Lord Reginald said quietly.

The King brought his hands together, touching fingertips. "So..." he said slowly. "There is indeed substance to thy claim for Wallenford, my lord Pendragon." Mallory did not move. "But. To this other matter. We must determine whether, indeed, it is madness that issues from thee. Or heresy and Satan's voice, or—the truth."

"There can be little doubt to that, Majesty!" Becket strode toward the King, his face taut with intent. "All witchcraft comes from Satan, and all madness likewise! This man is one of that kind, for it is both apparent in his appearance and in the beasts that companion him, familiars for the magics he would contrive!"

Mallory shook his head as he listened, and smiled grimly, extending an arm to invite the eagle from his shoulder. The weals on which the bird had been resting were very sore. Gently, he began stroking the fierce bird's elegant, unhooded head.

"These creatures," he said sternly, "befriend me for they know what thou will not! That I am not given to the practise of malice of any kind.

"Even the great Merlin, who was my father's brother, served as teacher and counsel to my brother Arthur, who was an annointed king. So it is with me, who am not the Pendragon. I seek the King's justice, in keeping with the honour and wisdom and powers of my heritage, and in the recognition of the King's true rule as Prince of this realm. The Lords of

Fairie, being got of spirit instead of clay, who were masters of the earth long before dominion was given unto men, well knew the laws of rule and destiny, and were supremely wise on all matters of order. And I, who am the last Prince of Fairie . . ."

"He condemns himself, my liege!" Becket growled outraged protest. "He must be given over to Holy Church for the purging of his soul and to the safety of us all before God."

"What dost thou fear in me, priest?" Mallory interrupted. "Is thy trust in the God whose servant thou profess to be so small that thou may not understand He is the Creator of all creatures, whether they be substance or spirit?"

Becket spluttered. The King flung back his head and roared with laughter.

"Aaah, Thomas. He hath caught thee out. Well said, Lord Pendragon!"

Becket spun about to face the blind man with feral suddenness. "And what of Satan, whose creature thou art?" he demanded.

Mallory again shook his head a little. "Aye, the Devil," he answered at once. "Who is Satan, beyond the consummate spirit of all intemperate and ungoverned passions and lusts, aye, even for power. Yet, even the Devil is an innocent, for in his chaos, he cannot know that the worth of power is to be found in the manner of its balance! Power is a servant of harmony, and not an end to be achieved for its own sake."

The King's face sobered as he digested this, his eyes never leaving the Archbishop's face. Aye, he thought. He liked the wisdom of it, and the statement correlated well with his own beliefs. But, Becket stood with flushed cheeks and clenched fists. His erstwhile friend were grown intemperate in his own fashion. In ambition, and zeal. In pride. Balance—aye, that was everything.

"Thou play ingeniously with words and logic, Lord Pendragon!" Becket pressed on. "Mayhap thou will answer me this. Whyfore, if thou art such as thou claim, have not thy— unnatural father, or thyself, undertaken to take the rule of the fiefs of Wallenford, as surely, he and thou have the power to do?"

Lord Mallory laughed. "Shall I summon the winds, my lord? Shall I send lightning to set fire to the earth? Or brew tempests of thunder fit to make the very heavens tremble?" His voice had deepened, shadowed with tones of power. "To what end shall I force the return of what is rightfully mine through the use of such power? To what purpose beyond making thee kneel in fear of me?

"Nay, priest. Shall I do less than my brother who brought unity and order to this realm once before? As King Henry strives to do now? I am well content to plead my case before the King, for the seeds of justice that he sows will endure into the future, transcending the brief generations that follow. I will place my trust in the King's judgment, for order is the balance on which the weights of power are set. Justice is the scale. And, in this, the King is annointed God's guardian!"

Henry Plantagenet grinned. Becket had been stripped of argument, for Lord Pendragon had brought the whole disputation neatly back to the point of origin. He shifted, watching the white fingers delicately stroking the feathers of the large bird, and knew himself to be feeling very favourably disposed toward this unique young man.

Mayhap, with time, Lord Pendragon could prove himself uncommonly useful. Like minds—and an uncontested grip upon the bridle. He looked at Becket, reluctantly acknowledging that it was now but a matter of time before . . .

And, the Earl of Wallenford, who stood, grim faced and aging. One of several lords he had been considering for the office of Chancellor since Thomas now was consumed by an unforeseen passion for Holy Church.

"It would appear, Lord Pendragon, that thy claim to be De Cheiney's heir is beyond refutation . . ." the King said slowly, standing. "But this other matter involving thine entitlement of Pendragon, and thy claim to be the brother of that most puissant Prince, Arthur, must, in some fashion, be proved."

Mallory nodded a little and stepped forward. "Majesty," he said. "It may be done without difficulty. I know where my brother lies entombed. I know the whereabouts of Avalon, where my brother lies under enchantment awaiting final release into the realm of spirits. No other save myself may uncover the crypt in which he is held."

King Henry considered the blind man thoughtfully, well aware of the silence that had gathered like storm clouds about him.

"We shall be satisfied by such revelation, my lord, for there are none who have ever found that tomb," he said slowly.

"Another deceit!" Becket muttered.

The King reseated himself and leaned forward. "Thou hast an uncommon interest in this matter of lies, Thomas," he said pleasantly. "We are troubled that it should be so close to thy heart."

Becket paled at the reprimand and mumbled something unintelligibly apologetic.

"Lord Pendragon shall prove himself as he has described," the King pronounced. "Then, we shall resolve this matter of his dispute with Lord Fulk over the fief of Wallenford!"

Sir Ranulf stepped briskly forward then, his mouth set. He bowed.

"Majesty? It is a long-established and fair practise to settle such disputes by contest of arms. I would gladly serve as my father's champion to the protection of his name and honour!" He glanced at the blind man. Lord Pendragon had no hope of . . .

Lord Pendragon stepped forward. "My liege. I am content to keep with the same tradition, and would be satisfied to such a match of skill at arms," he said with quiet confidence. "And, as fate decrees, mayhap I will win my spurs and the honour of knighthood that is given to other men!"

A murmur of astonishment passed through the hall.

"So be it!" the King said with stern finality, unable to perceive any predictable result.

"Majesty?"

"Lord Pendragon?"

"I must have my brother's sword." Mallory held out his right arm to the air, palm up in supplication. And, before the King could think to reply, that gleaming weapon that he had brought with him to the hall rose up into the air from its place beside him. Point down, it hovered, the dragons of its hilt unfurling their wings.

Then, it flew sedately through the air to the Pendragon's outstretched palm. A moment later, it was sheathed at his hip, and he bowed, turned away, and strode from the chamber, the wolf padding at his side.

It was an uncertain silence that followed his departure.

# NINETEEN

"My servant informs me that Lord Mallory's claim is, indeed, entirely just, my lord." Becket eyed the Earl of Wallenford with deliberation, secure in the privacy of his own, austere apartment. "De Cheiney's gift was endowed to include his heirs, and more. This Lord Wilfred of Wodensweir was recorded as so entitled in the document of the Domesday Book, the fief being held of him and his heirs since the time of Alfred. The King is well aware of this, and considers Lord . . . ," he hated to say the name, "Pendragon's petition to be entirely justified and fair.

"That, my lord, is the crux of the matter. For reasons of his own, His Majesty has discovered a liking for this cunning— blind man." It went deeper than that, Becket knew, being part of this conflict between them, on the dominion of God over the dominion of Princes. "Or else," he added deliberately, "our liege lord is seduced by sorcerous wiles!"

The Earl of Wallenford breathed deeply. For the first time in his life, his honour was open to doubtful review. His property was open to forfeiture, and the King's trust in him was rapidly evaporating. He should have killed the boy, he thought, when he had the chance. . . . Yet, how could he have known that the wolves would not have harmed Mallory De Cheiney as they did with all else? Or that the accursed old man would have rescued the lad. He shifted, deliberating on how to best utilize the single instrument remaining to him. The girl.

"My lord," he addressed the Archbishop carefully. "There are few men able to best my son in any of the skills of arms, and yet, I am brought to fear the sorceries that this lord Pendragon may have to command. Blind, or nay, I cannot but think it may be impossible to prevail against him. Other means must be found. . . .

"To that end, my son has in his possession the self-proclaimed daughter of this lord Wilfred of Wodensweir."

"A witch!" Becket leaned forward eagerly.

"Beyond being vile-tempered and proud beyond reason, her powers are not apparent. But, she claims to have proof of her right to Wallenford."

"Is she the true daughter of this—lord Wilfred?

"It may well be that she is his, gotten on a girl he wed some twenty years ago, or more. As I understand, Lord Robert De Cheiney raped and killed the woman, as he were wont to do among his serfs. Since that time, the fiefs of Wallenford have been plagued by wolves and such other curses." Becket rose from his chair to pace, frowning thoughtfully as his fingers wove through the beads of the rosary suspended from his waist.

"Were Holy Church," he speculated aloud, "to examine this maid and find her clean of witchcraft, my lord, then mayhap it would well serve thee to wed thy son to her and thereby hold Wallenford through the older claim of her rightful inheritance which is," he gave the Earl a penetrating look, "of greater legitimacy than that of De Cheiney."

Wallenford nodded a little. "'Tis said that Lord Mallory was born after that unsavoury incident, which would render him the younger of the pair."

"Just so, my lord!" Becket murmured. "A daughter's claim is not usually given preference, but for this case, there may be some precedent! As to thy son's betrothal to the house of Sussex, it shall fall to thee to contrive some manner of withdrawal! The King must be brought to see the folly, even sin, of his fascination with this red-eyed warlock!" His eyes narrowed as he studied the aging Earl. "His Majesty, who is an annointed prince, must be brought more closely into the fold of Holy Mother Church, for God rules all men through the blessing of His Son." Becket made the sign of the Cross, as if in benediction.

Or, the Earl wondered with new doubt, as another spectre of power . . . ?

Rosamund shuddered and clenched her jaws to keep her teeth from chattering. Muscles held to immobility for so long screeched excruciating protest at even the slightest movement, and sore pain seeped outward from that place inside that Sir Ranulf had used again. Punishment or lust, it had made no difference, for she had spat at him and refused to answer his questions, or to give him the passion he perversely wanted from her.

They had flung a cloak over her head, Sir Ranulf and his father, and had borne her along passages and down steps that stripped away any sense of direction through a series of nauseating changes. Then they stopped, and Rosamund was set on feet still bound together, kept from falling, only by the arm of Sir Ranulf.

She blinked as the cloak was whisked away, and stared at the slight, lean-faced man in a priest's robes who stood before her. She recognized him at once. The Archbishop, Thomas A'Becket. Was this the King's doing, then, she wondered? She stared warily about the large, barren chamber.

"Peace, my daughter," the Archbishop said in kindly tones, making the sign of the Cross over her. He smiled, and Rosamund stared at him mistrustfully. "I am given to understand that thou art the lady Rosamund of Wodensweir?"

"I am so named and titled," Rosamund agreed warily.

"There is naught to fear, my child. Lord Fulk and Sir Ranulf have, in their charity, brought thee to the guardianship of Holy Mother Church."

To Rosamund, the remark seemed more threat than reassurance, and Becket turned away so that she could not see his face.

He continued: "It would seem, my lady, that since Sir Ranulf has cast his gaze upon thee, he hath become bewitched by passion and hath forsworn to wed any other save thyself!"

Should she be impressed, Rosamund wondered sourly?

"Knowing thou art the child of Lord Wilfred of Wodensweir, the former lord of Wallenford, lends added sense to his suit, my lady." Becket turned to face her once more. "Sir Ranulf is a true knight and intent to the service of the lady who hath taken his heart."

Very clever, Rosamund thought bitterly, meeting the Bishop's gaze with unflinching sternness. Her experience of the knight had not led her to conclude he had any affection for her whatever!

"Sir Ranulf, being a chivalrous man, is angered to know that the Earl of Arundel hath defiled his guardianship and made of thee his mistress. And he wishes to make the restitution due the honour of thy name, through the sacrament of marriage. But—"

Aaah! There was a catch to all this, Rosamund thought.

"Holy Mother Church must be able to bless such a match before it may be made, and the Church has several points of concern.

"Firstly, it hath been pronounced by several witnesses of good repute that thy father, Lord Wilfred, was, or is, a warlock of no mean power. It is our concern, therefore, that our son in Christ hath not been seduced to vile passion by a witch!"

Rosamund snorted contempt, her temper flaring violently. "Seduction, Holy Father?" she sneered. "I had not thought it were possible, lying bound and subject beyond any defense, to another's use!" She glared at Sir Ranulf who flushed, and, surprisingly, looked away. "As for this knight! Pah! He is no more than a rutting boar!"

Becket met her look with undisturbed calm. "Nonetheless, daughter," he said more sternly. "Despite these protestations, it is well known that a woman may, through witchcraft, drive a man to a delirium of lust, and, thereby, seduce him into sin."

Rosamund ground her teeth, her face whitening at his next remarks.

"It is for Holy Church to determine whether or not thou art a witch, child. Thou wilt be put to the test. If all is well, and thou art innocent of those powers and marks of Satan, then, the Church will bless and sanctify thy union with this good and noble lord!"

He sounded almost happy, Rosamund thought in horror, biting back rage as she recognized her very real danger. She jerked to stare again at Sir Ranulf, who looked discomfited. He turned away. Was this her only opportunity to gain her inheritance? Under the lawful rule of this man?

Then, she was dragged forward and impelled to stand as her clothing was torn away from her. She clenched her teeth, resolving to silence, and stared at nothing as overly zealous hands poked and prodded at her body. She glowered at the humiliation of this nakedness, and at the insults of the touching. Aye—she knew. This was worse than rape.

And, without her powers, she was helpless in ways she had not known were possible. Rigid, she fought the terror of that truth with all the strength of her will, nodding meekly when the Archbishop chastised her for her boy's garb. Something else, she knew with shame, that she had never done before.

"The maid is free of mark or blemish, and is without apparent deformity. Now, we will ascertain if she is a witch!"

Becket announced to the pair of uncomfortable nobles at the far end of the chamber.

Lord Fulk merely nodded, fully cognizant of the practicability of such tests. But Sir Ranulf stared at Rosamund with disturbed fascination, at the dark hair that tumbled over her exquisitely curved back. At her dark eyes that shimmered like black pools of pain for the shame that he had never thought to see, at the hard line of her mouth, set in stubborn effort. He felt an uneasy shock pass through him, and thought of his sister, or others of his womenfolk in a like position, and knew he would never tolerate . . .

And it was the fire in Rosamund that made this even worse, for it was that which he liked above all else in her—so unlike the meek and coy demeanor of other highborn women. Yes, he had treated her ill, but a part of him still recoiled at her helplessness.

He saw her shiver violently as the same large monk that had probed her flesh stepped forward to pick her up, then set her to lie upon a long table, where he strapped her down.

"Witches, it is commonly known, do not burn!" Becket said with an edge of passion. "So we shall begin with the first test!" Sir Ranulf had not thought he were capable of cringing.

Rosamund screamed as the irons touched the soles of her feet and sent incredible waves of pain up her legs. She thrashed and bucked against her bonds, and did not notice as a lock of her hair was cut away and put to the torch. . . .

She screamed again as her breasts were viciously clutched and squeezed to see if the nipples yielded up milk, or witches' venom, or, as was the case, nothing at all. She must not cry . . . Her head tossed violently. She must not cry, she knew, for the tears would betray her—the tears of blood that were the heritage of the Fairie.

"Enough of this un-Christian savagery!" Sir Ranulf roared across the nightmare. "This maid is no witch! It is plain enough to see!"

To the sheer astonishment of both his father and the Archbishop, Sir Ranulf, his own features ashen and drawn, strode forward and flung his cloak across Rosamund's body, slashed away her bonds with vicious strokes of his dagger, then drew her close into his arms with infuriated protectiveness. Terrified of what her eyes might reveal, Rosamund clung and buried her face in Sir Ranulf's surcoat, and shuddered convulsively with pain, with the humiliation she felt.

"I will wed this lady, and gladly, my lord!" Sir Ranulf barked at his father. "But I will not sully mine honour by more brutality to this highborn woman! There is no proof, beyond a single man's word that this lady's sire is a warlock. But, that she is of proud and ancient lineage is beyond question, and for that I will not see her so defiled!" With that, he strode away, Rosamund held tightly against him.

Becket and Wallenford looked at each other with measuring gazes. For a time, their eyes remained locked, then a moment of flickering understanding passed between them. A single thought, expressed softly by Lord Fulk.

"Mayhap this lord Wilfred of Wodensweir was nothing more than an eccentric old Saxon hermit after all!" he murmured. "Mayhap," he said with greater deliberation, "all this talk of the Pendragon is most purely Mallory De Cheiney's contrivance? I think there is only one warlock in all this, and that is De Cheiney himself!" Becket nodded slightly. "'Tis certain that the troubled history of Wallenford does much to bear this out."

"There is one warlock, beyond question, my lord," Becket said softly, and they both recalled the dragon sword that had flown obediently to its master's hand. . . .

Sir Ranulf swallowed and shifted uncomfortably as he set Rosamund on the bed, saw her curl into a tight ball beneath the folds of his cloak, her face largely hidden by her hair. She gasped with excruciating pain. She had not uttered a sound as he had carried her back to his chamber, nor when he had set her down with unfamiliar care. More able to cope with action, he rummaged for clothing that would cover he until he could find her woman's attire, and, more importantly, water and unguents to tend her scorched feet. She did not move as he knelt awkwardly to put the soothing balm on her scorched and bloody soles.

"Lady Rosamund . . . ?" he rasped the clumsy plea. "I would not have brought thee to this. I am not given to such— ill usage."

"Then I cannot comprehend that which thou intended and did before." Her voice was a muffled, uneven hiss of anger. Sir Ranulf drew back.

"Thou made a fool of me," he told her honestly. "I am a proud man and scorn is hard for me to bear." She did not respond to this fragile apology. He swallowed. "I think thou art proud also. . . . ," he offered clumsily.

"Aye. I had thought so." Her voice was barely audible. Sir Ranulf flinched, more disturbed by the quality of that remark than by her other reaction to that which had been done. He reached for her, turned her to pull her into his arms, and gasped. Froze.

Blood. Drops of blood shimmered scarlet in the corners of her eyes, trickled down her face, and made a smear across one cheek.

"Mother of God!" he grated hoarsely and drew back further to cross himself. "It is said that only some of the Saints have ever wept thus!" He breathed his awe. Rosamund collected herself with grim effort, wrapping the cloak about her and sat up.

"Saints, my lord?" she asked brutally. "And witches!" His eyes widened further. "Aye. I am of Fairie blood, though I have no powers at all. Thou have naught to fear in me." The last was uttered with a bitter edge as she reached for the bowl of water and wiped away every trace of what he had seen. "What wilt thou do now, sir knight?" she asked, looking at him. "Give me up to that vile priest?"

"Becket is a holy man, my lady . . . a . . . " he retorted, stung.

"Nay, my simple lord. He is a schemer!" she retorted acidly.

Sir Ranulf ran his fingers through his curly brown hair. She said the truth, he thought reluctantly.

"What a coil this has become . . . ," he murmured, looking away for a moment. Then, at her. "Nay. I will not give thee over to Becket," he heard himself promise as their eyes met. Silence followed as he saw her recover her pride again, and felt a new, uncomfortable humility that were sprung, in part, from his still profound desire for her.

"What of thy father? Lord Wilfred?" he asked. Rosamund looked at him with all the regal assurance of a queen.

"He was the Pendragon, my lord. The High Warlock of this realm. But, not to fear. He is gone to rest among the shadows with the rest of Fairie."

"And Wallenford?" he asked.

"It was the Pendragon's demesne from the time of his own beginnings, from times long before the Romans. He nurtured it, keeping the forests and the abundance of wild creatures therein. He hath ever guarded it, for it is sacred land."

The wolves, Sir Ranulf thought. Aye, they were the war-lock's servants.

"Lady . . . ," he ventured cautiously, after a moment. "When thou art wed to me, then Wallenford will be fittingly restored to thee."

"Shalt thou be lord of both then?" she asked, her gaze unwavering, cool.

"Of course!" he said, a little confused. Rosamund looked away.

"Aye. Of course," she said with a disconcerting lack of tone.

Rosamund sat alone with feet that shrieked and throbbed bitter pain, clothed in the woman's garb that Sir Ranulf had found for her. It was a relief of sorts, his absence, time for her to grope through the courses open to her, though they seemed few enough.

Surely, this was not as her father had intended? Surely, he had not intended to deliver Wallenford into her hands by this —illusory means? And, if she were wed to Sir Ranulf? What then would become of her, for, like the land, she would be little more than property.

That was intolerable. She shifted, then winced at the consequence of her movement, her thoughts slipping along another path.

Would it not have been the same with Mallory as her lord? Unlike Sir Ranulf, he was blind, and given to gentleness almost unnatural in a man. And so lacking in her own fierce manner of pride as to be incomprehensible to her.

Wallenford's heir was as stiff-spined as herself. Sir Ranulf would be content only to rule her, his pride requiring it. He would hold her and own her. And she would resist.

As she did with Mallory. Yet Mallory seemed untroubled by her rages, seemed uncaring of her choices, even intent to make light of it all, like his seductive pranks with the crystal eye. And his smiles that were impossible to understand.

Rosamund frowned. Why were thoughts of Mallory haunting her mind? And, why had her father so dispossessed her to favour him? For the first time, she felt the need to find another kind of understanding.

* * *

"Where is Rosamund?" Mallory quietly asked the dreaded question of Lord Reginald early in the morning following his audience with the King. Lord Reginald shifted uncomfortably. He had searched the castle, and all the grounds thereabouts without success, finding only that her belongings were vanished from the chamber she had been given to occupy. His knights had scoured the town, but with the same lack of result.

"I know not, my lord," he answered, guiltily aware of having cuckolded Mallory by lying with his lady. Mallory stood up, his face shifting to troubled consternation.

"It is more like her to harp and rail than to keep away and husband silence!" he said slowly, setting his cloak upon his shoulders, and turning toward Lord Reginald. "I sense thou art troubled, my friend . . . ?"

"I have not seen the lady Rosamund these three days past," Lord Reginald answered, self-consciously aware that the way Lord Mallory cocked his head to focus his hearing was as disconcerting as the King's grey-eyed stare.

"And thou hast searched for her . . . I hear it," Mallory murmured. "But, I think there is more—something between thee . . . ?" Lord Reginald shifted uncomfortably, still acutely torn between his feelings, and his rigid adherence to the laws of honour and chastity. Then, beyond incredulity, Lord Mallory began to smile slowly. He shook his head. "I had thought it was so!" he declared. "But she is not for thee, Reginald. She would rule thee into misery. Thou art too gentle for her!" Lord Reginald spluttered both embarrassment and confusion. Coming from a man as passively screne as the Pendragon, Lord Reginald found the remark almost ludicrous, and strangled the urge to retort. But Mallory's expression had sobered again.

"Even if she has lain with thee, Reginald, it was not sufficient to bind her," he said softly, unhappily. "Rosamund is of the Fairie, as I am. We are like creatures, and not suited, I think, to mate with others." He reached into the pouch at his belt and withdrew the crystal sphere, his expression shifting to one of intense concentration as he passed the fingers of his right hand across its surface. Lord Reginald did not move or speak. Instead, he watched.

Somehow, he realized, Lord Mallory knew.

It was unnerving.

\*   \*   \*

His fingers slipped across the surface of the globe, probing the textures of the local geography with a minute attention to detail. Mallory searched the castle, moved around corners, along corridors and through doors, seeking out every smallest place, only avoiding any contact with those mobile densities that were the people of the court. High and low, he hunted through the vast structure, and frowned abruptly as he discovered Becket and the Earl of Wallenford bent together across an oaken table. Curious, he touched the vibrations of their conversation—focused it.

"Sussex must be brought to understand, my lord," Becket were saying, "that thy son is bewitched beyond reason, that he will bear no other course save that he wed this maid that is at least, thankfully, highborn.

"Once that is accomplished, it will be a simple matter to dispatch the witch to trial and to the stake for the cleansing of her immortal soul. Wallenford will be secured for I have found some proofs of her father's entitlements, and, likewise, her own origins."

"I thought she was not a witch . . . ?" The Earl's voice was somewhat puzzled.

"Her flesh burns, my lord, which is a good sign. But she did not weep as would be normal!" Becket's voice was vehement.

"What of Lord Pendragon?"

"That Lord Pendragon is a warlock of terrible power is beyond any question, my lord!" Becket's tone reflected his loathing. "He casts spells upon the King for His Majesty's favour, and therein lies a problem. But, he is blind, and cannot succeed against thy son, save by the use of conspicuous sorceries. Therein he may be caught in a web of his own contriving, and thus disposed of. Through Sir Ranulf's good arm, or our liege lord's enlightenment . . ." Mallory listened to a deep sigh, as Becket continued, "It is my task to dispatch all of these last heathen beliefs that linger, and to bring this realm to God who will rule through the Word of His Blessed Son, and through the Sancity of the Holy Church under the Pope, as it hath been ordained. The machinations of Satan will be purged away!"

"Amen!" Wallenford's response sounded a little wary, Mallory thought. He let the voices fade, and poised for a moment, his face grim.

"What has thy magic shown thee, Lord Mallory?" Arundel asked.

Mallory sighed. "It would seem," he said slowly, "that Thomas A'Becket confuses the God-given power of the Church with his own ambitions to achieve ecclesiastical sovereignty in this Kingdom. He seeks to rule the King as well, and the King, being annointed of God to his own rule, is being trapped carefully upon a point of logic and held between the horns of Faith. To this end, Becket intends to use Wallenford, and Lady Rosamund." He shook his head regretfully. "I could pity Lord Fulk, for he swims in deeper waters than he can manage!"

Mallory's fingertips moved again, searching across the portal of the surface of the crystal, guided by new knowledge that Rosamund had somehow fallen into Wallenford's hands. He moved upward, through winding, spiral stairs to the chambers of a distant tower, and found her, sitting taut and hunched over. His mouth tightened. Her posture was an unfamiliar reflection of fear, of confusion unnatural to her.

Then, he felt her pain. He touched the raw burnt places on her feet, and summoned a fragment of the power to soothe the agony. Then he drew his hand away, as he tried to govern his anger. This time, it was infinitely harder.

He slipped the crystal into its pouch and let his hand drop to the wolf's head.

"Now, my lord, we must seek the King!" His voice rumbled with the deep stern promise of thunder. Lord Reginald followed as the Pendragon strode from the chamber with all the sure briskness of a sighted man.

# TWENTY

Rosamund looked at the ghastly wounds in her feet. Drainage oozed from them, and the damage from the burning was more clearly visible as it spread into the surrounding tissues. Pain crawled with relentless persistence upward, through her legs to settle with sickening discomfort in her belly. It ate at her, the pain . . . combined with, and enhanced all the other things that brought her to feel so much despair. The shocks of intrusive abuse, the freedom that had vanished. The new and total absence of choice, for it now seemed that Sir Ranulf must have his way in the end.

She stiffened a little and shifted carefully, condemned by her wounded feet to unfamiliar and perpetual sitting. One man or another for her lord, what difference could it make? What difference should it make? For such was the lot of females. Yet, it was a form of intolerable damnation, she knew, for it was the nature of her own pride in herself to perceive no honour at all in such subservience that made of her property, thus depriving her of personhood, or considered her to be little more than a womb for the bearing of sons.

And, Sir Ranulf, for all his gentler words and solicitous treatment over the past hours, was no more than a proud and average man whose own sense of manhood would never tolerate any loss of power to her. Rosamund inhaled deeply and closed her eyes.

Why . . . ? Why, if this was as the Fates decreed, had not her father raised her to know only the content and limitations of a woman's lot? Her eyes flew open, and she froze, forgetting to breathe for a moment as she felt . . .

Felt . . . The air that touched her feet changed to become a caress of warmth, an aura of soothing relief. Then it stirred lightly to swirl around her like the heat of summer's brilliant sunglow, and she knew a fleeting sense of presence.

Mallory . . .

He had found her. And suddenly she knew he was employing his powers to ease the pain of the burns, and, to reveal himself with ingenious quiet.

An instant later only relief from pain remained, and Rosamund sat very still, staring intently at the bolted door.

Mallory, she realized slowly, who was not like other men. At all.

"Lord Pendragon?" Henry Plantagenet straightened from his studious perusal of the business that littered the oak table before him and noted the sober face of the silver-haired man as the other bowed.

"Majesty. I am come to seek thy will on another matter pertaining to rights and justice," Lord Mallory said, extracting folded sheets of parchment from the flat wallet at his waist, which he then held out with his right hand.

"How so, my lord?" The King stepped around the end of the table and eyed the pair of documents.

"Herein is written the contract of marriage between myself and the lady Rosamund of Wodensweir that has yet to be fulfilled. It was made and sealed of her father's own hand. The same lord Wilfred gave into my keeping this other document of entitlement. I pray thee, Majesty, read it, as I may not, and see that it is the lady Rosamund, who hath been given into my guardianship, who is the true claimant to the fiefs of Wallenford." With a sharp and curious glance at the Pendragon, Henry took the parchment sheets and opened them.

The marriage contract, he rapidly discovered, had been drawn up some nineteen years before, and was sealed with a swirling dragon such as comprised Lord Mallory's own insignia. He puzzled briefly over questions of relationship, then shifted his gaze to the second document. His eyes widened as he discovered its antiquity, and read the addendums that comprised half of its substance.

It was, beyond any refutation, a grant of entitlement and sovereignty to the lands that comprised Wodensweir, or Wallenford—to one lord Uther the Pendragon and those heirs of his body and of his devising for all future time.

The King frowned. Curiously worded—the use of the term sovereignty suggested that Wallenford was considered as something peculiarly apart from the rest of the realm.

But, the most astonishing thing of all, the King discovered, lay in recognizing that the document had first been signed by one Arturus Rex; then had been reaffirmed and sealed by every subsequent English monarch up to, and including, King Harold, who had died at Hastings exactly one hundred years ago.

The Conquerer's signature was noticeable by its absence, and Henry's frown deepened. So, too, were the signatures of his own grandsire, Henry the First. And Stephen.

The King looked up at the Pendragon who stood before him, waiting quietly. Wallenford had passed through several pairs of hands since the Conquest, he thought, with little claim to legitimacy, it would seem, in view of the endorsements and seals upon the document in his hands.

"We are a little puzzled, my lord, as to thy submission of these documents to us. The matter of the disposition of Wallenford is to be settled upon the field of battle as agreed," the King said slowly.

"My concern is not for myself, my liege. But rather, I fear for the safety of the lady Rosamund, who is given by betrothal to my guardianship. She has disappeared during the time I lay weakened from the—beatings I received. Therefore, I am come to seek that safe assurance that is the mantle given to all who are declared Royal Wards." From his place behind Lord Pendragon, Lord Reginald's eyebrows rose appreciatively. Very clever, he thought, realizing in the same instant that Mallory knew exactly where Rosamund was to be found.

"If we recover this maid, and declare her our ward, my lord, we have also the disposing of her hand and entitlements," the King said with narrowed eyes.

Lord Mallory smiled a little. "It were better so, my liege," he said calmly, "for mine own fate is not assured. But, as I have said, the wolves of Wallenford will not cease their stewardship until their rightful lord is returned!"

Was this last a threat . . . ? the King wondered.

"How is it that this marriage contract remains unfulfilled, my lord?" Henry asked suddenly.

The Pendragon's smile faded. His answer was very quiet.

"I do not tame the eagle with hood or jesses. Nor bind my wolf's loyalty with leash or collar. Nor do I goad my horse's courage with spurs. It is the same for her."

The King did not respond, but continued to look at the Pendragon with increasing interest. He thought of himself, and Elinor, of how he had won her from Louis of France—and how much he had gained.

Elinor, the lioness—so much more than the Acquitaine!

"So be it, my lord!" he said abruptly and spun away to bark terse orders. Mallory stood very still, listening as men scurried from the chamber to attend the King's will. He bowed his head, and his mouth thinned as he thought of where they would find her. And he used another fragment of the power within himself to slip suggestions to the men now searching.

Then he waited, contained to stillness.

Rosamund stood with teeth clenched on legs that trembled from the pain in her now bandaged feet. Sir Ranulf stood beside her, grim-faced with anger for the cold reserve she continued to show him. She did not look at him. Instead, she stared with unrelenting contempt at Becket, who stood before them both with the beneficent smile of a malicious child who had contrived successfully to get his own way.

Becket made the sign of the Cross.

"Now thou wilt be brought into the fold of God's lambs through this Holy Sacrament of marriage. The sins of fleshly incontinence are hereby absolved," he intoned majestically. "As Eve was brought forth from Adam's rib to be his handmaiden, so, too, my daughter, thou art given into the care of this good lord."

The door to the chamber was flung wide with a resounding boom, and six armed men erupted through it. Becket spun about. Wallenford did not move, recognizing both the King's livery and the stern-faced knight who led them. Sir Ranulf's hand flew reflexively to his sword hilt, then stopped.

"Put that aside, lad!" the older man advised him. "This is the King's business! We seek the King's Ward, the lady Rosamund of Wodensweir, who hath been wrongfully abducted from the King's household!" His blue eyes met Rosamund's. She nodded fractionally.

"This Lady is wed to Sir Ranulf of Wallenford, Sir Armand!" Becket stepped forward. The knight's eyebrows rose scornfully. He had never liked the arrogant and upstart Saxon.

"In this furtive haste, my lord?" he said coldly. "It is not resolved yet, I'll warrant!" He held out a hand. "My lady, do thou come with me to the King's summons!"

In the miracle of relief, Rosamund stepped forward, gasped, and felt her knees buckle at the excruciating consequences. Grim-faced, the knight caught her and scooped her up. Sir Ranulf jerked himself away from the iron hold his father had taken of one arm.

"I will carry my lady, Sir Armand!" He reached to take her, but the knight gave him a quelling look and turned on his heel.

"I think not, my lord!" he grated, and swept from the room. Wallenford seized his son's arm again.

"Have a care, Ranulf. The decree is not yet signed. . . ."

Sir Ranulf jerked his arm loose and turned on his father. "I care nothing for these manipulations of thine!" he snarled. "I want Rosamund. She is my bride and will remain so!" Then he, too, thrust his way from the chamber.

The Earl of Wallenford eyed Becket. "Evidently, she is the King's Ward," he stressed slowly.

"She was not so yester-eve, my lord!" the Archbishop retorted sharply. "I'll warrant the warlock Pendragon hath contrived this." He glanced down at the parchment on the nearby table that contained only one signature, his own, seized it, and strode from the chamber as well. The Earl of Wallenford followed closely, wondering.

It was eerie, the stillness with which Lord Pendragon had been standing for the past hour and more, the King thought uneasily, glancing up again from the documents and missives requiring his attention. Even the wolf beside him had not moved. He ignored the Earl of Arundel, who had retired to a far corner of the chamber, then looked down once more, seeking the inkwell for his quill.

But the sound of briskly marching, mailed feet caused him to set down the pen instead. Henry leaned back in his chair as Sir Armand, with three men flanking him on either side, walked briskly toward him, a woman in his arms.

"Majesty." The knight stopped and inclined his head, unable to bow further. "I bring the lady Rosamund of Wodensweir." Lord Pendragon stiffened, but did not otherwise move, and the King stared with masculine fascination at the rare beauty of the young woman with her long, luxuriant black hair and pale, exquisite features.

"How is it that this lady is unable to walk?" he asked, noting the bandaged feet protruding from the hem of her gown, and catching the approach of Becket and the lords of Wallenford out of the corner of his eye.

"The lady hath suffered torture and is damaged of the

same, Majesty," Lord Pendragon said with somber force as he stepped forward.

Rosamund looked at him and gasped, "Mallory!" But he did not turn toward her.

"Majesty, I must protest this seizing of my bride!" Sir Ranulf broke in, striding forward, his face taut with ire.

"The lady Rosamund is not for thee," Lord Pendragon said with the same stern command, and Becket likewise approached to bow, his features near apopleptic.

"This is witchcraft, Majesty! Surely thou have seen the spells that are conjured all about thee by this—warlock?" He crossed himself piously. "This woman is his creature, and I have brought her through tests of fire and through sacrament into the embrace of Holy Mother Church!"

"SILENCE!" the King roared. His complexion as ruddy as his hair, he stepped toward them and stood glaring, feet apart and fists set on his hips. "By God, we will bear no more of this snarling in our presence! We will not rule a realm of ill-trained dogs!" He paused to let the insult sink in, and focused his attention on Becket. "Thou, priest, presume too much authority by far!"

Sir Ranulf and his father behind him reddened. Becket stared back at the King with a combination of pallor and resolve. Sir Armand did not change expression by so much as a particle, and the girl simply stared as well, wide-eyed and tense. Henry cast a wary glance at Lord Pendragon, who stood with restrained calm, the suggestion of a smile touching the corners of his mobile white lips, then stepped toward the woman, still held in Sir Armand's embrace.

"What is thy name, my lady?" the King asked with a gentleness he reserved for women.

"I am Rosamund of Wodensweir, Majesty. The only begotten child of Lord Wilfred of Wodensweir, who were also known as the Pendragon."

"She is witch-got, my liege!" Becket pressed closer. Henry shot him a look of dislike and swung back toward the table to seize the two documents Lord Mallory had given him, spinning nimbly about to face the priest with a scowl.

"Then, it was unwise of thee, as a priest, to dispose of this lady's person and titles to the peril and keeping of a Christian man!" he snapped. "Likewise, my lord Archbishop, it was equally unwise of thee to dispose this, our ward, whose person has already been given to another lord," he said in silken tones.

Becket paled in earnest, his eyes flitting to the parchment in the King's hand. Sir Ranulf went rigid, and the King's eyes found the lady Rosamund's face.

"Nor were it wise of thee, my lady, to consent to this other alliance!" the King told her.

"I did not, Majesty!" Rosamund flared at once. "It was forced upon me, as was the person of Sir Ranulf of Wallenford!" The King's eyebrows rose as he moved his gaze to the named knight whose face went scarlet with fury at this accusation.

"Sir knight?" Henry asked in the same smooth manner. Sir Ranulf stepped forward and bowed, his shoulders rigid.

"Majesty, I did seek to rectify both mine own and this lady's honour by the sacrament of wedlock. I love the lady, and, finding her unchaste, even easy in the bestowing of her favours, sought to redeem her."

"Thou art generous, Sir Ranulf," Lord Pendragon's voice cut across this with astonishing smoothness. "To give honour that is not thine to bestow! I consider that there was little benefit to this charity and devotion beyond setting the seal of thy father's grip upon Wallenford."

Sir Ranulf ground his teeth and clenched his fists as Lord Pendragon, one hand searching the air before him, walked past toward the lady Rosamund, now seated upon a footstool that someone had found for her. Interested, the King did not comment, but quelled Sir Ranulf's reflexive reaching for his sword with a glance.

Reaching her, Lord Pendragon knelt and touched Rosamund's skirts. She stiffened, watching him with a wariness that were apparent to all. Then he spoke again.

"Do thou remember, my lady," he said in soft, melodious tones, "that time when we were virgin together, when thou said to me, 'thou art mine'? Did I not answer thee most gladly, 'I am thine'?

"So it has ever been, my lady, in keeping with thy father's will, and in keeping with mine own as well." His silver head bent as his white fingers passed delicately down her legs to her feet, discovering the bandages, gently unwrapping them. Rosamund bit back the retorts that sprang to her lips, her own cheeks flushed with discomfiture at such public intimacy, as

she caught the King's expression of intrigued, even enter-
tained fascination.

Then she gasped as Mallory touched the burns. He felt her
flinch and held up one of her feet.

"I cannot resolve in my mind, my liege," he said with
penetrating clarity, "that Holy Mother Church should cause
such suffering and brutal damage as all here may witness in
these wounds upon this lady's feet, while I, presumed a warlock and a creature of Satan, must seek the power to heal the
same?"

"Heresy!" Becket hissed, but the King stepped toward the
Pendragon and watched as Lord Mallory closed his eyes of
blood and passed his white fingers across the viley burned
tissue.

He focused, drew the pain into himself, and the damage—
and felt the tissues struggle, then draw together, closing and
banishing the broken places. He felt the injuries pass along his
fingertips, up his arms, and through his own flesh, down into
the tissues of his own feet. Aye—a simple replacement.

"It is a miracle." Sir Armand, who had stood guardian over
the lady Rosamund, was the first to utter exclamation, his own
expression a hushed whisper of awe. "A miracle! There is not
even a scar!"

"It is magic!" Becket thundered. "This sorcerer practises
enchantment upon the body of a witch! This is an evil seduction of the foulest order!"

The King did not move, but continued to frown thoughtfully. Rosamund, watching the way Mallory straightened, the
way the pain flickered across his face as he stepped carefully
back, knew otherwise, understanding what he had done.

"I have but moved the damage thou hast wrought in the
name of the Church to another place." Mallory said sternly.
"Away from this woman thou sought to torment because she
hath not the power to prevent it."

"What place is that, wizard?" Becket demanded.

"To myself, priest," the Pendragon told him with regal
calm. "As with creation, destruction cannot be undone. There
is only change."

"Majesty!" Becket turned to the King, this time in a more
pleading manner. "For the love of God and this Christian
realm, do thou dispatch this—unnatural creature, for he en-
dangers all Christian souls."

Henry Plantagenet, still frowning, turned slowly toward Lord Pendragon, who stood peaceably but a few feet distant, and considered the silence of the others gathered around him, awaiting his word.

Only the lady Rosamund reflected a like assurance to the Pendragon's demeanour. But then, he acknowledged with a start, she was got of the same sire.

"We are troubled by these magics, Lord Pendragon, though we perceive little to fault in their application," Henry said sternly, shifting to look at Becket. "Yet, we are reminded that Arthur the King was likewise surrounded by sorceries, having been taught and advised by that wizard Merlin who were endowed with great and wonderful powers. And, we mark that history bespeaks the glory of that same king who was a noble and Godly prince and brought great good to the realm.

"Magic, or miracle, we are persuaded to require that proof of kinship thou claim with this long dead king, before we resolve the direction of our justice."

"My brother's tomb . . ." Lord Pendragon said softly.

"Just so, my lord," the King agreed tersely.

"Near the place now called Glastonbury, my liege," Lord Mallory added.

"Glastonbury, then! We depart within the hour," the King said briskly. "To the rest. The lady Rosamund is our ward, and this marriage to Sir Ranulf is declared void. The lady's hand shall be bestowed upon the lord who will rightfully hold Wallenford of us!" With that, the King spun on his heel and strode from the chamber with his usual ferocious vigour, barking orders that sent servants scurrying in practised urgency to his bidding.

Sir Armand bowed and offered the lady Rosamund his arm as she stood.

"To the Queen, my lady," he murmured politely. She stood up on bare and painless feet, and glanced at Mallory, who stood so very still, so self-contained within his own peculiarly striking beauty. She felt a curious sense of wonder as she let the knight draw her away.

Mallory did not move as he listened to the others depart, catching the distinction of Lord Reginald's footsteps amid the others, their hesitation, and disappearance also.

Only the venomous presence of the priest remained as Mallory touched the wolf and began walking in the direction of the door, each footstep costing him dearly.

"I will see thee destroyed, warlock!" he heard Becket's muttered promise and frowned.

"The King hath far more to fear from thee than from me!" he gave dismissive reply, finding the arch of the doorway with his fingers, then passing through it.

# TWENTY-ONE

The dark eagle soared high in the radiant blue of the clear summer sky, sometimes becoming a mere speck, sometimes swooping through the air to describe vast spirals on the updrafts with a raptor's miraculous dominion over the winds. And, it uttered eerie cries from time to time that echoed melancholy spaciousness back to the horsemen riding across the rolling, lush green land below.

The wolf loped easily beside the wonderful great blue stallion that Lord Pendragon rode. The horse's ears pricked ever forward, the reins lay slack upon its neck, and it moved lightly across the earth for all its massive size, with a strange confidence, as though it knew the direction that had been chosen. . . .

It was impossible, at times, the King thought with admiration, to realize that Lord Pendragon was, indeed, completely blind, unable to see any of the ditches, or banks, or hills, or drops that passed beneath him. And, yet he sat his horse with fluid ease, seeming to accommodate any move the animal chose to make. Good horsemanship was one of the King's passions.

Curious, likewise, the King observed, were the suggestions of pleasure he perceived in the scarlet-eyed lord who seemed ever intent upon numerous and incomprehensible subtleties in the land about him.

Behind the King and Lord Pendragon, Rosamund rode her silver horse amid the substantial retinue, keeping to her place behind the Queen as she had been instructed to do. She was well guarded now, no longer feeling disposed to irritation at the presence of the Earl of Arundel on the one side, Sir Geoffrey on the other, and the austere Sir Armand at her flank. Yet, as she rode she studied the patches of forest longingly, and thought of the silver horse's fleetness, of escape, of the home that was the solitude and safety of her father's tower.

It seemed remote now, as she was likewise impelled to search through the array of feelings and experiences that had occurred since she had last seen that hidden place. And, from time to time, her eyes were drawn to watch Mallory, who rode ahead, as she struggled to understand the elusive cunning that he seemed to have developed. Tried to understand why he did not seem to wish to woo her as those others had so assiduously undertaken to do.

Curiosity and an agile mind moved the King to establish frequent conversation with the pale young man beside him as they journeyed across the southern part of England. Like the examination of a particularly unique gemstone, conversation exposed facets of enlightenment, or reason, or questions for further perusal. . . .

Henry Plantagenet learned much, discovering Lord Mallory to be disposed to his peculiar trait of quiet not only because of his need to listen, but because he, like the wild creatures, shared a subtle communion with the patterns and flow of natural things. For a prince of intense energy, given to strenuous scholarly appetite, and to the indulence of vigourous passions, this was a new and intriguing mental exercise.

It had been the love of philosophy that had first brought the King to seek the friendship of Thomas A'Becket, and then, to elevate him. Good days, those had been, Henry knew. . . .when Becket had been his honest and trusted friend, ever loyal to his purpose, and often a source of sound advice.

It had been trust that had caused him to elevate him further to Archbishop of Canterbury, the highest ecclesiastical office of the realm, and then to Chancellor of the realm. He could not have predicted the outcome of steadily escalating conflict. He could not have known that Thomas would take his vows so seriously as to discard all other consideration, even that primary loyalty—to the King, who Thomas himself had once fervently proclaimed to be God's own appointed guardian of His earthly kingdom.

Loyalty? It was become hypocrisy now.

But, Henry knew with the same sure conviction he had for the presence of blood in his body—he was God's annointed royal servant. It was for this he had been born and nothing else. Bitter lessons too were learned by princes, for he was coming to know that a king, in all things, is a man alone. Friendships must be qualified. Love was a thing to be contained. Power required distrust. . . .

Now, he set about to know the reach and depth of Lord Pendragon.

Lord Mallory, his wolf inevitably beside him, had wandered away from the encampment shortly after the site was chosen where all would spend the last night before reaching Glastonbury. Glancing at the lady Rosamund, who sat with meek posture and far from meek eyes near the Queen, the King turned away from the scattered gathering and walked into the woods to pick his way along a trail, brushing past ferns and shrubs flecked with the gold of evening.

Down a hill, and across a tiny brook, he walked with increasing content, then veered south up a long rise. Abruptly spotting a fallow deer, he wished he had thought to bring his bow. She poised for a moment, then bounded away, shimmering soundlessly through the underbrush to disappear over the crest of the hill ahead of him. The King followed, and reached the top of the rise to stop and stare in amazement.

Some fifty yards ahead, Lord Pendragon sat cross-legged in the tall grasses near the edge of a small clearing, his hand outstretched toward the deer. She trembled warily, ears flickering, then approached, and touched the white fingertips. Even more wonderfully, she then relaxed and moved closer to lie down in front of Lord Mallory, allowing his hand to fondle her ears, stroke her dappled back.

Lord Pendragon raised his head slowly and smiled as he cocked an ear in the King's direction.

"Majesty . . . ?" Quiet-sounding, his call, yet clear. The King strode through the undergrowth toward him.

"How couldst thou know, my lord?" Henry asked. The Pendragon's smile widened.

"I have learned recognition, my liege," he said gently, then murmured to the nervous doe. "My friend knows thee for a hunter, Majesty. She is wary. . ." The King squatted down on his haunches a little distance away and watched the way the Pendragon's white hand moved with sensual delicacy along the animal's back.

"Do thou hunt, my lord?" he surprised himself by asking. Lord Mallory shook his head.

"I dislike the killing, Majesty," he said. "Nor do I find any

satisfaction in the consuming of meat." The King frowned
thoughtfully, putting a blade of grass between his teeth, and
remembered the vast forests of Wallenford.

"There are other fiefs for a gallant and loyal liegeman that
are in our gift," he suggested deliberately. Lord Mallory's expression became very sober.

"I must recover Wallenford, Majesty," he said firmly. "It is
there that my obligations lie." Henry stiffened.

"Is not thy first duty to thy Liege Lord?" he asked more
sharply. The pale face before him looked regretful.

"Aaah, my king. I am caught between a pit and a snare in
this! I must live in the world of men, and for that, I have given
my life into thy hands. But I am, in accordance with my
father's will, the last Prince of Fairie, and to that office, I am
impelled to the stewardship of Wallenford, which is a most
special place in this realm thou art given to rule." His tone
softened to a particular melodiousness. "Understand, it is a
sanctuary of a kind, Majesty, being the last true virgin land in
this realm. Likewise, and for that, it harbours the resting place
of the Pendragon, and of his brother Merlin, and of other lords
of the Fairie from long-forgotten times. It is a haven for those
of the spirit. And it is a focal point for those powers that
remain within the natural earth of this kingdom.

"For the present, the wolves are the guardians," he continued. "But, without their lord, they cannot prevail, and so I am
obliged to undertake this stewardship, for I am likewise endowed of my father with that knowledge that is needful to the
sustenance and preservation of that forest." The King chewed
another blade of grass.

"It is a mystery," he said at last. "But we wonder at this
contradiction, Lord Mallory, between thy duty as our vassal
and this high estate and other duty thou additionally profess."
Mallory's fingers reached out to touch the grass, then lower to
grasp a fragment of earth. He held the soil up in his palm.

"There is no contradiction with appropriate understanding," he said quietly. "This—the earth, is the source for all
substance, for men, and for the beasts, and for the Fairie
also."

The King frowned. "We do not perceive thy meaning."

"Life is got both of spirit and substance, but spirit most
chiefly. And, in those few, especially chosen places on the
earth where the spirits of the Fairie may yet reside, there is
created another power. It is a wellspring from which the na-

ture of spirit is loosed to seek out substance and become manifest life." Lord Mallory breathed deeply. "Mortality is no more than a simple change, Majesty, that occurs when that which hath been drawn from the earth must be returned to it. It is then that spirit seeks new forms to occupy."

"What of Heaven and Hell?" the King asked, interest overruling his recognition of the potent heresy of Lord Mallory's discourse.

"Those are conditions of spirit, my liege, not locations in space. Mayhap, Heaven is wisdom, and Hell is ignorance?" Henry Plantagenet shifted restlessly as he considered the subtle truths of that, the conditions within his own soul that drove him. Toward knowledge, toward understanding. To—what purpose? Even now, knowing himself to be the most powerful prince in Christendom, he was yet driven to accomplish— what? He knew the answers. Yet, in a fashion, they eluded him as well. Pursued him, made him press his flesh to exhaustion, then arise and try again.

"We wonder," he enquired slowly, half to himself, half to Lord Pendragon, "to what purpose are these compulsions of the spirit?"

Lord Mallory smiled thoughtfully. "Mayhap, toward that attainment of the completion that is a total life in the spirit, such as men have inherited from their ancient union with the Fairie. So it seems, that the path of destiny pursued by men who have been given sovereignty over the earth, follows a troubled, but appropriate direction. It is a matter of choice."

"And what is the other, my lord?"

"Absence by the loss of spirit. No life at all!"

Henry Plantagenet kept silence for some considerable time, then. He watched the silver-haired young man before him, increasingly radiant in the descending nightfall, with the deer beside him, and the wolf, now entirely at rest with its nose reclining on neatly folded forelegs.

It is an example of flawless harmony, he thought.

"Where is God in all this?" he asked suddenly.

The Pendragon moved a little and sighed deeply. "As I perceive, my liege, God is life itself, the essence and consequence of spirit. Both the power and the freedom of the choice that is its absolute license."

That was a statement fraught with awesome implications, the King thought, yet, it was not entirely inconsistent with the teachings of the Church.

"And thou, Lord Pendragon, hast placed thy fate and life in our hands, when it becomes increasingly apparent, that thou art endowed with the power to do otherwise?"

"In accordance with destiny, Majesty, thou art the King. This realm is thine inheritance. It belongs no longer to my kind. Therefore, I, too, must yield myself to thy choices as is fitting."

"And, should we choose to see thee die, Lord Mallory? What then?" the King tested.

"I must submit myself accordingly," the Pendragon said with calm acceptance.

Henry shot him a wary look. "We mistrust this absolute assurance of thine, my lord!" he said more harshly.

"It is an expression of the extent of my bondage to mine own honour, my liege," the Pendragon told him.

The King thrust himself to his feet and stood for a moment, looking down upon the other, then, without answer, frowning still, he turned and strode back through the woodlands to the encampment.

The great eagle abandoned its flight to rest upon the Pendragon's shoulder as the considerable group of the King's retinue undertook the last mile toward Glastonbury.

An uneven mixture of large manor, hamlet, and small township, Glastonbury lay nestled in the gentle loop of the river Brue that passed around its western side. The remains of an ancient church and monastery dominated the clustered gathering of cottages and other low, thatched buildings. All around the area were well-tilled strips of planting interspersed with commons plentifully littered with grazing sheep. Smoke spiralled upward from the center of a few of the thatched roofs, and serfs, about the endless daily tasks that comprised their livelihood, stopped to stare in fascinated awe at the Royal entourage—to stare, likewise, at the silver-white skin and hair of the lord who rode by the King's left hand.

The blue stallion picked its way steadily toward the clustered buildings, then, with a sudden tensing of its muscles, it flared its nostrils, pricked its ears and veered south toward a low wall that extended outward from the ruined church.

Said to be constructed by Joseph of Aramithea in ancient times, the King knew, if remotely, of the ruin. He turned his own animal to follow Lord Pendragon, his eyes scanning the crumbling mortar and stone, half-buried beneath the surrounding tall grass and underbrush. A few jutting beams were all that remained of the roof of the church, along with a raggedly melancholy wall half-smothered by bushes that served as a reminder of the cloisters and monastery that had once been here, extending its erratic form from the southern end of the church. Immersed in the lush, wildly growing vegetation thereabouts, the ruins exuded an aura of almost dreamlike serenity.

The blue stallion halted of its own volition, and the Pendragon dismounted, turned a little toward the King, and extended the fingers of one ungloved hand toward the church itself. A sense of peculiar quiescence pervaded the afternoon air as the rest of the company brought their horses to stillness, and waited.

"There lies Avalon, my liege," Lord Pendragon said quietly. The King frowned, for he had always thought of an island. But Lord Pendragon turned, and moving the eagle to his saddle, began to walk, for once without the wolf beside him, toward the church. He felt his way through the tall grasses, down a wide gully of considerable depth, and up the other side.

The King remained astride his horse, watching Lord Pendragon grope and stumble awkwardly through the uneven ground, then turned to see the slowly gathering mob of common folk and others that had begun to form a half-circle about his retinue. He signalled Elinor to bring her horse up beside him, and again, turned to watch the Pendragon as Lord Mallory reached a small, swollen rise in the heavily vegetated ground amid the ruins and stopped to stand very still, his fingers remaining outstretched.

Then he grasped the hilt of the sword called Excalibur, and drew it from its scabbard to hold it aloft, its blade glinting with unnatural brilliance in the afternoon sun.

Mallory felt the warming of the interwoven dragons that comprised the hilt, felt their shifting beneath his palm, and moved to hold the blade of the weapon. With a delicate hissing, the dragons came to life, spreading their wings to pull against his grip.

They knew exactly where to go.

Mallory loosed his hold, felt the sword rise into the air a little above and before him, and listened to the softly beating wings as he followed the sword, uncaring of the gasping exclamations of the mass of people gathered some distance away. He struggled over the inconsistent ground, pushing through bushes, and half-tripping over unpredictably fallen rubble, concentrating his attention on the feel of growing stillness in the patch of air ahead toward which the sword was guiding him.

He stopped, suddenly enfolded by an aura of empathy, and listened as the sword raised itself to an even greater height above the ground. It poised—then plunged suddenly downward to bury itself in stone with a strange, clarion reverberation of sound. He held out his hand and took another step toward it, feeling the power inside him reach out in recognition to touch a kindred mood.

"King Arthur lies here, my liege!" he let his call rumble like thunder across the charged atmosphere.

The King did not glance about him, but flung himself from his horse and strode boldly in the direction that the Pendragon had gone.

Some crossed themselves. Sir Ranulf met his father's eyes, then dismounted to follow the King. Arundel did likewise, and others. Rosamund, still astride the silver horse, stared at the great lintel rock in the grass at the southern end of the ruined church, the sword still gleaming above it, the blade half-buried in the stone, at Mallory, who continued to stand very still.

She felt a sense of summoning, an elusive beckoning of power, and touched the silver horse with her heels, catapulting him through the gully, over the rough sod of the illusion that was all that remained of the Isle of Avalon, and halted the animal beside Mallory.

"Where is Arthur?" she asked.

Mallory's white hand pointed toward the sword. "He lies below. Only Excalibur may release him," he said quietly. Rosamund stared at him in some confusion, and frowned.

"Do it then! Take the sword. Thou art the one with the power!"

But Mallory shook his head. "Nay, my lady. It is not for me. Thou art the Pendragon's blood daughter, and this task is for thee!" Rosamund's mouth tightened and she glared bitterly at him.

"Thou mock me! For I am no different from any other mortal now!" she said harshly.

Mallory's face turned upward, half toward her. "Nor was

Arthur, Rosamund," he said in the same quiet tone. "Yet he was the Pendragon's begotten son!"

"What passes here?" the King demanded sternly as he approached and stopped on Lord Mallory's other side. "We see but turf and rubble, Lord Pendragon."

"Do it, Rosamund!" Mallory urged. Slowly, Rosamund slipped from the silver horse, and, as soon as her feet touched the ground the beast turned and galloped away. She gathered her skirts in one hand, stepped onto the mound of broken stone, and reached for the dragon sword.

"It is for the Pendragon's daughter to loose the bondage that has held our brother imprisoned for so long, my liege," she heard Mallory say behind her. There was a gasp or two. Lord Reginald watched, thinking that it was no longer possible for him to find amazement in anything Lord Mallory said or did.

The King merely nodded.

Almost hesitantly, Rosamund reached for the hilt, touched it, felt and saw the dragons furl their wings, bow their heads and became still as her fingers closed around them.

Power glowed. Power tingled as it passed up her arm, impelled her to pull. She smiled a little. Humans were something to fear, but this was not. She took a deep breath, releasing her skirts to put her other hand upon the hilt of Excalibur, and pulled with all her strength.

There was a slight, hesitant slipping. She closed her eyes and focused her will, and felt . . . Felt the power in Mallory stretch toward her, envelop her. She pulled again, and the sword slipped upward, easily, into her hand, drawing power into itself.

The air began to shimmer, and the earth trembled delicately.

"Now, Rosamund," Mallory's voice was little more than an urgent whisper. Her eyes still closed, she felt the sword come alive in her hands, and let her arms guide it in the great, swooping arc it craved.

The air formed a funnel of energy, a foil of another sort, and she grunted as she drove the blade toward the earth with all her might.

There was a violent cracking sound that rent the air, and lightning from the sword dove into the earth. Her eyes opened suddenly, and Rosamund jumped back, releasing her grip on Excalibur.

Rumbling gathered from below, and the ancient church began to crumble at its southern end. Cracks split the great stones that had formed its construction. They fragmented, and evaporated into dust that vanished into the violent wind that blew with sudden frigid cold across the frightened company to disappear a moment later like an illusion.

# TWENTY-TWO

The air was stiller than before, and sunlight glowed with brilliant radiance. And, the southern part of the ancient church had vanished as though it had never been.

Enclosed within the fragmented walls that remained, the turf had disappeared to reveal a floor of flagged marble squares some twelve feet below the former surface. The King suppressed a shiver as he stared at the sword Excalibur that hovered on lightly fluttering wings above a pristinely white, ornately carven tomb in the center of the nave. Then, he read the inscription that was so clearly engraved beneath the feet of the effigy thereon.

"Arturus, Rex Britaniae," he inhaled sharply. "God's Blood!" he whispered and glanced about at the tense, pale faces of those around him, pausing to watch as Lord Pendragon held out his hand toward the lady Rosamund. She took it, and the pair of them walked down toward the tomb, separated, and stopped to stand, one on either side of the sarcophagus. The King followed, pausing at the foot of the tomb.

Above them, the sword poised, shimmering in the air, then, suddenly slipped point downward, to pass through the very center of the marble effigy.

It disappeared.

The effigy began to crack, the marble carving splitting into a thousand fragments that fell away to lie in another kind of rubble around the tomb. King Henry shivered a little as he leaned forward, and stared in awe at that which lay within.

The dragons of Excalibur closed their wings as the sword settled across the loins of what appeared to be a sleeping man of late, middle years.

Dark hair, liberally strewn with silver, lay in thick profusion about a fair complected face, that, save for the lines across the brow and about the mouth, was exactly the same as Lord Mallory's.

Armour of an ancient design covered a muscular body, the rings gleaming beyond the borders of a tunic of purest white upon which was embroidered a rich profusion of red and gold dragons. Roman greeves covered the loose, cross-gartered hose on the legs of the sleeping man, and a simple crown of gold held back the long hair and bound the wide forehead.

The man sighed deeply, and stirred. His brows flickered, and, very slowly, he opened eyes of brilliant green.

"So many dreams..." he whispered in a deep voice that was likewise reminiscent of Lord Mallory, but reflected as well an eerie, ageless exhaustion. He turned his face a little, his eyes coming to rest on the snow-coloured features and red, sightless eyes of the young man standing before his right shoulder. He smiled wearily.

"The last Pendragon..." he murmured softly. "Merlin told me of thy coming, my brother. Aye, I see the stamp of our father's handiwork upon thy face. The purity and the blood made flesh..." He closed his eyes again briefly, licked his lips. "My colours... Merlin told me it was a blind man who would loose me to final peace." His brows gathered into a pain-filled frown. "Mordred...? I could not pass it to him. He was given to such misuse of the powers."

Mallory's fingers found the brow of Arthur and touched lightly. "There is but one King now, my brother."

"The dreams are unclear—Our father?"

"The Pendragon hath passed to his rest. His destiny was accomplished, save for one thing, and that is given into my hands."

Arthur nodded faintly, his fingers groping to touch the sword that lay across him. "I feel Excalibur," he said. It was uncanny, King Henry thought in complete awe, how alike their voices were.

"It is returned to thee. The Pendragon sought it from the Lady. It is with her, he hath gone to sleep."

"Aaah. Aye... The Lake," Arthur said with remarkable softness. His brows flickered again. "Yet, my brother, I think I will have little need for the sword." He turned his head slowly, stiffly, in the manner of one who has forgotten how to move, and then, his green eyes widened as they settled on the woman to his left.

"Guenivere!" he breathed. "Sweet Jesu—beloved Gueni-vere..." Rosamund gasped and paled. And shivered violently.

"I am Rosamund of Wodensweir," she said unevenly, glancing at Mallory. "I am the Pendragon's other child."

Arthur continued to study her face. "Aye. I see it now. Yet thou art so like." His face became gaunt and drawn with the burden of ancient griefs. He looked away.

"The lady Rosamund is the grandchild of thy Queen, my brother," Mallory said then. Rosamund's dark eyes widened to enormity as this thing that she had never known was revealed. "Her mother was Launcelot's daughter."

Arthur's head tossed a little, his voice tinged with unhappiness. "I dreamed there must be issue of that union..." he whispered. "My loins would not provide—save that once..." He closed his eyes again. "So much pain we did endure. I tried...I loved them both so well...." A drop of scarlet appeared in the corner of each eyelid, shimmered on the dark lashes, swelling as another joined it. "Do thou set me free, my brother! Let me find relief from this arousal. From this perpetual imprisonment..." It was an exhausted plea.

"Tears of blood?" Behind them Henry Plantagenet whispered in awe, shifting closer.

Arthur's eyes opened, shimmering green and scarlet. "Whose voice do I hear?"

"Henry Plantagenet, my brother. He is the King of England now," Mallory gave answer. Arthur's breathing was shifting into a pain-filled gasping.

"A man...?"

"Aye. And a fit and honest prince!"

"It has come to that then..." Arthur's breath rattled in his throat. "To men entirely..." His face twisted in agony, the lines upon it deeply etched, the pallor of his skin becoming grey. "Merlin had said..." he gasped. "That, when the last Pendragon—gave his life into—the hands of his chosen king ...Then, there would be no more need of me...That my tasks would be completed for all time.

"Take Excalibur. Let me pass into the sanctuary of spirit..." This last issued forth as a barely audible, hoarse shivering of sound.

"God give thee peace, my brother," Mallory uttered with clear and gentle solemnity as he reached for the sword. He grasped the hilt and drew it away from the man who now lay very still.

King Henry crossed himself with the gracefulness of true

reverence as Arthur Pendragon's breathing faded into silence.

"God keep thee, noble king," he murmured, then froze to
stare at the changes that were beginning to occur before him.
Grey now, the flesh of Arthur began to shrink and dry, the skin
shifting to a deep parchment yellow. The scarlet liquid in the
corners of his eyes dried, went dark. And where the startling
green eyes had been, the flesh sank away into gaping holes in
a skull now defined by skinlike wrinkled, sepia leather.

The rich dark hair fell away. Armour rusted, and the splen-
did clothing lost its brilliance and colour as it sank inward to
lie against the bones of the ancient King. Cloth, like flesh,
that rotted steadily away, fraying in an accelerated decay, then
crumbling into fragments. Finally into dust.

The King gagged despite himself as brown shards of tissue
fell away from teeth, from what had been a face, leaving no
other sight than dry white bones.

Even these shifted, collapsed to lie discarded against the
smooth inner base of the sarcophagus, and crumbled into a
white dust so fine as to be lost in the slightest movements of
the air. . . .

The only sounds to interrupt the silence that followed were
the soft hissing of Excalibur as Lord Mallory slipped the
weapon into the scabbard resting against his left hip, and, the
rustling soft sounds of grass erupting through the seams in the
marble flagging of the stone beneath the tomb, growing with
determined and unnatural insistence in its haste to cover.

"It is time to leave, Majesty," Lord Mallory spoke, his
voice breaking through the frozen incredulity of those around
him. But King Henry, compelled by things beyond his own
comprehension, dropped to his knees.

"This is a sacred and most blessed place!" he intoned with
deep clarity. Others followed suit, bowing their heads as they
murmured a prayer, crossed themselves. All save Sir Ranulf,
who stared at the lady Rosamund with hypnotized fascination.

Guenivere and Launcelot . . . ?

"Mallory?" Rosamund murmured helplessly. He felt his
way around the empty marble sarcophagous, over which thin
new vines were already beginning to grow, and groped for her
hand. Now, she gave it to him thankfully and felt his warmth.
Only he could understand it all, for he was a part of the same
thing.

"Come away now," he whispered gently. "Arthur is free

and at peace, and there is more yet to be accomplished." Mallory began to move, but it was Rosamund who guided their steps across the encroaching foliage, away from the weeds and from the ruined church.

Rosamund stopped walking when she came abreast of the silver horse, peacefully cropping grass alongside Mallory's blue stallion.

"How can I be my father's daughter and the grandchild of my brother's Queen?" She asked the question uppermost in her mind.

"Thy father loved thy mother dearly, and he wove spells to give her longer life than other humans."

Rosamund frowned at this. "I had thought she was descended of the Druids?"

"Aye. Through Guenivere." Mallory inclined his head and reached out to touch the neck of the blue horse, stroking it gently. "Launcelot was of the Fairie blood, as were many of the lords of the Round Table. Thereby such longevity was possible to contrive."

"If I am all these things, why did my father give thee all his power?" Rosamund's voice hardened at the recollection of the Pendragon's bitter reprimand. "Power that I could well have used to my preservation. Or, is it for my womanhood, that I am not equal to thee in rights and may not be so endowed?" Mallory sighed, his expression becoming unhappy. "My father even made a gift of me to thee. Am I never to be free as thou art? As are other men?"

"Thou art freer than thou know. . . ." he began quietly.

Rosamund flared. "How so, Mallory? Do thou tell me. I am a woman, and all of mine entitlements and properties belong to whomsoever is my lord. What manner of self-possession is that? Thyself, or some other, it makes little difference. I am condemned to the same fate!"

"Is that how thou determine to perceive me, Rosamund?" Mallory asked softly.

She glared at him. "How art thou so different, Mallory? Am I not given to thee? Is not Wallenford thine?"

Mallory's face tightened. "Hast thou never paused to consider, Rosamund, that thy father's thinking was upon a different and more ingenious course? I have tried to tell thee before, but I think thou hast not understood, that I am thy father's gift to his daughter!"

Rosamund paused warily. "How so?" she asked sullenly.

"It is upon my shoulders that the Pendragon placed the burden of his power. Aye, be assured on that, it is a burden! Likewise, the task of regaining thy stewardship of Wallenford, *within* the framework of the King's law," he stressed, "has fallen to me. He knew that day when I did answer thee by telling thee, 'I am thine', that I would be his servant in all matters concerning thee." He turned toward the blue horse with a deep, regretful sigh. "Thy father, my father likewise, understood me well. He also knew well this world of men that thou and I must live within. The Fairie are gone, their realms are not available to us. And, so, I am become thy safety."

Rosamund did not answer, but stared at him, uncertainty and something else pushing the old resentments back.

Mallory did not have that same, fierce warrior pride that stamped her own disposition, the temperaments of other men. He was content with little, subtle things. She understood, of a sudden, the breadth and reach of his capacity for patience. Understood other things with new wisdom got of her own recent experiences. Mallory was indeed a most fitting guardian for the forests of Wallenford.

The Pendragon, she acknowledged for the first time, had chosen his successor well.

"Now, thou must fight Sir Ranulf for Wallenford," she said.

"Aye."

"He is strong and well skilled."

Mallory turned toward her, his scarlet eyes staring past her at nothing resolvable. He smiled slightly.

"I do not doubt it!"

"Thou wilt have need of those powers my father gave thee," Rosamund began carefully, thinking . . . But he shook his head.

"Nay, Rosamund. There will be no use of them. I will fight as a man."

"But?"

"I am blind," he finished for her. "Aye. So I am told oft enough. It is a disorder that hath no real meaning to me. Think, rather, that I were well taught at arms."

"Not well enough, Mallory," Rosamund said then, recalling her own encounter with the knight.

"Mayhap thou taught me better than thou realize!" He

smiled cheerfully, his hand reaching toward her. "Rosamund," he whispered intently, his head cocked a little, expression become serious. She swallowed, stiffened. "For love of thee, do I not always accomplish miracles?" he finished softly. She fought for control then, fists clenched.

"I am soiled goods, Mallory," she managed unevenly.

"Nay," he denied, stepping forward to find her with his arms and drew her against him.

"God's Blood, but my soul is in chaos!" she rasped, heaved a shuddering sigh, and fought for self-control as he drew her closer still, bent his head, and set his face against her hair. Feelings that groped as he did, he thought, and wrapped the caressing softness of another aspect of the power about them both, content, for the moment, to be contained within it. Her tension eased then, and she fit against him at last.

Walking away from the tomb, already near-vanished beneath the stranglehold of smothering and rampant growth that had moved back into the ruins of the ancient church, the King raised his head as he stepped beyond the confines of its shattered walls. He saw Lord Pendragon and the lady Rosamund locked in each other's arms some distance ahead.

Aye, he thought. They belonged. He held out a hand to Elinor, and smiled a little as her fingers slipped into his grasp. He continued another few steps, then stopped to look back at the others who had followed him into the sacred ground of Avalon. Solemn faces, all. He saw young Sir Ranulf raise his eyes to see the pair still some distance away, saw, as well, the jealousy that made a raw movement across his features.

"The lady Rosamund is not for thee, sir knight!" the King murmured as Sir Ranulf strode within earshot. He flushed abruptly and looked at the King. "They are not entirely of this world," Henry said, not unkindly. Sir Ranulf's expression became grim.

"And Wallenford, Majesty?" he asked after a moment. "My father's honour. My own?"

King Henry sighed deeply. Lord Fulk was a worthy lord in most things and not to be undervalued. Somewhat avaricious, perhaps, but not uncommonly so.

"As God wills," he let his voice ring out across the still afternoon to encompass the entire population about him. "The disputation over the fiefs of Wallenford shall be resolved upon the field of battle tomorrow! Sir Ranulf. Lord Pendragon! Do thou both gird thy loins with honour for the fulfillment of our just decree!" Sir Ranulf bowed and strode away to join his sire.

Lord Mallory seemed not to hear, but bent his head further and caught the lady Rosamund's mouth with his own.

# TWENTY-THREE

"I would squire thee, my lord," Sir Geoffrey offered gruffly.

Mallory smiled. "Thou doest me great honour," he accepted warmly, groped for the cup of wine that had been set before him, found it, and sipped lightly. The campfire crackled and popped, heat flowing from it to waft like contentment over them, and Mallory shifted to an even more comfortable position.

Rosamund sat silently near the fire, watching—thinking. Lord Reginald moved about with restless unease, also thinking, of his own half-smothered feelings for the lady he had known, and the liking he had conceived for Lord Mallory.

And that which lay before them all on the morrow.

He watched the way Lord Mallory's wolf now divided its attentions between the Pendragon and Lady Rosamund, soliciting affection from each in turn, as though discovering . . . He watched the way her hand reached to fondle the animal's fur, and thought that Rosamund was greatly changed. Her wild, defiant air was gone, and the sullenness. Now, she had of a sudden acquired a self-contained dignity that made her beauty truly awesome.

Lord Reginald sighed as he forced himself to settle down and lean back against a saddle, his gaze passing across Sir Geoffrey, who had undertaken the tasks of cleaning armour, to the Pendragon. Lord Mallory's face was serious, composed, seemingly stronger than it had appeared before, and his silver hair gleamed in the fireglow in a manner suggestive of a halo.

The eerie scarlet eyes were almost black in the night, deep and unreflective. He sipped wine slowly, and without apparent tension for the concerns the morning would bring. Lord Reginald lay back and closed his eyes, seeking the diversion of attempting to find rest.

Mallory continued to sit unmoving through the night, feeling every facet of the power that stirred restlessly inside him, hungrily in search of release through a fastidious probing of the weaknesses in his character. It was particular, this undertaking of preparation for the morrow.

Sir Ranulf rose stiffly from his knees, aware that he had long moved beyond the usefulness of prayer. Yet, beyond faith, his vigil had extended to encompass much more as he had undertaken a detailed examination of himself, of his considerable abilities as a fighting man, of the unique aspects of this combat that lay before him.

Aye. He knew himself, his strengths, the nature and applications of his own cunning, his capacities for self-rule. But there were troubling, unknown, and impractical considerations to the unique battle that lay before him. His first confidence, got of Lord Pendragon's blindness, had dissipated into uncertainty for all the other's claim to fight as a man. Unknighted, Lord Pendragon was not even bound by the same oaths and honour, and he was a sorcerer whose abilities were unknowable and beyond defense. How, he wondered, could he prevail against such a sword as Excalibur?

Sir Ranulf looked up from the dark ground away from the campfires where he had chosen to isolate himself, and strode to his father's tent, brushing through the flap to see Lord Fulk rise to meet him, his face stern with the sobriety of a clearly aging man. Sir Ranulf stopped.

"I would know, my lord, why thou took Wallenford from Mallory De Cheiney all those years ago?" he demanded. Lord Fulk shifted and looked away. "Am I not owed some explanation, Father?" Sir Ranulf pursued. "For, it is on thy account I am not like to see the setting of tomorrow's sun!"

Lord Fulk breathed deeply. "It was a den of madness when I came there on the King's business," he spoke slowly, almost reluctantly. "Lord Robert—" his revulsion was plain—"his lady, Edwina, my own sister, had become a tormented lunatic wraith. Destroyed. He had destroyed her. Lord Robert had well nigh destroyed all of it. His vassals were in terror of his brutality, his rages. It was all refuse and disorder. Carrion in the halls. Neglect and decay of appalling proportion.

"And the boy? Lord Mallory—he was a blind mad thing that howled with the dogs in the hall. I had thought it better so, to let him wander, to let the wolves find him and finish him, for I knew I could bring Wallenford to order. And," his tone were briefly defensive, "for the most part, I have done so."

"It was wrong of thee, Father," Sir Ranulf said after a long silence.

"I could not have known that the wolves guarded so much magic there. I have never been prone to superstition. I thought to dispose the strange tales and such . . ." Lord Fulk turned back to meet his son's look.

"I seek ever to increase the honour of my name," Sir Ranulf said after another pause. "But, I have been wise enough to learn the distinctions between proper rule and contrivance by deceit. I do not soil my hands! Thou hast mismanaged this by dishonest practice," he sighed. "And now, this warlock brings us all to justice!"

"How could thou fail against this—blind man, Ranulf?" Lord Fulk demanded, scowling.

Sir Ranulf stared at him, his mouth drawn in a thin line. "I have not scoured my soul these past hours," he said acidly, "for my conviction of triumph, my lord. I may well be the one to die. . . ."

"Then I will see Lord Pendragon burned for the witch he is!" Lord Fulk snarled.

Sir Ranulf shot him a look of contempt. "With Becket's aid, my lord? Nay. I think not. The King's ear is not bent in his direction. And what of Wallenford? It will be lost in any case. The wolves will have it after all!" He swung on his heel and strode away, ducking into the night.

The bright morning light was softened by a scattering of soft white clumps of cloud that floated high across the sky, intermittently obliterating the sun. A breeze blew across the meadow that had been chosen for the battlefield, making the tall grass ripple like the surface of a green lake.

The King sat loosely in a chair that had been brought from the manor house and set upon a dais that had been quickly, roughly erected during the night. The Queen sat by his right hand, and beyond her, the lady Rosamund sat with her head bowed and her hands tightly clenched together in her lap.

Behind them stood a crowd composed of the population of the King's retinue, serfs, and others from the manor and hamlet nearby.

At each end of the meadow were minor centers of activity

as the two men, preparing to fight, made ready for the battle
that was shortly to begin.

Lord Mallory did not speak as Sir Geoffrey touched his
armour, checking the mail, then set his helm over his head,
strapping its laces to his gorget. Casque and coif muffled
sound and made it hard to hear properly. Mallory breathed
deeply. All he could feel was the small fragment of air that
touched his face through the cross-shaped slit in the front of
the helm. He groped with his fingers along the stallion to his
left, found the stirrup, and swung himself up into the saddle of
the blue horse. He heard the distorted screech of the eagle,
discontent with its perch of wood some yards distant. The
wolf—he had sent to Rosamund.

"The lance, my lord."

He heard Sir Geoffrey's voice and held out his hand, closing his fingers as he received the weapon.

"The shield."

He felt the knight slip the moon-shaped device onto his left
arm and bent the elbow to grope for the reins.

"All is in readiness, my lord."

Mallory did not answer, but listened intently instead, seeking the sounds that gave direction to space. He touched the
blue stallion and he cantered forward, toward the noises that
were some distance ahead, a little to his right.

He heard then, the increasing thunder of other hooves, and
knew it was Sir Ranulf's destrier that approached. Then, it
suddenly changed gait and direction, veering toward the
sounds that gave location to the presence of the King.

The blue horse veered of its own volition, and came to a
halt likewise. Mallory bowed from the waist.

"By our will," the King's voice rang out clearly to penetrate space, "all disputation over the fiefs of Wallenford shall
be brought to honourable resolution by combat. It is proclaimed that the gift of Wallenford shall be bestowed upon
whichsoever of these two lords prevails in this contest of
arms. Good, my lords. Do thou serve each other and us with
all thy might and honour for the accomplishment of God's
Will!"

"Majesty?" Mallory heard Sir Ranulf call out from the
confines of his helm.

"My lord?"

"I would request to wear a favour of the lady Rosamund, in

hope that I may win her hand as well as mine own inheritance!"

Silence followed, and Mallory heard the knight's horse move restively. He set his lance down against the blue horse's side and drew Excalibur from its scabbard, shifted his hand to grasp the blade and held the sword out, hilt first. He called out then.

"My liege. I would give into the keeping of the lady Rosamund this enchanted sword, and I pray that I may receive another weapon in its stead." He heard a rippled murmur, felt Rosamund's hand draw the weapon from him, and knew that she had reseated herself with it in the silence that followed.

"I will give the use of my sword most gladly, Majesty!" Lord Reginald stepped forward, drawing his own precious and unpretentious weapon. He held it out. Lord Mallory's hand groped awkwardly, found the hilt and slipped the new weapon into his empty scabbard. He took up his lance, and the blue stallion spun about and galloped to one end of the meadow.

Sir Ranulf stared in brief amazement after the blind man, then bolted his horse away in the opposite direction, his request for a favour never granted.

The King looked at Lord Reginald.

"It was honourably done," he murmured approval, glancing to where the lady Rosamund sat, Excalibur across her thighs.

The horn sounded, and the blue stallion bolted forward with all the force of a whirlwind. Mallory crouched and lowered his lance, shifted his shield and listened with all his concentration. He heard the horse that was sweeping toward him, the slight shift in the rhythm of its hooves. He raised his shield and ducked as he felt the tip of his own lance slither off Sir Ranulf's shield, and the jarring blow along his left arm as the other man's lance hit his own shield with well-placed forcefulness.

He swung the blue horse about as he reached the end of the meadow, and the beast lunged forward once more, into the muffled patterns of approaching thunder. Mallory shifted his head, unable to hear as he needed to. Echoes—Again, his lance tip slithered, and Sir Ranulf's weapon crashed into him with terrible force, nearly propelling him from the saddle. Mallory reeled and clenched his thighs, heard the crack of splitting wood as his horse caught his imbalance and swept him on.

Again. This time he shifted differently just before the intensity of the approaching horse's hoofbeats spoke of contact. He heard his own lance shatter and felt the reverberations that stripped it from his grip. Then, the stunning shock as Sir Ranulf's lance slid inward from his shield to catch him under the arm and draw him upwards.

Space became chaos, spun . . . And Mallory felt the ground slam into his back. Vaguely, he heard the other man's horse come about. He gasped and reached for the laces of his helm, tore the thing off, and flung it away. He rolled, and reached for the hilt of Arundel's sword, jerking it free just as a light thud told him that Sir Ranulf had leaped from his horse a few feet to the right.

Mallory thrust himself to his feet. Now he could hear! Aye, all the details of movement that he needed to perceive. Footsteps that were light thuds on turf, the metallic synchrony of chain mail. He felt the air move, and leaped away as the other man's sword swept close past his face. He brought his own weapon up with lightning speed, heard and felt the reverberations as the two swords met.

Nothing else mattered so much as the sounds that told of the sword's location, its direction expressed through the other man's movements, his breathing, his swiftness and strength.

Mallory countered and leaped, and touched Sir Ranulf's shield several times. He managed by momentary agility to elude Sir Ranulf's lethal blade, or to force it away. Panting with exertion, he heard the other man do likewise, information that revealed the precise location of his opponent's body.

He felt pain tear across one thigh as the other man's sword swept just under his guard, and lunged back to trip over something on the ground—his own helm. He fell and rolled away with a gasp as Sir Ranulf's blade bit air and turf a fractional distance from his face, and jerked to swing himself to his feet, lunging in a counterstroke.

He felt the tip of his own sword bite steel mesh in the vicinity of the other man's arm, and spun lightly on his good leg, pulling his sword back to bring it down across the horizontally hissing arc of Sir Ranulf's weapon.

He thrust closer, tried to force the other weapon from Sir

Ranulf's grasp, and cried out involuntarily as a pinpoint of steel drove through his own mail and screeched along his ribs.

A dagger, he knew. He reeled back and swung his sword in an oddly angled arc that bit along the other man's shield, jerked his sword free and stepped back again, half stumbling on the uneven ground. He ducked away as Sir Ranulf's sword slammed against the upper part of his own shield, then slashed into his shoulder. Blood and sweat mingled, and pain joined with a violent gasping for air.

Mallory drove forward suddenly, in a move that was entirely new, and sent the point of his weapon diving forward as he aimed low. He heard a cry and felt resistance, and, jerking back, felt another violent blow across his left shoulder. He gasped in agony at the snapping of his collarbone and reeled away to let the shield fall from his useless left arm. He managed to swing his sword up just in time to divert yet another blow.

He dropped to one knee, and with all his strength, dived again with the point of his sword, straight for the panting sounds before him. He heard a gasping sound as the tip of the weapon lodged itself, scraping past steel into deep, soft flesh.

The belly . . . ? He did not know. He heard the thud of a shield, and then, a peculiar groaning whisper.

"I am a dead man . . ." He heard the rumpled buckling of a falling body. "God keep my soul . . ." Mallory poised as he heard the rasping breathing change to a hideously moist gurgling, then cease altogether.

He let the sword fall from his hand, and stood for a moment, very still, trying not to become lost in the pain and weakness that was enveloping him.

Sir Ranulf was dead, Mallory realized, dimly aware of voices, of running feet and the bodies that were gathering around him.

"Sir Ranulf is dead, my liege!" It was Sir Armand's voice that made the pronouncement.

"Lord Pendragon is the victor, then," he heard the King's firm voice. "Wallenford is fairly won!"

But Mallory was enveloped in something else, something beyond the pain, beyond the blood that drained against his clothing, and the threatening exhaustion.

He had killed. Wallenford was recovered by the death of another man at his hand. It could not be so. It must not be so. . . . He jerked forward, shaking free of the fingers that reached to touch him and dropped to his knees, using his teeth to rip away the gauntlet from the hand he could still use.

He groped, and, biting back a groan of pain, shifted closer. He moved his fingertips up along the skirts of a surcoat, above the belt, and found the place where his sword had entered just below the sternum. He probed, aye, and felt the place where the weapon had pierced diaphragm and lung and nicked the heart.

"Nay!" His cry was a loud keening across the air. Voices stilled as he bent closer and bowed his head. "Nay. . ." It was another pain that overflowed in the knowledge that this death was wrong. The honour of men was not the same as for the Fairie. Wallenford could never be secured upon a grave.

He felt the touch of a hand and shook it away.

"My lord, thy wounds need care!" It was Sir Geoffrey's voice.

"Nay!" he rasped again and reached his fingertips into the rent flesh before him and summoned . . . Felt the powers shiver loose from that place deep in his soul where he had bound them down . . . Become a pulsing reflection of his own heartbeat, that stretched to flow down along his arm, a force so unlike the fading strength of his own damaged flesh. He searched through his reeling wits for an incantation from the vast well of his father's memory, and cried out again, uttering words that sounded as though they came from far away.

And, beneath his fingertips, he felt a violent shuddering, a sudden pulsing movement that was hesitant at first, then strong. He let his fingers slip back, closing the passage that his sword had made, and felt his body crumple in a spiralling song of unmanageable pain.

With a sigh, he surrendered to it in absolute relief.

No one stirred. Stunned onlookers gazed in awed confusion across the twisted, matted grass, across the blood and scattered weapons, at the body of Sir Ranulf, which had begun to breath again, blood no longer oozing from that deadly place where his mortal wound had been.

The Pendragon lay crumpled on his side, surcoat rent, blood bright fresh and everywhere upon him, his strangely pure face completely still, save for a faint, slow breathing.

The King crossed himself.

Rosamund, galvanized from frozen horror, flew to Mallory's side, dropping to her knees with Excalibur still held in one hand.

"Thou shalt not die, Mallory!" she called out. "Do thou hear me, thou shalt not die!" Helplessly, she shifted back as Sir Geoffrey, together with Lord Reginald, and Sir Armand, picked him up with all possible care, and followed as they carried him away.

His face grey, Lord Fulk stared after them for a moment, then dropped down beside his son to loose the helm and draw it away.

Sir Ranulf groaned and rolled his head, then opened his eyes and blinked slowly. He gasped, confusion crossing his face.

"I had thought I was dead . . . ," he whispered slowly, and raised a hand to touch his upper belly where he could clearly feel deep, grinding pain was. It was the King who stepped forward to stand above him. Sir Ranulf looked up at the somber, regal face.

"Thou were fairly slain, Sir Ranulf," King Henry said. "And, by some miracle, Lord Pendragon hath returned thee to the living."

"He is proved a warlock beyond question now!" Lord Fulk said unevenly.

Sir Ranulf turned to look at him, seeing an ill-gathered effort to collect some manner of dignity. The King frowned.

"His claim is fairly won, my lord!" Henry Plantagenet growled. "Lord Pendragon hath proven himself a gallant and chivalrous lord!"

Sir Ranulf watched his father retreat before the King's rebuke, then glance down to meet his gaze before striding stiffly away from the new-got contempt in his son's face.

It was with a silent and preoccupied thoughtfulness that Sir Ranulf lingered near the place where Lord Pendragon lay recovering slowly from his wounds over the next several days. Then, finally, on the fourth, he ventured to approach the tent that had been set up in the same meadow where they had fought.

He stiffened as he sought entry, past the clear assessing gleam of Sir Geoffrey's watchful eyes. He stepped inside and saw the lady Rosamund sitting beside the couch of furs on which Lord Mallory lay, his red eyes closed. She stiffened and glowered at him mistrustfully.

"How art thou come here, Sir Ranulf?" she demanded. The knight stared at stained bandages that made a peculiar contrast to the extraordinary whiteness of Lord Mallory's skin, and thought of the unnatural healing that had occurred within himself. He found it difficult to speak.

"Sir Ranulf?" Lord Pendragon called out softly, his eyes opening to gleam unfocused scarlet, and his hand lifting weakly to reach out in a blind man's groping manner.

"My lord . . . ," Sir Ranulf managed.

Lord Mallory smiled. "Thou live. I am glad to know it!" he said quietly. "I could not find honour in holding Wallenford of thy grave!"

Sir Ranulf swallowed, abruptly humbled. It was true then.

"My life belongs to thee, Lord Pendragon!" he said stiffly, seeking dignity, aware of the lady Rosamund's watchful eyes.

Lord Mallory shook his head a little then stopped the gesture, wincing at the pain from his collarbone. "Nay, Sir Ranulf. Thy life is thine own," he managed softly.

"My service, then?"

Again, Lord Mallory smiled a little. "Nay, not even that. I would prefer friendship rather."

"Gladly offered, my lord!" Sir Ranulf exhaled a sudden and great relief.

"I am honoured." Lord Mallory's voice dropped to an exhausted whisper. His scarlet eyes closed and he sighed.

Sir Ranulf looked at Lady Rosamund then. He knew himself, and that he still wanted her. He stiffened. But, she was not for him.

"Lady," he said with proper formality and bowed. She nodded, and he turned away and strode from the tent.

He knew, as he walked away across the meadow, that he would wed Sussex' daughter, and that he would remove himself to Petworth. And, that he would feel no dishonour at all.

# TWENTY-FOUR

1171 A.D.

Mallory stirred beneath the soft weight of the furs that covered the bed, stretched luxuriously, and reached for Rosamund. She shifted with a grunt that told him of her reluctance to be disturbed, and he grinned. As with everything, Rosamund's sleep was not done by halves.

Content to lie still for the time being, simply feeling her warmth beside him, Mallory tucked his arms under his head, and thought of all that had occurred during the five years that had followed his recovery of Wallenford.

So much.

Recovered from his wounds, he had found himself accorded particular honour in the knighthood he had received from the King's own hand, both recognition and a statement of Henry Plantagenet's seal of feudal guardianship over him.

Likewise, at Winchester, he had wed Rosamund in the Christian fashion, his name and hers written together on the documents of entitlement that were the other testament to the possession of Wallenford.

Then, together, in a time of new discovery, they had ridden home, lingering in the heart of the vast forests, coming to that ancient tower where only the memories of a now distant childhood lingered.

Mallory had summoned the wolves then with songs they understood, and had released them from their bondage of duty, loosing them to live again as the free natural creatures they were.

Then, with Rosamund beside him, Mallory had walked for the last time through that now barren hall that had once been alive with both magic and magnificence. He had touched the dust and cobwebs that lay upon that great circular table and covered the array of shields, the other things that fell to dust beneath his fingertips. It was in that place at last, that Rosamund had finally come to accept the power that lay still profound and coiled within him, to give herself up to the destiny that her father had prepared for her.

The serfs of Wallenford had been terrified by the first appearance of their blind lord, and by the wolf that was ever at his side. But, both time and persistent applications of generosity and justice had brought those fears to melt away.

The somber, decayed gloom of Wallenford Castle were slowly dispelled by carefully conjured artifacts. Bright tapestries were hung upon grey stone walls. Rugs were scattered across floors once strewn with lice-infested straw. Torches bestowed warmth from the sconces, and industry began to reap the harvests of plenty as new prosperity was discovered.

Mallory moved restlessly, shifting his arms to trace fingertips along Rosamund's back, grinning again, as he found her neck with his mouth and began to trail kisses along the silk of her skin. She murmured, rousing to slow sensuousness. He felt himself harden deliciously and touched her hip gently.

"Thou art a man of prodigious appetite, my lord!" she grumbled drowsily, then turned to wrap her arms about him.

"I but find pleasure in serving thee!" he murmured that which had now become something of a jest between them, and moved over her to capture a nipple with his lips, tasting it with his tongue, inhaling deeply to drink of her scent.

Rosamund sighed and opened for him, pleasure that had become familiar, yet was ever freshly tantalizing, delicately new.

"Is it not time to be about the begetting of heirs?" Mallory asked softly.

She started at that.

"I thought it was inevitable . . . ?" Puzzled, she felt his sigh as he found her mouth and moved between her thighs to caress her with both fingers and loins.

"We are Fairie enough to contrive our children by choice," he said then. "I thought to wait until thou should wish it."

Pleasure faded a little as thought became dominant. She touched the faded scar that crossed his ribs in a diagonal line, the other upon his left shoulder—and lay quietly as he continued to travel over and within her.

"Aye . . ." Rosamund whispered at last. "It is time to beget a son!" She clutched at him, and Mallory moaned in urgency, moved eagerly, deeply into her. She welcomed him and closed her eyes, and felt something more than pleasure pass from him to her as he carried her upward along an elegant spiralling wave of shimmering sensation.

Life . . .

"This way, my king," Mallory said quietly some considerable time later, as he nudged the blue stallion to center forward, up the steep hill that lay ahead, winding between the thick profusion of ancient oak trees that comprised the better part of the forest.

The King followed, and felt the quiet in the air around him, as though he were being watched by a thousand pairs of eyes, all invisible. He stiffened a little as his mount halted upon the crest of the hill and stared with curious wonder as he thrust aside a low branch.

Before him, surrounded and concealed by the dark, impenetrable greens of vast and twisted ancient trees, lay a small lake.

Not a ripple stirred upon the dark, marble-seeming surface, despite the fresh breeze that brushed against his face. And, the water seemed to gleam with a thin layer of liquid reflectivity over an obsidian darkness of incalculable depth. Eerie, the King knew. Something more than natural.

"The Lake, Majesty," Lord Pendragon said, and his horse moved forward the pair of steps needed to bring it to the very edge of the precipitous embankment. Then, Henry Plantagenet watched as Lord Mallory drew the sword Excalibur from its scabbard at his side and held it up.

"I do return thee now to the Lady," his voice rang out deep and sure across the waters, to echo strangely as it rebounded off the enclosing trees beyond. "Go now!"

The golden dragons of the hilt came to life as the King had seen before, stretching out their wings to fly from Lord Mallory's pristine and outstretched white hand. The steel blade glinted with blinding radiance as sunlight shattered upon it, and the sword moved out over the Lake, to poise in the air directly above the very center.

An instant later, an ancient hand, gnarled, and with twisted, skeletal fingers, reached up through the surface of the waters, and the dragons of Excalibur's hilt folded their wings. The blade dulled, and the weapon plummeted down into the grasp of that outstretched hand, then disappeared.

A single ripple moved outward from the center of the lake

from the vanishing point of sword and hand, and in its wake, the water changed to rich, translucent blues and greens. Henry Plantagenet described the Cross upon his breast.

"It is done," Lord Mallory said softly. But the King continued to stare at the Lake, able now only to see things he understood as purely natural, as though what he had just seen had been no more than an illusion conjured by an overwrought imagination. The leaves on the trees all about ruffled lightly in response to an unperturbed breeze, and the surface of the water before him sparkled its reflection of the sunlight as it rippled in natural response.

"Wallenford is, indeed, a sanctuary. . ." he said, beginning to understand that which had been ambiguous before. Lord Pendragon reined his horse back until he was abreast of the King.

"Aye, Majesty," he affirmed quietly, but Henry Plantagenet shifted restlessly in his saddle, and glanced about him with the uneasy knowledge of the turmoil that had brought him to visit Wallenford, had brought him to seek the relief of even a few days of peace. The weals of self-ordained guilt still nagged his back.

"Sanctuary . . . !" He exclaimed suddenly in another tone. He had endured much of late. "Becket is dead. And I am his murderer! And now, they make of him a saint . . ."

"His death was inevitable, my liege," Lord Mallory said with serene conviction.

The King looked sharply at him. "How so, my lord?" he demanded.

"In this realm, there can only be one King, Majesty. And that office is given unto thee!"

Henry Plantagenet felt his breathing cease for a moment. His eyes narrowed briefly as he continued to stare at the other, then widened slowly as the blood drained from his face. He exhaled violently. "Is thy power so great, Lord Pendragon . . . ?" he asked.

The silver head of the young, white-hued lord cocked a little as silence gathered with incredible force between them. "It is, my liege," Lord Mallory said at last.

Henry thought suddenly that he had been foolish to ask. Again, he breathed convulsively as he thought of Becket's demise. "Why. . . ?" he rasped, compressing many questions into a single word.

Lord Mallory shifted in his saddle, turning his face more

directly toward the King. Sightless red eyes . . . What, Henry wondered, did their bloody, unfocused gaze really perceive?

"As it were begun with Arthur, Majesty, so it will continue. As I have said, there shall be but a single prince to rule this kingdom. None other. As this realm was sundered from the rest by the encroachments of the sea and brought to its own unique definition, so too, that which hath been given of the Fairie shall be realized in a most particular destiny."

"Thou knowst the future . . . ?" the King asked. Lord Mallory shook his head.

"Nay, Majesty. That is forbidden," he answered at once. "Impossible to perceive. I have but the wisdom of my father's profound and ageless memory within me. His knowledge. It is from that same well of experience that I am given to draw mine own understanding." He smiled with an intriguing expression of content. "He knew . . . and it comes to pass accordingly," he added softly.

The King continued to stare at the other, and thought of all the details of experience that had compounded his rule, his life, in the past five years. And of the strong sons he had gotten, promise for the future. Then he bowed his head, absorbed . . . and understood.

Not even a saint could manage a prince's estate. Aye—It was secured.

"Come, my liege," Lord Mallory said softly. The King looked up abruptly and saw satisfaction on that pure white face beside him. He had been read, he knew. "A feast awaits us at the keep, and 'tis a long ride to return!"

"Aye. So be it, my lord!" Henry Plantagenet declared firmly, and spun his horse about to spur it forward through the est. Away from the Lake. Toward his destiny.